THE DEVIL'S CUT
(Penumbra Papers #3)

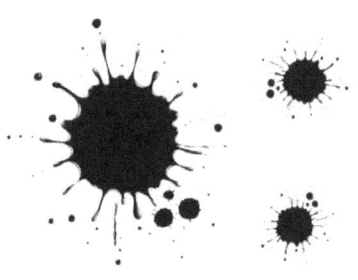

Silver James

Contact: silverjames@swbell.net

Cover design © by *Clary Carey*, clarycarey@gmail.com
Image: www.bigstock.com, Red Calm © M.P.T

Edited by Gregory Alan

Published in the United States of America
First Edition Print

ISBN-10: 0989921786
ISBN-13: 978-0-9899217-8-7

DEDICATION

To everyone who believes in magic
and isn't afraid to dream.

ACKNOWLEDGEMENTS

Writing is the one profession where the voices in my head mean I'm only a little crazy when I talk back to them. I love the creatures living in my imagination, even when they argue with me. Which they do. Way more than they should. Silly critters.

I have my dad to thank for encouraging that imagination, and for fostering my love of reading and books. I miss him every day but hopefully, wherever he is in the afterlife, he knows I'm doing what I've always loved best—making things up.

As always, many thanks to the Wild Warriors on my street team, friends, and family. Y'all are the reason I keep writing the stories in my head.

I truly appreciate the help I receive from my critique partner Heidi, beta readers Siobhan and Beth, and cover artist Clary for the many "do-overs" until we get things right. I couldn't write without the support and cheerleading by my wonderful husband, Greg aka Lawyer Guy. Last but definitely not least, I want to recognize my readers. Each email, Facebook comment, tweet, and visit to my website convinces me that I must be doing something right.

One last caveat: Any and all mistakes are my own.

THE DEVIL'S CUT
PENUMBRA PAPERS #3

PROLOGUE

Chicago: February

"SADE, CALEB IS MISSING."

Sade's first thought was, "So?" Then she sat straight up in bed—an interesting exercise considering the extremely sexy vampire next to her who was rather intent on keeping her in his arms and otherwise occupied.

Caleb had gone "walkabout" before. He did it when he purportedly resigned from the FBI, and she'd spent a couple of months tracking him down. This time, though, she had a Really Bad Feeling™. She swatted at Sinjen's hand as it tried to get fresh. The resounding *smack* and his resulting mutter was gratifying. The question was— did Caleb disappear on purpose? Or was he actually in trouble?

"Dammit, dammit, dammit." Sade growled into her cell phone.

"Language," Sinjen reminded her with a sigh. His effort was rewarded with another stinging slap against the back of his hand as he caressed the silken skin of her abdomen.

"How long?" she demanded of the caller, FBI Director George Bailey and her boss.

Sinjen gave up trying to lure her back to more pleasurable pursuits. His beautiful FBI agent had

1

turned all business on him. Throwing back the covers, he got up and padded naked into the kitchen to start coffee for her. While he couldn't drink the brew, he enjoyed the scent and the taste of it on her lips and tongue. He'd also been with her long enough to know a cup would earn him a kiss. Returning to the bedroom a few minutes later, his smile turned sultry as he recognized the light in her eyes as she openly admired him.

With a great deal of reluctance, Sade pulled her eyes away from the prime specimen of sexiness standing beside the bed and gratefully accepted the steaming mug he held out. She swallowed a gulp of the hot, black coffee and asked. "So he was on a case? Or did he go undercover?" Sade knew Caleb tended to immerse himself when he went "dark," sometimes not surfacing until time to make a bust. She listened for a long moment, and her hand started to shake. "Gawdammitalltohell."

Sinjen rescued the mug from her hand before the contents spilled over his silk sheets. Setting it on the nightstand, he eased onto the edge of the bed and gathered her into his arms. His lovely spitfire wasn't yet as strong as she pretended to be. The memories of how close he'd come to losing her washed over him, and he couldn't suppress the shudder that surged through him.

Sade's eyes narrowed, her face looking like it had been carved from ice as she growled into the phone, "If he's dead, I'm going to kill him!"

She left his bed—their bed—with alacrity as she said those words and ended the call with a promise. "I'll find him."

With her declaration, Sinjen's world changed. Again. After centuries of darkness, Sade had arrived to shine light into his black soul. How was it possible that this brittle woman with her lean frame, her bottle-green eyes, with her dogged determination would be given the key to his salvation after all this time? Those words she spoke would steal her from him. Take her from his arms, his bed, perhaps even his heart. His wounded warrior would face the demons of the world, fighting any assistance he might offer, even his very existence at her side, every step of the way. Very few held her loyalty. He feared he was not one of them.

She snatched up the thick robe tossed across the foot of the bed and stormed through the glass door leading from his bedroom to the railed balcony. Outside, Sade faced the frigid, ice-capped waves of Lake Superior. A dark aura radiated around her. Loneliness. Despair. Both swamped her. Sinjen hated the words he had to utter, wanted to spit them into some black void to be swallowed and forgotten. Instead, he stood behind her and pulled her into his embrace.

He didn't want to speak the words so he whispered them against her hair. "I can't go with you."

"I know." She pushed away and stepped toward the railing, keeping her back to him. "No big deal. You aren't an agent, and this is official business. Besides, I'm headed to Arizona. Or New Mexico. Somewhere in the desert. Not a good place for a vampire. All that sun and stuff."

Sinjen reached for her, but she jerked away. "Sade, look at me."

She twisted her head, and light glinted in her bottle-green eyes. Her chin lifted in the show of defiance he'd come to know so well. "You aren't invited anyway."

As if that would stop him? Nothing could keep them apart—nothing but the demand for his appearance at the Conclave—a command he'd received upon awakening and ignored in favor of staying in bed with Sade. Mathias issued the Conclave's edict, and he could not disregard it for long. Not only was the master vampire the Conclave's *Veşnic*, he was also Sinjen's sire. He could not deny a direct order from either entity for long. Though time was short, he curled a lock of Sade's silky hair around his index finger and gave a little tug. "Come here."

"No."

He stepped closer, only relaxing once she turned toward him. Her arms circled his waist, and she buried her face against his neck. He kissed the top of her head. "I've been summoned to the Conclave. I'll catch up to you. When I'm done."

"Yeah. Sure."

Sade hadn't cursed since getting off the phone, a tell-tale sign of her depressed mood. It worried him so he prodded. "Don't do anything until I get there. I'll find Caleb."

Her head jerked back, anger flaring in her gaze. "The hell with that. I don't need your fucking help."

"Ah, there's the woman I love."

"Fuck you."

"Yes. You will. Right now."

CHAPTER ONE
STANDING OUTSIDE THE FIRE

Six months earlier, Carlsbad, New Mexico
"RIGHT NOW, I'D GIVE ANYTHING to be somewhere else." Caleb muttered the sentiment as he gazed around. There wasn't much wind to speak of, and heat waves shimmered around the headstones making them look ghostly despite the solid, salt-of-the-earth granite squares delineating each gravesite. He was surprised at how many trees dotted the cemetery, though their leaves were the color of dried sage. The grass beneath his feet was brown. This was desert country—hot, desolate foothills pushing toward the Guadalupe Mountains. This part of New Mexico was Apache territory—the stuff of western movies and penny dreadful novels. As the crow flies, he wasn't all that far from Lincoln County, of Billy the Kid and the Lincoln County cattle wars fame.

A friend of a friend had called, asking if Caleb had seen the news. He hadn't. When he tuned in, he learned a buddy had died. A Border Patrol officer. Shot and killed in the line of duty. The guy was human, wearing a vest, looking for coyotes at the border. Someone sliced Bear's femoral artery. He bled out right there on the scene in a matter of minutes. Left behind a pretty little wife, two boys and a baby girl. So here he was, on a hot August day, watching the internment of a man whose life he'd valued.

Bear's widow and her family sheltered beneath a dark green canopy. White folding chairs squatted in formation atop a square of Astroturf. As many

5

mourners as could fit under the false shade crowded in close. The flag-draped coffin hovered over the open grave, a mound of flowers and ribbons sending odors into the air that reminded Caleb all too much of the Fae. On the opposite side of the grave, almost hidden by the flower arrangements, the honor guard stood with rifles grounded at their sides. The color guard propped up limp flags and tried not to sweat through their dress uniforms.

Caleb stood back from the crowd. He'd found a nearby tree and leaned a shoulder against its sturdy trunk. His jeans and boots were clean, his dress shirt pressed. A few men wore suits and ties and looked miserable for it. The women at their sides were dressed in their Sunday best. Marrying and burying, Caleb thought. Why folks always dressed up when they knew it was going to be a long, hot day of standing on their feet was beyond his comprehension.

He wasn't alone in the circle of shade provided by the tree. A few other men and a couple of women migrated over. As each one stepped into the relative cooler temperature of the leafy canopy, he checked them out as they assessed him in return. Law enforcement personnel were unmistakable to the knowing eye. Their eyes moved constantly, watching, weighing, planning. A cop always had an exit strategy in case things went wrong. They could gauge a person with a quick glance. Even when relaxed, cops looked ready, just like the small group flocked around the gnarled trunk of the tree nearest the gravesite.

"Did you know him well?" an old veteran with a face weathered by the sun asked Caleb.

Caleb nodded. "Long ago and far away. We worked a couple of cases."

The man nodded. "Roy was a good kid." He stuck out his hand. "Tucker Moran, Texas Rangers."

Grasping the old ranger's hand in his own, Caleb nodded. "Caleb Jones. FBI."

A loud wail followed by a small commotion near the grave ended the conversation. Bear's widow had collapsed, and people gathered around her to help. A small figure in a dark suit darted out from between the legs of the adults and took off at a run. No one in the knot of people around the family realized Roy's oldest boy had taken off for the hills. The group under the tree glanced around, the women mostly studying the ground in front of them. Caleb flashed an easy smile.

"I'll go round the boy up," he murmured. Without waiting for a reply, he turned and headed in the direction the kid had fled, his long-legged stride quickly making up lost ground.

Caleb tracked the boy to the Community Center located across from the cemetery. The child was pulling on the locked doors and banging his fists futilely as tears streamed down his round cheeks.

"Good way to break a hand," Caleb said with quiet certainty.

The boy jumped a mile, whirling around. "Who...who're you?" he stammered, trying to swallow the lump of fear in his throat.

Caleb didn't move any closer. "My name is Caleb. I knew your dad. What's your name?"

Wiping his tears with the back of a hand, the boy squared his shoulders. "If you really knew my daddy, you'd know my name," he declared.

"Your dad called you RJ," Caleb told the boy. "Your name is actually Roy Edward Montoya, Jr. But Bear, he called you RJ."

RJ nodded solemnly. "He did. Ever'body called him Bear 'cause he was s'big. But he told me that Big Bear and Little Bear sounded stupid, and while bein' a junior was an honor, bein' called Junior would probably suck too."

Caleb's smile remembered better times. "Yeah," he agreed. "That was your dad's logic. I was with him when you were born. It broke his heart he couldn't be there for you and your mom."

The kid tilted his head back to stare up at Caleb. He had to shade his eyes to see the man clearly. "Daddy's never comin' back, is he?" Caleb shook his head solemnly but didn't speak, sensing the boy had more on his mind. "Grandma says I have to be the man now." Caleb ignored the squeak in RJ's voice. The boy sighed. "I'm only nine," he complained softly.

Turning his head, Caleb glanced back across the cemetery. There was movement around the grave. "Looks like they're finishing up. Think we might better head back?" RJ nodded so the two of them slowly retraced their steps. "You don't have to be grown up, RJ. Be a kid for as long as you can," Caleb advised. "There'll be men who step up for you and your brother and sister. That's one thing about what your dad did. It's a family. You have a problem, you can go to one of your dad's friends. Your mom needs something done around the house, somebody will be there. You do what you can. You look after the little ones. But like you said, you're only nine."

RJ nodded slowly. "Then it's okay?" he asked with a slight hitch in his voice. The boy blinked rapidly as his eyes filled with tears.

"Yeah," Caleb said. "It's okay." *Damn*, he thought. *What's wrong with the world that a nine year old has to ask permission to cry at his dad's funeral?* He slowed his steps even more. Caleb's sharp hearing picked up the droning of the preacher at the graveside. Once he was done, there would be the flag folding ceremony and presentation and then the twenty-one gun salute. A bugler and a piper stood with the color guard. That

8

meant both "Taps" and "Amazing Grace."

The boy's soft sniffle drew Caleb's attention back to him. He reached in a pocket and pulled out a clean handkerchief. He'd stopped at Wal-Mart and bought a package the night before when he'd rolled into town. Caleb held it out for the boy without looking at him and hid his smile when the handkerchief was snatched from his hand without a word. Studiously avoiding looking at RJ, Caleb started reading the names on the grave markers they passed. One in particular caught his attention. BUJAC, the staid granite marker declared. Caleb paused, looking closer. "Etienne Pelissier Jacques de Bujac" the inscription read.

"You ever watch John Wayne movies?" he asked RJ. The boy glanced up, his eyes red-rimmed now. "One of the guys in a lot of his films is buried here," he explained with a nod of his head. "His Hollywood name was Bruce Cabot."

RJ's head nodded like a bobbin head doll. "He was in 'Hellfighters'. That's my favorite movie of all time. Daddy and I watched it over and over."

Caleb blinked, a bit taken aback. "I figured you for an Iron Man kind of guy."

The boy shook his head emphatically. "Naw. Those movies are for kids. Daddy loved the Duke."

"He did indeed. An interest we both shared. That's how I knew Cabot's real name."

RJ flashed a hesitant smile. "I'll bring flowers for him when I come to visit Daddy. That way he'll be remembered, too."

When a murmured "Amen" from the crowd drifted through the arid air, Caleb started walking again, RJ keeping up easily now. "Do you know what comes next?" Caleb asked. The boy looked up, a question reflected in his eyes. "Part of the color guard will fold up the flag, and give it to your mom. You should be beside her when they do." He glanced down. RJ gulped but looked stoic. "Then the honor guard will fire their weapons. Three times. Your dad was a hero. He gets a twenty-one gun salute." Caleb was surprised when a hand crept into his but he gave it a reassuring squeeze. "Then either the bugler or the piper will play followed by the other one."

RJ squeezed back. "Taps," he whispered. "I *hate* that song."

Caleb understood the boy's reaction. "Taps" always made his chest tight, too. "Yeah."

They parted ways at the back of the canopy. RJ slipped around to the side to rejoin his mother. Caleb stood watching for a moment, a quiet smile on his face as the kid settled in the chair beside his mom, reached over and took her hand. "You'll do, Roy Edward Montoya, Jr.," he murmured before striding back to rejoin the group of law enforcement professionals under the tree.

"Little britches gonna be all right?" the ranger asked.

Caleb nodded. "Yeah. He's gonna be just fine eventually. A lot like his dad, that one."

The ranger nodded. "Roy was a fine man. I hope we catch the sorry son of a bitch who bushwhacked him."

Cutting his eyes toward the other man, Caleb tried to bite his tongue. He wasn't a Fed any more—at least not to these law enforcement professionals. This wasn't his jurisdiction or his job. Not at the moment anyway. "They know who did it?" he asked despite his resolve.

One of the two women in the group nodded. "Yeah. A coyote drug runner by the name of Santos Santana. Roy had been staking out some of the bastard's trails." She growled low in her throat. "Marti Atkins. Border Patrol," she added by way of introduction. "Santana has been in our sights for years, but we can't ever get

THE DEVIL'S CUT

anything concrete on him. I swear the guy is made of Teflon."

Caleb searched the databank in his memory. "Santana. Wasn't he a low-level coyote working out of El Paso?"

Atkins nodded. "He was. A year ago, we started picking up whispers. Now the guy has a big hacienda out in the desert. A private jet. Hell, last I heard, he just bought some fancy French helicopter."

"You talking about the long-range chopper built by Eurocopter?" Caleb asked.

One of the men nodded, and Caleb realized he was wearing pilot's wings on his uniform. "Yeah. Santana got an EC 130 B4. Damn thing is faster than my Bell 206 Long Ranger. He sends it up just to tease us."

Caleb nodded, considering. "But he's still using mule trails to transport?"

"The aircraft is just for fun, apparently. And giving us shit." Atkins spat, the wet glob sending up a puff of dust from the dry grass before disappearing. In the desert, any moisture was a blessing.

The men around her all nodded.

"How'd he move up the food chain so fast?" Caleb kept his voice low so the conversation didn't drift toward the mourners.

One of the men shrugged. "Santana has always been around, hanging out there on the outer edges and flying under the radar."

"Until a year ago," Atkins interjected. "All the sudden, everybody's whispering Santana's name."

The man nodded. "Yeah. Suddenly, Santos Santana's shit don't stink. DEA sends a boy down there to check things out. He reports back about the new house, the fancy cars and fancier women, and planes. Santana built his own airstrip. Then put in a landing pad for that swanky French helicopter."

Atkins broke in, her frustration bubbling over. "But he only uses the aircraft to run to Vegas, or his place up in Aspen. He's so cocksure of himself we don't even have to get a warrant. He invites us in to search. The plane and the chopper both are clean as a whistle. The little pipsqueak thinks he's an international playboy now. "

The blue New Mexico sky faded to white under the heat of the sun. The group grew silent, unconsciously coming to attention as the color guard stepped into place to remove the flag draped over the coffin. Slowly, each step of the procedure was carried out meticulously as two men folded the American flag into its familiar triangle shape, stars on top. One member of the color guard smartly paced over to a tall, lean man wearing the dress uniform of the US Border Patrol—tan slacks with stripes up the outside seam and an Eisenhower jacket. Presenting the flag, the color guard saluted, executed a precise about face and returned to his former position. The man in uniform, most likely Roy's commanding officer, stepped to Mrs. Montoya, and bent from the waist to place the flag in her hands. She remained ramrod straight in her chair, the black veil hiding the woman's tears. Straightening, the man nodded to the honor guard.

Seven rifles pointed to the endless blue sky. Seven fingers pulled triggers with a surety born of hours of practice. Seven gunpowder reports echoed across the cemetery. Acrid smoke drifted on dead air as seven more shots rang out, then seven more. Caleb winced, unable to hide the involuntary twitch of his shoulders. Every professional under that tree did the same.

The others drifted off but the old ranger dallied. He studied Caleb unblinking. "Find the sumbitch, Mr. Jones. Find 'im for little britches and them tykes. Find 'im before we have t'bury another good man. Or woman."

Caleb stared at the man, convinced the ranger knew—knew he was more than he appeared. "I will," he vowed.

He waited until the mourners had all departed. He waited until Roy's coffin was lowered into the ground, and a backhoe filled in the hole. He was nothing if not patient. The cemetery was empty at last—empty but for the souls of those confined there. A breeze kicked up, the heated breath of the desert, and it teased Caleb's hair with ghostly fingers as he stood at the foot of the fresh grave and contemplated the scene.

Colors. Red roses looked like blood splattered against the pale tan of the grass. The blinding blue sky stretched toward forever. He closed his eyes against the assault to his senses but saw only the black of the widow's dress outlined by the white chair in which she slumped. An American flag, left in a stand beside the grave, snapped like a gunshot as the wind kicked up a dust devil.

Standing alone, he raised his right arm, his hand angled ramrod stiff across his forehead in salute. He lowered his hand to his side and spoke from his heart. "I'm sorry I wasn't there for you, Roy. But rest easy, my friend. I'll take care of it." He turned away and trudged toward his car. "I'll give the devil his due."

TIME TO GIVE THE DEVIL HIS DUE. Caleb was back in New Mexico after only a month. Maybe August's heat had cooled with September's arrival. He strode through the Albuquerque airport with a martyr's air. Until the girl brushed past and halted him in his tracks. A dancer. She had to be. Shoulders square, chin high on a neck stretched as elegantly as a swan, making her look taller than she was. She passed down the concourse with a gliding step, arms swinging a graceful arc in counterpoint despite the backpack negligently hanging from one shoulder. Men turned to watch her pass. Women looked down their noses at her, both jealous and admiring.

Caleb followed, quartering the girl's back trail so she wouldn't notice him. His nostrils flared ever so minutely as he caught whiffs of her scent. Magic. It cloaked her in verbena and ginger, masking her true fragrance.

She tossed her head, sending her hair flying in a silken arc, and looked over her shoulder, as if giving him a come-hither glance from under fringed eyelashes. Busted. But he didn't care. His werewolf senses strained at the leash his humanity clutched in tight-fisted control. So focused on the woman, he missed the flash of magic roiling up his rear until it flashed over him, singeing the tips of his hair.

Nothing like the smell of burnt fur to shake a man out of his daydreams. He whirled and grabbed the magick by the front of his high-dollar shirt.

"She better be with you, and the both of you better

have more control than what you just showed me." Caleb growled the words, knowing they'd made the appropriate impact on the young dragon he'd collared. He could see the red feral gleam of his eyes reflected in the kid's pupils. He laughed. Kid? The dragon was probably a hundred years old but compared to human growth, he was barely twenty. The dragonet sputtered until Caleb flashed his FBI badge.

"Not in this airport," he growled again. "Don't make me go all furry on your ass."

"Yessir. I mean, no sir. I mean…We'll be good, sir."

Caleb turned the kid loose and watched him run to catch up with the female. Yeah. She was a dancer all right. A fire dancer and way too hot for him to handle. Good thing Sade hadn't been tasked with this assignment. If she had one more run-in with the Drakon, human and dragon relations would be set back a century or two. He continued toward the baggage claim, chuckling. Nikos Constantine continued to sniff around his FBI partner and foster sister, Sade Marquis. She didn't take grief from anyone, much less an arrogant dragon enforcer. He lined up at baggage claim, and his suitcase was the first one on the conveyor. He snagged it and headed to the car rental desk.

In a better mood, he stepped out of the Albuquerque airport and sniffed the air. He appreciated the desert. Things were cut and dried out here. Clean. He collected his SUV at the car rental lot and headed toward Buhmfuch, New Mexico. The town wasn't on any official map, but he found the place from the directions he'd received by email. The hand-painted city limits sign was befitting the little hole in the wall too small for any of the national chains to have a motel. The local place was clean enough and looked like it should have been the subject of a 1950's postcard…or would have been before the neon sign got busted.

The TeePee Motor Court was one of those iconoclastic places—a motel left over from the days of the great Mother Road, Route 66. Square adobe cabins connected by carports marched around a square courtyard with an empty pool—empty of water, anyway. It was brimming with tumbleweeds. The office was just a tiny bit bigger than the cabins, with living space behind the postage-stamp sized lobby for the owner, a crotchety old woman with wispy gray hair and watery blue eyes that didn't miss a thing.

The woman snapped at him as he entered. "Rooms are twenty-five a night, thirty-five if ya run the window unit. I'm Marjorie Dawson. That's Missus to you. You want somethin' I ain't got, tough shit." She pushed a clipboard at him, with a card stuck on it. "Fill it out."

After he checked in, Caleb placed his credit card on the scarred Formica countertop. Mrs. Dawson stared at it like it was rattlesnake. Snorting in disdain, she asked if he didn't have cash or a check. Before he could reply, the office door opened, the bell above it jangling like an old-time telephone. The dude that walked in was about twice Caleb's size. At 6'1" and two hundred pounds, Caleb wasn't exactly undernourished. The newcomer wore a dingy, red-plaid Western shirt, faded jeans and scuffed cowboy boots. The guy's belt buckle was hidden beneath his beer gut, and greasy brown hair straggled out from beneath a battered baseball cap.

The man pressed up against Caleb and all but smelled his butt. Evidently satisfied, he stepped back and nodded to the old lady behind the counter. "Evenin', Miz Dawson. This feller is a guest of Orrin's. Put 'im in yer best room." The woman nodded and pushed a key—a real, honest-to-god key on a ring with a plastic tag—across the counter. In chipped white paint, the numbers 101 stood out against the scratched black background of the tag.

Caleb picked up the key and waited for the big guy to move. They stared at each other for a long, tense moment. Caleb didn't blink. He could take the fat slob in a heartbeat, letting that fact show in his expression. The other guy blinked first, backed down, and let Caleb precede him through the door. Caleb's lip curled. Damn but he hated werewolf politics—all that posturing and "I'm bigger and badder than you" swagger. Like Romulus, his pack Alpha, Caleb's physical appearance was wiry and therefore misleading. Even without his werewolf strength, he would have been able to pick up the other man and toss him. And like Romulus, he had developed The Look™—that unblinking stare of a stone-cold alpha predator. He didn't have to use it often. Even humans had a tendency to recognize he was something more and backed away from picking fights with him. Mostly easy-going, his reputation as a badass amused him.

Out in the barren courtyard, Caleb watched a little dust devil kick up its heels. "I take it the bossman wants to see me now?" he asked the lump behind him without turning around.

The big man sneered and tried to sound tough. "Yeah. He said to fetch you."

"You got a name?" Caleb wasn't intimidated. In fact, he had to bite back a snort of laughter. Fetch? Was the guy a dog or a werewolf?

"Buddy. Buddy Johnson." He added the last name like that was supposed to impress Caleb.

He shrugged. So the big lout was related to the Alpha. Big deal. He'd lay odds that the whole pack was related one way or another. Isolated packs tended to inbreed. It was bad for the species but what could you do about it? Caleb looked around. His rented Ford Explorer was the only vehicle in the lot. "You hike in?" he asked, eying the big guy incredulously. Since he was fully dressed, the man hadn't shifted and run in.

"Naw," Buddy confirmed. He spat into the dust, the glob of phlegm landing about an inch from the toe of Caleb's boot. "Garth dropped me off. Figured I'd ride back with you."

Caleb stared at the gooey mess near his boot then slowly raised his head to stare at the man standing a few feet from him. One sardonic eyebrow arched. He didn't have to say a word. His brown eyes had gone flat but with a flash of reddish gold deep within them. Buddy took an involuntary step backwards.

"C'mon, then. Orrin don't like t'wait," Buddy muttered grumpily, trying to hide how much Caleb intimidated him.

With a curt nod, Caleb turned on his heel and strode purposely to the Explorer. The surface of the SUV was coated with a fine layer of dust, and it was all Caleb could do to keep from sneezing. He remembered now why he was a city wolf, and it had nothing to do with cable TV, the internet, or indoor plumbing. He slid in behind the wheel and allowed himself a momentary chuckle. Who was he kidding? It had everything to do with those things, plus restaurants and pubs, and, if he were perfectly honest, pretty women.

Buddy climbed into the passenger seat, and Caleb was glad this was a rental instead of his personal car. The dude smelled ripe—not in the way that an apple or orange smelled ripe, full and sweet with a hint of musk. No, Buddy smelled ripe like week-old garbage does—or a pro wrestler who forgot his antiperspirant. Caleb hated those little cardboard evergreen trees people hung from the rearview mirrors to cover up odors of a host of sins from cigarettes and weed to BO, but he would have to buy one somewhere once Buddy got out of the vehicle. Despite the dust, Caleb rolled his window down and leaned toward the dribble of fresh air that wandered in.

"Where to?" he asked as he started the Explorer.

Without looking at Caleb, Buddy pointed. "Hope you got four-wheel drive in this buggy, city boy," he growled.

Caleb followed the direction of Buddy's finger which was pointing out toward the middle of nowhere back behind the motel. He could make out the vague outline of a road snaking up the hill. It looked more like two scuffed tracks heading out into the desert than a road. He put the SUV in gear and pulled forward, engaging the four-wheel drive as he did so. Caleb might be a city boy but he wasn't stupid. There was a reason he had a satellite phone. Out in the desert in pack territory microwave cell phone towers were few and far between. He'd been warned that his client lived in the boonies.

Aiming the nose of the SUV through a gap in the cabins, Caleb had to pull hard on the steering wheel to miss the fenced-in satellite dish behind the motel. This touch of civilization seemed incongruous but he kept his sardonic smile to himself and kept driving.

After about an hour of grudging silence on Buddy's part and careful negotiation of the ruts and rocks that comprised the so-called road, Caleb was thinking about calling the whole thing off, going back to Albuquerque, checking into a real hotel and ordering up a cold beer from room service while he caught the Cowboys and Jets game on the tube.

"Stop," Buddy snarled at him.

The nose of the Explorer had just tilted up to make a fairly easy climb up out of a dry wash. Caleb eased the SUV to a stop and set the parking brake.

"Wait here," the other werewolf ordered. Climbing out, Buddy slammed the door and trudged up the hill. He topped the rise and disappeared over it.

The hair on the back of Caleb's neck prickled. He

looked around carefully and suddenly felt like he was in a John Wayne movie surrounded by Indians. He couldn't see anybody but instinctively knew he was completely surrounded. He now wished he'd gotten the supplemental insurance from the rental agency. Running over a werewolf did a lot of damage to a car's bumpers and paint job. Wolves tended to dent the fender, bounce, and leave long scratches in the finish.

Despite his uneasiness, Caleb waited. The Alpha had contacted him, after all, and he was here under the leader's "flag of truce." Werewolf packs were funny, even the civilized ones. They just didn't cotton to outsiders sticking their nose into pack business. Whatever was going on out here in the desert, it had to be bad enough that Orrin Johnson was willing to suffer an alpha from another pack in his territory.

Caleb chuckled. Folks just didn't get the distinction. There was the Alpha in a pack. Alpha with a capital A. This was a werewolf who fought his way to pack leadership and was the smartest and the strongest. Usually. Sometimes, just the strongest. The pack got their *flavor*—their personality from the Alpha. Then there were alpha and beta wolves, and omegas. Caleb was an alpha. He was strong, had good senses, shifted easily, and wasn't afraid of fighting or doing what needed to be done—in either form of his "self".

Betas were weaker. They cowed and went belly up when an alpha looked crosswise at them. And then there were the omegas. In the wild packs, omegas often got drowned at birth. They were the weakest. In an unhealthy pack, the alphas picked on the betas, and everybody picked on the omegas. Civilized packs took care of the omegas but kept them hidden away. Omegas wet the bed and couldn't control their changes, no matter how old they got. They were born whipped and never got over it.

It said a lot about both Orrin Johnson and his pack that his second in command was a beta. Either the man didn't want a challenge, or the pack was weak. Either way, he would be wary.

Not for the first time, Caleb wondered if he'd bitten off more than he could chew. All he knew about this case was that a couple of pack members had gone missing. Problem was, this was a pair of young'uns—15 and 17. Two brothers who wandered off to do some hunting hadn't come home, and nobody had seen hide nor hair of them or the ATV they'd been riding. If a werewolf from their pack couldn't track those youngsters, they were well and truly gone. Caleb's contact said it appeared the boys had just disappeared off the face of the planet.

When the Old Man got wind of the situation, Caleb had no say in the matter. Pack territory bumped up against land claimed by a certain drug lord with expensive tastes and a penchant for murdering law enforcement personnel. Caleb hadn't forgotten his last trip to New Mexico a month earlier so he didn't whine with Director Bailey sent him undercover.

He sat inside his SUV for thirty minutes before he started getting really antsy. All the hair on his neck remained at attention and ready to salute, and his palms itched. That was a sure sign of trouble to come. The old wives' tale talked of itchy palms predicting money. To a werewolf, it was an indication that fur was bristling right below the surface. Before it got too bad, Buddy came huffing back over the top of the rise, waving an arm, urging Caleb to drive forward. As he put the Explorer in gear, the sense of being watched vanished. "Guess I'm in, then," he muttered.

Just over the hill, Caleb found a settlement, for lack of a better term. Campers, RVs, a couple of ramshackle cabins and even an old school bus were scattered around a loose circle. He pulled past Buddy and didn't stop, chuckling as the other man jogged to keep up. He drove slowly. As much as he wanted to, he didn't kick up a cloud of dust or spin the tires to pelt Buddy with loose rocks. The man's huffing and puffing, and red face in the rearview was payback enough.

Pulling up next to a battered old pickup, Caleb shook his head. "Frankentruck," he muttered, getting out of the Explorer. A Chevy bed had been grafted onto a Ford cab—or at least, that's what the model marquees pronounced but you couldn't prove that by him. He strode across the open space between the structures, his gait loose-limbed and loping. As he approached the man sitting in a lawn chair in the center of the open square, Caleb noticed wolves literally coming out of the woodwork. He slowed down, finally coming to a stop about ten feet from the man. He took off his sunglasses.

"Alpha." Caleb greeted him with a quick nod and a brief lowering of his eyes.

"Took ya long enough," the man growled at him.

Putting his sunglasses back on, he stood quietly facing the man, his arms loose at his side. The Alpha was almost as big as Buddy, but while Buddy just looked dumb as a stump, there was a wily glint in Orrin Johnson's eyes. Caleb watched the other man from behind the dark lenses of his shades, quietly assessing. The Alpha had spent a lot of time in werewolf form as evidenced by his ears, which were slightly elongated and pointed with hair growing in them. He wore a denim shirt that had seen better days and his chest hair spilled out the vee of the plackets of the snap-front shirt. He hadn't shaved in a couple of days, and as the wind kicked up again, Caleb was thankful he was upwind. The Alpha hadn't bathed at least since his last shave.

"So, boss...you plan to keep wasting our time or are you going to tell me what's happening that's got you worried enough to bring in a stranger to deal with your business?" Caleb remained loose, at least on the outside. Inside, he was coiled tight ready for fight or flight.

"Somethin' weird's goin' on 'round here," the Alpha drawled. "Got two come up missin'." He brazenly looked Caleb up and down. "But you know that. We can't find no sign. You know what that means?"

Caleb nodded. "Yeah. They've been snatched." He deliberately took off his sunglasses and looked around the desolate settlement. "I don't care one way or another, mind you, but I gotta ask, boss. Any of your boys running...contraband?" Caleb fixed his gaze on the man in the chair.

Orrin shook his head emphatically. "Fuckin' druggies," he spat—literally. The glob landed about six inches in front of Caleb. Impressive range. He'd do well to remember that. The man continued. "We're too far north for the coyotes but yeah. We get low flyin' planes now and again."

Lips pursed, Caleb considered. Orrin's reference to the coyotes had nothing to do with the four-legged variety, and there were no werecoyotes. He was talking about the two-legged varmints who trafficked in illegals—people, drugs, and guns. The fact that smugglers used the area didn't surprise him much. The Mexican border was like Swiss cheese—easy to cross if you knew where the holes were. Santos Santana sat about twenty-five miles away, as the crow flies.

"You know what it's gonna cost you?" Caleb finally replied.

"Your room's taken care of." Orrin waved a fist the size and shape of a small ham. A girl of about 15 or 16 slunk out of the crowd and approached Caleb. She pulled a wad of cash out of her cleavage and held it out to him. "That's the first thousand. More when you say so." Orrin hacked up another glob and spat, this time between his own scuffed boots. "An' that's Mimi. She's one'o mine. She'll treat you right." He leered at his daughter. "Or else."

The girl flipped her father off and headed toward the Explorer. "C'mon, dude." She huffed an aggrieved sigh before blowing and popping a chewing gum bubble with a smack of her lips. "Let's get this over with."

Caleb wisely held his tongue. He liked his women older and more enthusiastic, but he wasn't going to turn down the Alpha's offer—not in front of him anyway. Very bad form, especially since the girl was one of the man's daughters.

"I'll be in touch," he called over his shoulder as he followed Mimi to the SUV.

"I'LL BE IN TOUCH."

Caleb ended the call, unsure if he'd hear back from the DEA agent but the guy had always been a solid source before. Being patient under these circumstances wasn't easy. His best guess was that drug runners had stumbled across the kids, shot 'em in the head, and left 'em out in the desert. Yeah, wolves were pretty impervious to gunshot wounds except for silver bullets, or a head shot. Oh, yeah. A heart shot might take a werewolf out too. To be positive, werewolf hunters went for the head shot and then cut off the head just to make sure.

Werewolves could regenerate but not like portrayed in movies or books. Most of the stories about werewolves weren't exactly literature. Pulp—pure and simple—and filled with misinformation. Some of that was intentional. No. Werewolves didn't automatically heal when they changed forms, though they healed faster than humans. Fire was a bad thing. Burn scars didn't heal. If someone shot Caleb today, he'd probably come back in a couple of days to rip the shooter a new one. He wasn't partial to being shot. It tended to piss him off. Royally.

While he waited for the call back, he interviewed all of Johnson's pack. Talk about an exercise in frustration. By the time he got to the old man, he was starting to wonder if the whole pack had a combined IQ of a hundred. Seriously. They weren't just narrow between the eyes, they were well into uni-brow territory. This happened when your father's sister was your son's

25

mother. Sadly, Caleb wasn't kidding when he sketched out that family tree.

A month before, he'd received a call. "Can you come to New Mexico?" the voice on his answering machine requested. "Friend of a friend is in trouble. Sorta needs your kind of help." Curious, Caleb had returned the call. Word on the street said he was a freelancer and no longer part of the Bureau. Director Bailey himself set Caleb up in the undercover role, and he while he couldn't walk away from a case, he now found himself regretting it. He was promised retainer fees up front and expenses, plus a "bonus" thrown in by the Alpha—a thousand in cold cash and the Alpha's daughter for the length of his stay. Not that he'd be accepting any of it because the FBI frowned on its agents taking money or favors while on duty.

Mimi was only 15 so Caleb installed her in a motel room happily watching reruns of the "Jersey Shore" while he went out sniffing for clues. She was a typical hormonal teenage girl and not the brightest bulb in the box—which meant he might come back to a snarly werewolf, or to a bitchy teen. Caleb didn't do jail bait even though the wolves had the same idea of "age of consent" as the fae. Not only he was almost old enough to be her father, but the more important fact was they had nothing to talk about. You could only screw for so long, and then it was either roll over and start snoring or talk.

Caleb was a talker—or more precisely, he was a listener. He'd learned that particular skill a long time ago. The things to be learned by simply letting a person ramble on never ceased to amaze him. Even strangers would pour out their life story to a sympathetic ear. So far, though, he hadn't had much luck getting the pack to open up. He had one last stop to make.

The old man sat on a rickety chair that had once

been a ladderback but was now missing a couple of rungs. Sort of like the old man. Kicked back against the side of a decrepit Winnebago, the guy propped his bare feet on an upended bucket. Somebody had tossed down an old sheet of plywood to use as a patio. The man glared at Caleb through rheumy eyes as he scraped a big-ass knife against a piece of wood. A trail of tobacco juice dribbled down his chin. Caleb squared his shoulders and stepped into the shade cast by the trailer.

"Got nuthin' t'say t'ya, boy."

Caleb had gotten a lot of that sentiment today. He propped a booted foot up on a plastic crate. "Hot day."

"Yup."

"Gonna be hotter tomorrow."

"Yup."

Staring out over the desert, Caleb didn't speak for a few minutes. Despite talking to everyone in the pack, he was disheartened by the fact he hadn't learned one iota of information to help him locate the two kids. He didn't hold out much hope for them, unless they'd been able to shift and were out there hiding in furry form. Problem was, they were pups. He didn't have complete control over his shift until he was almost 18, and he had good genes. A 15-year-old and a 17-year-old from this pack? He doubted they had any control at all.

"Anybody new hangin' around?"

"'Sides you?"

"Besides me."

"Nope."

"When was the last time new blood joined the pack?"

Caleb looked around as the chair's front legs thudded against the plywood. The old man stared at Caleb, his expression blank. After a blink and hacking up a hairball, which he spat between his own boots, the old dude finally shook his head.

"Not in my lifetime."

Caleb did the math. This pack had been inbreeding for over a hundred years. Scary thought. He needed to get back to the motel and get the Alpha's daughter sorted out. He was not about to become a sperm donor, especially not to a gum-popping, underage Lolita who was narrow between the eyes.

"Not sure why the Alpha dragged you into this. Them young'uns are gone."

"You sound pretty sure."

"Yup. Pups go out, don't come back. No skin off my nose."

"You think they went rogue?"

"Nope. What lives out there got 'em."

"What lives out there?" Caleb's wolfy sense prickled.

The old man stared out into the desert, his thoughts miles away. Caleb gazed in the same direction. Sweat gathered high on his back and trickled down his spine, but he remained silent and alert. Oh yeah, he had a really bad feeling about what might be out there, said premonition confirmed when the man spoke.

"Bad shit, boy."

Caleb turned his head to look at the guy, and jerked when he recognized the fear etched on the old man's face. "The devil himself lives out there. He's been quiet a long time but he's stirrin'. You mark my words. Them boys are just the first."

Devil? There wasn't any such thing. Demons, oh yeah. But devil? Nope. Before Caleb could ask further questions, the man continued.

"The devil's comin' and if we don't give 'im his due, he'll take his own cut." With that, the old man pushed up out of the chair, stripped and shifted. The grey-muzzled werewolf curled his lip into a snarl, flicked his tail, and trotted off into the desert.

"Huh." Caleb had effectively been put into his place.

With those parting words playing in his mind, he climbed into his rented SUV and headed back to the TeePee. He needed to find someplace with Wi-Fi, and he needed to get shed of Mimi. He could do a Wi-Fi hotspot with his SAT phone, but he needed some serious bandwidth to dig into the sites he needed to check.

He'd never heard of a demon in the New Mexico desert, but that didn't mean there wasn't one. The old werewolf had to be pushing a 100 and he seemed to know something, even if he wasn't exactly willing to share much information. Back at the motel, Caleb got lucky. The Alpha's daughter was in human form. He made a deal with her. She'd go home with a smile if Caleb took her with him to Albuquerque for a trip to the mall and a Hot Topix shopping spree. The girl spent 200 dollars of his retainer but it was money well spent to get her out of his hair and back into the bosom of her family.

While she was trying on everything in the store, Caleb nursed black coffee at the Starbucks across the way. Surfing the net only pointed out the holes in his investigation. He did discover, according to a Most Wanted website, that there was a "devil" in the desert— a two-bit drug lord who called himself El Diablo. The Devil. Every time Caleb thought about the guy, he laughed himself silly thinking about the character, Muerte, from the movie, "Undercover Blues."

Sadly, the mere presence of a guy with the eye-roll-inducing nickname would send him nosing out into the vast hinterlands of cactus, sand, and scrub that comprised New Mexico's desert landscape. He glanced at his watch and decided Princess Werewolf had spent more than enough of his time and money. Swigging the last of his coffee, he shut down his laptop and strode across the mall. He caught Mimi just before she headed back into the dressing area with another armload of clothes.

"Yo, buttercup. Haul yourself and whatever junk you're buying to the register. You have five minutes before I walk and you're left holding the price tags."

The girl manning the register stared at him, glanced at Mimi, then returned her gaze to stare at him some more.

"Doesn't seem your type."

"She's not." That got him a smirk and a raised eyebrow. "Cousin. It's her birthday. Her family owes me big time."

Another clerk slid up next to him with a little hip bump. "I'd sure like to know what your type is."

Caleb studied both girls and wondered how he managed to get into these predicaments. He sure could use Sade about now, but he'd never admit that to her. "I like my women old enough to drink without getting carded."

That left these two out and they knew it. Mimi arrived with both arms full of clothes and smirked at the clerks. Caleb growled at the total and handed over his credit card with a grimace. "They didn't exactly teach you to add, did they."

Since he didn't ask a question, Mimi didn't answer. Instead, she batted her lashes at him. "I'm hungry. I want steak. Rare."

"You'll get burgers from the drive-thru while I'm taking you home."

"But—"

"Shut it, Mimi."

"I'll tell my dad."

He expected her to stamp her feet but preempted her tantrum by grabbing the massive bag and striding out. He called back over his shoulder, "You do that. There's a charity shop on the way. We can drop these clothes off."

Mimi bolted after him. "You wouldn't dare!"

"Sure I would."

The kid sulked all the way back to Buhmfuch. Caleb stopped at the motel long enough Mimi could grab her stuff and jump back in the SUV before he headed into the desert. He dropped her off at the pack's compound and she was immediately surrounded by her jealous cousins. Before Caleb could turn around and get gone, the old man sauntered up to the driver's side window.

"Where ya off to, boy?"

"Gonna go see a man about a horse."

The old geezer snorted, hacked up a noogie, and spat. "You do that, ol' son. And tell the sumbitch out there he still owes me a favor."

Caleb worried the question of what the blazes the geezer was talking about all the way back to the TeePee. He refused to make the obvious comparison that he was like a dog with a bone. First off, wolves didn't worry bones. They crunched them up to get the marrow in the middle. Still, he didn't like the answers pinging around his brain. Two pups didn't just go missing—not unless it was a boy and girl with more hormones than sense. And despite the idea the old werewolf was yanking his chain, Caleb had a bad feeling whenever he looked out into the desert.

Something was out there. Something old and malevolent. Something with the patience of a born predator. Something so steeped in evil that every hair on his body was standing on end. He'd just pulled up at the TeePee and parked when the man called him about that horse, only in this case, it was the illegal drug kind rather than the four-legged. Copying down the info the DEA agent passed along, Caleb didn't like the feeling settling deep in his gut. Devils and lost pups and a darkness creeping over the desert. The time for talking was over. It was time to get down and dirty.

New Mexico Desert

IT WAS TIME TO GET down and dirty. Caleb had a list of names and locations to check, but he knew which would be first—El Diablo, aka Santos Santana, the man who'd killed Bear Montoya. His wolfy sense twitched, and a spot between his shoulder blades itched like someone had a hunting rifle trained there. As he drove into the middle of nowhere, he relied on the GPS coordinates he'd received rather than the rental SUV's navigational system.

The desert stretched far and wide. Red sandstone cliffs loomed off to the south. Scrub brush, clumps of buffalo grass, and mesquite dotted the landscape like some haphazard connect-the-dots game. The sky was a blue-white so brilliant it seared the eyes if one looked too closely or too long. Taking to high ground, Caleb lay in the shade of a scraggly mesquite tree, his tongue lolling out the side of his muzzle. His gray and black brindle fur provided unique camouflage as he surveyed the flat valley floor below him. From this height, the rudimentary landing strip hidden at ground level was obvious.

Bored, he resisted the urge to chase a lizard that had tremulously crept too close. The little critter froze. When Caleb didn't move, it skittered off. The werewolf yawned and resisted the urge to lift his leg and nose in. He chuckled, though it came out as a whuffing growl. He remembered the first time he'd changed from wolf to boy and Sade's reaction. Sitting there on the edge of her bed, he'd glanced down at his lap, demurely hidden beneath a sheet.

"Ewww," his sister had sputtered. *"Don't even think about it!"*

At the time, he'd been far too embarrassed; his nakedness overwhelming and disorienting. No fur. No clothes. And that particular action was a comfort gesture for all canids. Besides, it felt good. He'd retorted that he could no longer reach that particular part of his anatomy. While other werewolves reverted to the habits of their wild brethren when shifted, he'd resisted, the look on Sade's face looming in his memory.

The wolf's ear perked at the low, droning whine of a small plane. His eyes tracked to the far horizon, focusing in on the tiny white speck. The dot grew larger as the sound got louder. Caleb momentarily lost sight of the plane as it flew map of the earth and dipped below the sandy hills to the south. Instinct had him crouching behind the mesquite tree, his ears flattened against his skull.

As he watched, the single-engine plane touched down and bounced along the rough landing strip. Caleb thought the plane was a Cessna, but all the markings had been removed, including the tail number. *Bad boys,* Caleb's human persona whispered in the wolf's brain. *The FAA is not going to be very happy.* The ruff on the back of his neck bristled as the plane slowed to a stop. An ancient military Jeep, its olive drab paint coated in the red and gray dust indigenous to this part of the desert, raced up out of an arroyo.

The pilot and the driver of the jeep spent about thirty minutes unloading wrapped bales from the baggage compartment and passenger area of the plane. The men conversed while they haphazardly stacked the bales in the jeep and a canvas tarp thrown over them and lashed down. The driver helped the pilot turn the plane then followed along side. At the far end of the runway, the jeep idled while pilot and driver got the plane turned around again, its nose pointed into the wind. Shading his eyes with his hand, the driver watched the plane take off, bank sharply, and disappear back over the sand cliffs to the south. The man climbed behind the wheel, put the jeep in gear, and headed out across the desert.

The wolf got up and stretched, his hips in the air, shoulders low, his nose between his front paws. Unless a rare desert rainstorm came along, he'd be able to track the jeep in his human form. With a desultory wag of his tail, Caleb trotted over the top of the low hill and headed down the other side. The rental was parked ass-in to a clump of cottonwoods holding on tenaciously near a dry stream bed. The wolf closed his eyes, concentrated, and a few moments later, with a loud popping of bones snapping back into place, Caleb appeared in his human form. Kneeling beside the Explorer, he took a few minutes to catch his breath and reorient. Wolf to man was not always seamless; the instincts and character of the animal overshadowed that of the human. Caleb rose from hands and knees to upright in one graceful move.

Popping the hatch on the back of the SUV, he snagged a plastic tub of wet wipes. Using several, he wiped down his whole body, depositing them in a plastic grocery bag. While the wipes didn't completely remove the smell of wolf, it did cut down on the wild muskiness left behind by the morphing. Cotton boxers, a pair of jeans, and a white tee shirt made him look human. He shrugged into a chambray shirt before sitting down on the edge of the cargo space to don socks and hiking boots.

Running his fingers through his wavy hair, he pretended he was presentable. Caleb settled sunglasses over his eyes to disguise the wolfish glow he knew would be visible to anyone who looked. Behind the wheel, he glanced in the review mirror. His hair was starting to curl along the hairline, making him grimace. At one time, back in the nineties, he'd let the natural curl have its way. He hated it now.

Pulling out of the draw slowly to keep down the dust, Caleb headed up and over the rise. Paralleling the rough runway, he followed as closely as possible in the tracks left by the jeep. Though the sun beat down relentlessly, Caleb left the windows open and didn't run the air conditioner. Periodically, he stopped, stuck his head out the window, and pulled a deep breath in through his nose. Satisfied his quarry wasn't too far ahead, he continued on. As the high desert began to flatten out, Caleb became more cautious, often parking the vehicle and getting out on foot to scout ahead.

One of those scouting trips led him to a cluster of run-down buildings. Lying flat on his belly, he watched for signs of life. A few minutes later, the Jeep he'd been trailing pulled out of a metal barn. The vehicle was empty of cargo. The driver pulled around to a shack and sat, the vehicle idling. A few minutes later, another guy exited the shack, climbed in, and they headed off vaguely in the direction of Albuquerque.

Caleb settled in to wait, as patient as the predator he was. An hour ticked by. Two. The Jeep was long gone and there'd been no activity around the place. Easing up to a crouch, he waited awhile longer. Nothing moved below him. He stood up, and using what cover was available, managed to get down to the barn without an alarm being raised. Caleb was a bit surprised there'd been no booby-traps. These drug runners were very sloppy, inexperienced, or cocky. Caleb snorted softly. Most likely, all three, he decided. He slipped along the side of the barn toward a hole where the tin siding had been bent back. There was just enough room for him to squeeze through.

The interior of the barn was lit dimly by sunlight filtering through holes and gaps in the metal room and sides. Dust motes danced across the shafts of light with every step Caleb took. He fought the urge to sneeze. Bales stacked in one corner reeked of marijuana. Bundles approximately the size of a cinder block, wrapped in plastic and duct tape, were stacked on a series of makeshift tables. He didn't have to cut one open to know it was cocaine. He prowled around but found nothing that would lead him to the missing boys. The sun was sinking in the westm, and the sky erupted into an artist's palette of purples, salmon pinks, and magentas. Caleb slipped out of the barn and checked a shed before approaching the ramshackle building that apparently provided living space.

The house wasn't locked so Caleb slipped in the back door. His nose wrinkled, and he gagged. The stench of lye, acetone, and iodine slammed into his olfactory nerves like a freight train. The kitchen was set up with all the paraphernalia needed for a working meth lab. With the overpowering odor of the chemicals hindering his sensitive nose, Caleb checked the rest of the small place. A living room with a ratty couch stumbled into a tiny bedroom. The bathroom was tinier still. Peeling linoleum on the floors and paint on the walls gave the place a tattered look. Caleb sniffed around but still couldn't detect any scent of werewolf pups. Standing at the bedroom window, he realized there was one more place to look. A battered truck with a homemade camper shell was parked beside the house.

Using his shoulder to prop the door open, Caleb slipped through it and trotted around the house to the truck. His nostrils flared but caught only the dry, acrid smell of mesquite and sand. The truck was a derelict, devoid of oil or gasoline. Caleb carefully peered through the dirty glass that passed for windows in the camper shell. The bed of the truck was stuffed with tarps, paint and paint thinner cans, and wads of paper trash, but no missing teenage boys. There was no sign of an ATV either.

Caleb checked his watch. It would be hard dark soon, and his headlights would be visible for miles. It was time to hit the road. He kicked at a pile of rags heaped around one of the flattened truck tires. The unmistakable odor of toluene wafted up. Caleb's eyes narrowed speculatively. He pulled an old Zippo lighter out of his front jeans pocket, flipped the top cover with his thumb, and stared at it. He flicked it once, and the flame flared to life as the spark from the flint met lighter fluid fumes above the wick. Caleb leaned down, and the flame licked hungrily at the rags. One smoldered, sending up a thin waft of greasy smoke, and then, like the flame before, it flared. Tongues of flame danced through the pile of rags and reached for the tire and the undercarriage of the truck. Tumbleweeds had gathered under the truck, and they blazed to life.

Without a backwards look, Caleb ducked into the house. A coffee filter with dried crystals in it flashed, shooting sparks to land among other combustibles on the wooden table. The whole place would explode in a matter of minutes. Unhurriedly, Caleb's loping stride took him back to the barn. He gathered up an armful of tumbleweeds, bunched them next to the dried bales of marijuana and flicked his Zippo. He stood there a moment, watching the hungry flames. As the first marijuana bale caught, Caleb turned and strode off into the gathering darkness. If the drug runners came back, they'd be too busy to follow him, even if they saw his lights.

Driving back toward Buhmfuch, Caleb allowed a contemptuous sneer as he watched the thick column of smoke rising just over the horizon. He figured he'd owe the DEA a few favors after this, but he wasn't too sorry those drugs would never hit the streets. Caleb checked his GPS, adjusted his direction and after a bit, he hit a secondary road. The Explorer's tires slapped against blacktop, grabbed and held, hauling the vehicle up onto the roadway.

Just over an hour later—Caleb had been delayed by a slow moving farm truck hauling hay—the lights of the TeePee glowed in his windshield. He pulled up in front of his cabin, climbed out, and locked the vehicle's doors. The lights in the office were out though the vacancy sign was stuttering off and on in the front window. The soft, ghostly glow of a television screen illuminated one of the back windows. His car was the only vehicle in the place. All senses alert, Caleb slipped up to his door, listened a moment, then slipped the key into the lock. He opened the door an inch and checked for the thread he'd attached up by the security chain. It was intact. Caleb pushed through the door and secured it behind him.

A few minutes later, he was in the shower washing off all the grit, grime and musk under the trickle of a shower. One of these days soon, he was going to head into Albuquerque, get a real hotel room, and spend an hour in a hot shower.

FOR THE NEXT TWO WEEKS, Caleb was out in the desert every day. He figured the kids had been discovered by the drug runners, since they'd been operating practically in the pack's backyard, and silenced. Some days Caleb searched as a man, some days as a wolf. On the days he was in wolf form, he noticed that he had company. He would often look up from quartering the ground for a scent to find a horse in the vicinity—the same horse. An old paint, roan and white, with tangled mane and tail and no halter came to watch him. The first couple of times Caleb didn't think much about it. The third time he looked up to find the horse standing about a hundred yards away staring at him, Caleb started to wonder.

The wolf morphed into man, but the horse didn't move. Tilting his head, Caleb stared at the animal. "You have a name?" he asked out loud.

The horse pawed at the ground, tossed his head, and nickered softly. The animal turned to stare off to the west. He pawed the ground again then turned back to stare at Caleb.

"Lassie you're not," Caleb groused. "Are you trying to tell me that Timmy's down the well?"

The horse tossed his head again, mimicking a human nod. Once again, he turned his head, nose pointing to the west.

Regarding the horse seriously, he sniffed the air, but his nose could detect no trace of the supernatural. He took a couple of steps closer, heartened when the horse didn't move. "Too bad you can't talk," he murmured.

Says who? A voice tinged with amusement echoed in Caleb's head.

Growling, Caleb shook his head. "Why didn't you say something?" He stared at the horse. "You got a name?"

His mind filled with rich laughter. *Aye, an' were ya never taught about the true power of names, laddie?* The horse whinnied.

"Oh, crap," Caleb mumbled, figuring out what the creature was. "Your kind is supposed to be extinct." He inhaled deeply again, finally caught the faint trace of ancient magic.

That brought another laugh in his head. *Aye, indeed, boyo. So we've led the world ta believe.*

"Ah...you want me to head west?" Caleb was more

than a bit skeptical. Pookas were known to lead the hapless traveler astray.

A deep rolling chuckle replaced the laughter in his head. *I'd not be leadin' another magick astray*, the pooka replied. When he spoke again, his voice was quietly no-nonsense with a hard edge and no trace of accent. *The humans went too far this time. The werewolves were young, and while wolves are seldom completely innocent, these had no misdeeds in their pasts.*

Caleb nodded slowly. "They're dead then?"

If it were possible for sadness to register on the face of a horse, that's the emotion that showed, though the pooka's eyes blazed angrily. *They are. Tortured first.* As the pooka spoke, his hoof pawed at the ground. *You will need your carriage to fetch the bodies. Their people will want to mourn them and send them back to whence they came.* He backed away a few feet and gestured with his head. *You will find them here*, the horse added, dropping his head and snorting softly at the earth his hoof had dug up. *Watch your back*, the pooka added.

Caleb nodded. "I will. Peace, horse," he replied.

The pooka tossed his head, pranced into a half-rear, turned, and galloped off to the south. Caleb waited, watching until the magick disappeared into a wavy heat mirage dancing off the desert surface. Then he waited a few more minutes before carefully padding barefooted over to the spot where the pooka had been standing. A drawing in the sand, every bit as clear as a printed road map, charted the trip for him, culminating with two small Xs.

Firmly fixing the map in his mind, he hunkered down and erased the drawn lines with the flat of his hand. Closing his eyes, he turned his focus inward, concentrated, and began the metamorphosis from man to wolf. His fingers and toes shortened, nails hardened and thickened into claws. His face elongated, jaw and nose lengthening into a muzzle. His ears, slightly pointed even in human form, grew and moved to the top of his skull. Fur sprouted through the pores of his skin, and his tail seemed almost to unfurl from his tailbone. In actuality, those bones simply lengthened, stretching to form the wolf's plumed tail. Caleb rolled his head on his neck, a quite human movement, and the bones popped into place. Tongue lolling slightly, he loped off in a ground-eating gait designed to get him back to his SUV in the quickest time.

When Caleb reached his vehicle, he reversed the process. This time, he didn't bother wiping down. This time, the more like wolf he smelled the better. He had a good idea what his reception would be when he brought the bodies of the two pups home. Unerringly, he drove straight to the area depicted on the pooka's map and stopped. The stench was overwhelming as he stepped out. Two blackened lumps lay about six feet from each other. Overhead, vultures circled, but none had dared approach the burned bodies. Reluctantly, Caleb approached, his nose filled with the scorched odor of burned fur, roasted flesh, and magical death. There was no doubt in his mind that he'd found to the missing teens.

With a heavy heart, Caleb hauled out the two plastic tarps he'd tossed into the cargo area of the SUV, just in case. Carefully wrapping a body in each one, he picked up the first and reverently carried the remains, stowing the bundle in the back. The second quickly followed.

Caleb made the drive back to the Johnson enclave in record time. He used roads when he could, but much of trip was made across open country. He occasionally crossed a barbed-wire fence line. If there was a cattle guard and gate, Caleb used it. If there wasn't, he cut the wires, drove through, and then repaired the cuts. This was cattle country. While much of it was open range belonging to huge ranches or local Indian tribes, one never left a fence down. Caleb made it back to Johnsonville, the name with which he'd tagged the packs' commune, just about sundown. Clouds had collected on the western horizon and the sky was ablaze with melting golds, vibrant burnt orange, and blood reds. In the east, the slim crescent of the moon rose, its pale, pearly-white opalescence almost lost against the stars popping out around it.

As Caleb pulled into the middle of the compound, Orrin Johnson strode out to meet the vehicle. Feet planted firmly his shoulder's width apart, meaty fists cocked on his hips, the man waited. Caleb stopped and wearily climbed out. More wolves trailed out of the shacks and campers and RVs until Caleb and the SUV were ringed by anxious faces. The odor coming from the back of the Explorer was unmistakable. A woman collapsed to her knees, wailing. The cry lifted to a mournful howl, raising the hair on Caleb's arms and neck. Not for the first time he regretted that Sade wasn't here to cover his back. He could feel in his bones there was a bad moon rising.

Evergreen, Colorado

"BAD MOON RISING. SERIOUSLY?" Technical Investigator Adele McCoy adjusted the radio and muttered. "Not in the mood for Creedence tonight." She'd been working late in the lab when the call came in. Evergreen Police Department had a crime scene that was above their pay grade. They were asking not only for investigative help from the Colorado Bureau of Investigation, but also for some expertise to process the scene. And that was her cue to go to work.

"I should know better than to answer the phone after hours," she groused to the October twilight. "If I hadn't answered, they would have tagged the on-call tech."

She was headed into the mountains, and because it was coming up on nighttime, she couldn't even enjoy the turning aspen leaves. The GPS in her Jeep droned out directions. She missed a turnoff, had to stop and back up before she could pull into the drive between massive stone posts. She applied the brakes and double-checked her notes. Yeah, this was the place.

Driving carefully up the winding road, Adele had to admit that she was impressed. First, the drive was concrete—the height of luxury for a rural retreat. Second, the views, even through the jaded eyes of a Colorado native, were stupendous. The house, located near the top of Clear Creek Canyon, had panoramic views of the Soda Creek valley and foothills. Hidden among majestic Ponderosa pines and aspen groves, the log home exuded rustic elegance and big money. The parking area closest to the house was clogged with a couple of police cars and a nondescript white Ford panel van.

Despite the incongruity of the vehicles out front, the house was a masterpiece of logs and glass. The fact it was new construction didn't diminish the impact. The place looked like it had been handcrafted by old-world craftsman. The drive circled beneath a portico, which was blocked by the van, but there was a pass around with just enough room she could squeeze the Jeep through. She pulled to the side of the drive and parked. Adele wasn't too surprised to find a local cop giving her an unfriendly glare as she stepped out, even though EPD had called CBI. He pushed right up into her personal space, cutting her off from her vehicle.

"Adele McCoy, Colorado Bureau of Investigation," she announced, fishing in her back pocket for her ID. She flipped open the case and showed the officer. The cop took her ID and read it carefully before comparing her picture. He actually held her ID next to her face. She bit back a retort, but then caught the name on the side of the white van. She'd thought it was the ME's. It wasn't. It belonged to a maid service.

"Please tell me you guys haven't released the scene!" She waved a hand toward the van.

"The cleaners are here. Mr. Parker's family asked that we let them in."

"What?" She screeched the word and had to fist her hands at her sides to keep from slugging the idiot. He ignored her outrage and handed back her ID but didn't move out of her way. Adele finally stepped back and sidled around him when he didn't back up. At the rear of the Jeep, she lifted the hatch and grabbed her kit. The cop followed her and she almost clobbered him in the head with the hatch before he moved away. "I'm here to process the scene," she explained.

"Why?" the cop asked suspiciously.

"Because it's my job." Adele snorted and performed an eye roll. She couldn't help herself nor could she help the muttered, "He can't seriously be this stupid." Slinging the bag over her shoulder, she turned on her heel and headed toward the front door, the cop hot on her heels.

As she approached, she let her gaze roam over the exterior making a quick assessment. Though the house appeared to be one-story despite the presence of dormer windows, Adele bet this floor had vaulted ceilings, and since the house was built on the edge of the ridge line, she suspected there was a lower floor built into the side of the mountain. The residence looked huge and she guessed it was in excess of 10,000 square feet. She didn't even want to consider what it cost.

"Five point six mill," the cop growled, as if reading her mind.

"Real 'Lifestyles of the Rich and Famous,' huh?" Adele tossed over her shoulder as she stepped up on the flagstone porch and approached the massive double doors made of an unfamiliar wood. She brushed her fingertips across the carvings and they tingled. *Alder wood,* a little voice whispered deep in her brain, but she had no clue how she knew that or why it mattered. One door swung open at her touch, and she stepped inside. The cop didn't follow her.

The interior walls were the same golden red as the logs used to build the house. The floors were polished marble laid in haphazard squares ranging in size from 18 inches to three feet. The foyer was small, simply a build-out with wide eyebrow windows to let in light. Within six steps, the place opened up to the soaring rafters of the great room. A natural stone fireplace and two-story windows dominated the opposite wall. On her left, an open staircase made of logs climbed to a large loft above. After looking again, she realized stone steps led down to the level below as well. The assumptions she'd made outside were correct. To the right, a dining room melted into the kitchen, a utility area, and the door to what she figured was a garage probably big enough for six vehicles. Beyond the stairs, the other wing of the house stretched out.

Adele could hear at least two women talking in the kitchen. Were these the maids? The top of a head was barely visible over the back of the large, overstuffed couch facing the fireplace. She walked over, her steps alternating between clicking on marble and being muffled by thick Persian rugs. The head she was stalking didn't move. Coming up behind the couch, she leaned over.

"Which way is the body?" she asked the cop sitting there. She had to cover her mouth to keep the chortle from escaping as the cop woke up, erupted off the couch, and tripped over the coffee table. He teetered for a moment, arms and one leg akimbo as he fought for his balance. The man finally got his limbs coordinated, righted himself, and turned to glare at her.

"You aren't supposed to be here. Get out," he ordered. "I'm going to skin Dykes,"

That got a raised eyebrow from her. "This is a crime scene." She flipped open her state ID. "I'm the technical investigator from CBI. Wanna explain why there's a cleanup crew at my unprocessed crime scene?"

The cop shook his head. "Not a clean-up team," he explained. "The regular maid service. I think."

"You think?" Adele rolled her eyes. Again. She couldn't process all the stupid. "Who called in the body?"

The guy shrugged, his brow furrowed as he taxed his brain. "Some female called it in. Said the vic didn't show up for dinner or something. She came out. Found him downstairs."

"Who was she?"

"Girlfriend. I think."

"There you go thinking again. Is your homicide guy here?"

"In the kitchen."

"Have any of you touched anything?"

The cop scratched his head. "Not the body. One of the gals made coffee for us. They're in the kitchen playing poker or something to kill time. We told 'em they couldn't leave."

Fighting her sigh, Adele said, "Just point toward where the body is, Barney, then you people can get back to doing whatever it is you're doing here. And don't touch anything!"

The cop pointed toward the stairs. "The study is downstairs." She walked off shaking her head. "Hey," the cop called after her retreating back. "My name's not Barney."

"Could have fooled me," she muttered. "The stupid, it burns."

Heading down the stairs, she was faced with a darkened hallway that served as an art gallery by the looks of all the paintings hung along its length. Adele wandered down the hall. She passed a room that could be used for cards or crafts or whatever really rich people did with rooms that had no real function beyond a repository for more furniture. The next room was a game room with a bar, pool table, and wet bar. The next door was cracked open.

Adele bumped it with her shoulder and looked in. She could smell death lingering in the air. Pushing on in to the office, she stopped just inside the door trying to get a feel for the place. A large desk fashioned from stripped pine logs sat angled in a corner so that the occupant could see both the outdoors through a wide window and the wood-burning stone fireplace. Overstuffed armchairs covered in coordinating Indian blanket prints ranged before the hearth. A chandelier and lamps made of deer antlers graced the ceiling and side tables. Wool rugs, reminiscent of Pendleton blankets were scattered haphazardly across the marble floor.

Her nose flaring at the rusted iron smell of human blood, she set down her kit and simply looked around. The suede desk chair, its back to the door, was a color the catalogs described as "palomino." The marble floor beneath the desk was gummy with a thick pool of blood, the edges starting to dry and crack. The desk was clear but for one piece of paper. She opened her kit and took out a pair of latex gloves. Pulling them on, she retrieved her camera and took photos. Leaving it hanging on a strap around her neck, she returned to the kit to grab a notebook with a pen stuck in the spine, a handful of biologic swabs, a Sharpie marker, and evidence bags.

Adele leaned over the desk from the far side to look at it and take a photo. Only one spot that was possibly blood stained the printed page, a computer generated receipt from a pawnshop with a Pueblo address. She made notes of the name, address. and phone number of the shop, slipped the paper into a bag, sealed and labeled it with contents, a number, and her initials. The voucher only listed an "Old Indian Artifact" as the item purchased, with no description. Weird.

She stepped around the desk, staring at the chair. The body hadn't been removed. Even having an idea of what she'd find, Adele wasn't quite prepared for this. Granted, the chief of Evergreen PD *had* mentioned the victim had been skinned, but she didn't anticipate the guy was speaking literally. She had to take a moment, her whole system temporarily shocked by the sight. She stared out the sliding glass doors, but she didn't really see the star-studded vista spreading out before her.

The quirky part of her brain that removed her from the immediacy of crime scenes eventually kicked in, noting the front side of the leather desk chair was no longer palomino. An interior decorator would describe the color as ox blood now. The pooled blood beneath the chair was undisturbed. No foot prints, no roller tracks. Huh. That meant neither the maids nor the local cops contaminated the scene.

How much blood would a human lose while being skinned? She thought it had to be more than what was here. The room appeared pristine. She wasn't a blood splatter expert by any stretch of the imagination, but she'd had the requisite courses and could make an initial assessment of a crime scene with a certain amount of confidence.

One of two things had happened—either Drew Parker had been dead when the skin was peeled from his body, or he'd been killed and skinned somewhere else before the body was deposited in the chair. This room did have an outside door to the back deck. And it was possible that the perpetrator or perpetrators, because she didn't believe one person could have done this, had cleaned up any blood trail from moving the body. A quick spray of Luminol would show what she needed.

Squatting down, she scoured the dark marble floor looking for splatter. Adele suddenly sat back on her heels as a terrible thought occurred to her. "Holy carp, Batman," she muttered. She grabbed her cell phone and hit a speed dial button. "Carl!" she barked, when her lab partner picked up. "Did the Parker file come in? Check the fax machine." She heard the phone receiver thump against the lab geek's desk, the faint shuffling of paper, and then a soft exhalation of air as he picked up the phone again.

"What am I looking for?" he asked.

She took a quick breath and asked. "Skin. Is there any mention of his skin?"

There was more rustling of paper and a series of hrms, haws, and a soft "That's interesting," before he spoke directly into the receiver. "Other than the complete absence of it, right?"

Adele nodded then remembered Carl couldn't see her. "Yeah. Parker was what, just over six feet tall?" Her brain tapped into her trivia retrieval file and came up with the fact that skin was the largest organ of the human body. The skin of an average adult covered about 3000 square inches and weighed approximately six pounds. She'd learned in her college human biology class that the skin received about 1/3 of the blood circulating through the body. She blinked and asked in a hushed tone. "Carl? What do you do with over six pounds of human flesh?"

Her question received a nervous laugh in reply. He finally spoke. "That's a rhetorical question, right? Because...uhm...I'm not Hannibal Lector."

"No," she mused. "No, you aren't. But, it wasn't completely rhetorical."

"Ewwww, Addie! Damn, girl. That's just...freaking gross. I swear your mind goes to the weirdest places sometimes."

She could tell Carl was seriously squicked and like her, he'd seen a lot during his tenure with CBI.

"Yeah, it is but... Where's the skin, Carl? Did the perp take it with him? And the skin accounts for 1/3 of the blood in the human system. Unless the desk chair is sopped with it, there's not enough blood here. Was he skinned somewhere else? Dammit, this scene is almost too clean for what supposedly happened here. How the hell do you skin a human and only have one drop of blood splatter in the room? There's blood in the chair and a puddle on the floor but..."

Her question was greeted by a long moment of silence. Carl finally cleared his throat. "Plastic tarps? I don't know. Give me a break here, Addie. You're the wannabe investigator, not me. I just look at the evidence, run the tests, and write the reports."

Adele snorted. "You know what your problem is, Carl? You have no imagination."

"I don't need an imagination," he retorted. "In fact, in this job, the less imagination the better. We deal in facts, Addie."

"There's nothing wrong with imagination and applying it to an investigation." Her voice heated as she made the declaration, and added, "And don't call me Addie. I hate that."

"Jacobson is headed your way."

"Crud. Is that the investigator who's assigned?"

"'Fraid so. Sorry, Addie."

"Argh, Stop it. Look, I need to go, Carl, so I can get finished here at Parker's house. I'll get back to Denver as soon as I can." She clicked off her cell before he could say more. Adele tucked her phone in a back pocket

After photographing the scene, bagging evidence, and determining with a spray of Luminol and a special filter on her Maglite that there was no trace on the floor that had been cleaned, she paused to survey the room again. When she looked up, Adele saw something she'd missed during her previous examination. On a shelf in the built-in bookcase next to the fireplace, a group of figurines collected dust. Curious, she walked closer to get a better look. The collection included clay figures, silver pieces, stone, even a crude painting on leather. Lizards. Everything on the shelf represented a lizard in some form or another.

A shiver skittered up her spine, skipping along each vertebra in her back. "Ugh," she murmured. She hated lizards. They skittered. On little pointy feet. And they shed their skin. Which creeped her right the heck out. Had ever since her high school biology class when one of the geckos had gotten out and shed its skin in her backpack.

Still creeped out, and with a great deal of reluctance, she turned her back on the display and moved into the hallway. She was convinced there was a secondary crime scene somewhere in the house. The master bedroom was her next stop. She met the transporters from the state ME's office on the stairs.

"You done, McCoy?"

"Yeah, though I'd double glove and have the body bag ready."

"That bad?"

"The vic's been skinned."

"Dude, seriously?"

"Seriously."

Back on the main floor, she turned toward the master bedroom. Her footsteps echoed hollowly as she paced to the end of the hall. The door was standing open so she stepped into the room. The covers on the bed were disheveled, but the rest of the room appeared to be in order. The western motif carried into this room as well. Like the great room, it had log-vaulted ceilings. The custom bed was made of stripped pine logs and looked big enough an NFL cheerleading squad could sleep comfortably.

This room, too, had a native stone fireplace, this one double-sided. Curious, she checked the master bath to make sure it was on the other side of the fireplace. It was. Limestone, wood, granite, and a soaking tub big enough to drown in made this room luxurious enough for a potentate. The bathroom was bigger than the living room in her apartment. It would make sense that Parker had been skinned in the tub or the limestone-lined shower after he was killed. Adele checked them both out closely. Nothing. This room was as clean as the proverbial whistle.

Back in the main part of the bedroom, Adele slowly turned in a circle looking for something that would set her gut to rumbling. But for the bed, the room was pristine, like a show house.

"Bingo!" She'd figured it out.

The vic didn't live there. The place looked staged, like a photographic spread in "Architectural Digest." Padding across thick flotaki rugs to the bed, she discovered the one thing out of place. A deck of playing cards tumbled across sheets that looked like satin but were twelve hundred count Egyptian cotton. All the cards but four were face down. The Ace and eight of Spades along with the Ace and eight of Clubs stared up at her. Only one word came to mind and it wasn't a word she said easily, but this time it burst out with no hesitation. "Fuck."

This was the poker hand that, according to legend, Wild Bill Hickok was holding when he was murdered in Deadwood, South Dakota. Aces and eights with, depending on who one asked, the nine of diamonds, the five of diamonds, or the queen of diamonds—the two pairs all poker players dreaded getting. Adele subscribed to the unofficial theory about Wild Bill's hand—that he had tossed one card to draw the fifth, but he was shot and killed before the fifth card was dealt.

What the heck was going on here? She was about to photograph the bed when the cop she'd left sleeping in the living room yelled.

"Yo, CBI! ME wants you downstairs."

"Yeah, yeah. On my way." She paused to snap a picture of the cards before stomping downstairs, wondering why the ME needed her. She found out quickly when she stepped through the door.

"You gotta see this!"

As Adele stared at the small pouch tucked between Drew Parker's thighs, she wondered two things—how had she missed it during her first examination of the body, and what the hell had this guy done to so totally piss off a person they'd do this to him. It was dreadful enough the bad-boy heir to the Parker fortune had been skinned but to have his testicles cut off and replaced by a bag of marbles? That was beyond harsh.

She couldn't meet the gazes of the two men standing with her. The ME's investigator was about to split a gut from holding in his laughter. Jacobsen, the assigned CBI investigator who'd finally arrived just looked pained. She didn't know what the deal was, but she would. She gripped the pouch with two fingers and tugged. It came free easily, and she reached into her kit for another evidence bag. With a deft flick of her wrist learned through constant practice, the bag popped open and she dropped the pouch in then folded the bag's top over several times. She grabbed the stapler she kept in her kit, and secured the bag before labeling it.

"Well, all righty then. I'll just get the evidence back to the lab."

Jacobsen called after her. "I want the reports ASAP."

CHAPTER SIX
MONSTERS

Colorado Bureau of Investigation Lab

JACOBSEN'S ASAP MEANT HIS PARTNER was waiting for her. The drive back to Denver had been uneventful but creepy. Adele couldn't put her finger on why. Well, she could—feelings of someone watching her, weird cold drafts washing across the back of her neck, the nagging idea that if she whipped her head around she'd find some specter looming in the back seat of her Jeep ready to pounce made for a white-knuckled grip on the steering wheel. The sun was peeking over the eastern plains as she lugged her gear from the parking lot.

She'd barely had time to unload the evidence and set up her work counter so she could process what she'd collected. The CBI agent standing there glaring at her didn't help her mood. At all. Who did he think she was? Evidence-R-Us? Did he believe she could just click "download" and the reports with all the right answers spewed out before she even started examining the evidence? Good grief. She was good, but she hadn't walked on water in...well...never. That would be her dad. Big Jim McCoy, the legendary homicide detective, the man who had a clearance rate of a hundred percent on his cases. Adele was pretty sure she was a big, fat disappointment to her old man.

But that was neither here nor there. Not today. She was good at her job, which was processing crime scenes and collected evidence. At the moment, she had a murder on her hands. Drew Parker was old money. The Parkers had ranched up and down the Front Range for over a hundred years. The family spawned a whole host of movers and shakers. And then there was Drew. In addition to the house in Evergreen, he had a residence in Aspen and another in Palm Springs, California, though "house" was mostly a misnomer when it came to describing his monster mansions. To describe Drew Parker as a spendthrift was almost too kind. And what was really sad? The guy was nice looking, though it was hard to tell in the crime scene photos. Of course, it was difficult to recognize it was a human body in that chair rather than a slab of meat.

Jacobsen's partner stood there pestering her about the pouch found between Parker's legs. She'd only started on the leather—most likely deerskin—bag, but she hadn't run any tests to find out exactly what the material was. The thing was so dried out and crusted, it was hard to tell, and she hadn't even opened it yet.

"Look, Daniels, I know this is a priority case." She glanced at the clock. "I'm working on twenty-four hours with no sleep. Do not push me. The reports get done when they get done. The more time you spend aggravating me, the less time I spend on the evidence. Now go away. I'll call Jacobsen as soon as I'm done." She crossed her arms over her chest and glowered when agent's eyes dropped. "Dude, my face is up here. Don't let the door hit you in the ass on your way out."

The door slammed behind the little jerk as she returned to the work table covered in white butcher paper. She had a procedure. And she never deviated from the order in which she processed evidence. Nothing got missed that way. Nothing got messed up. First things first. And that meant downloading the crime scene photos from her digital camera, sorting, labeling, and saving them to a disc to preserve chain of custody. After that was done, she could enlarge, enhance, and otherwise change the photos to see the minute details. While she might save those photos, she still needed the untouched originals so some scumbag of a defense attorney couldn't get the monster who'd done this off on some technicality.

By midmorning, she figured one more cup of bad coffee would strip off her stomach lining. Her eyes were gummy, her sight blurry. She desperately needed a nap. But first, she had to examine the last bit of evidence. She rubbed her eyes then pulled on a fresh pair of latex gloves. Tearing off a new piece of paper, she set the bag down in the center. The top of the bag had slits cut in it, and a leather drawstring with rough-cut, turquoise beads on the ends had been threaded through the holes. Adele hefted it in her palm, testing the weight of it before she dropped it on the scale for a precise measurement. She jotted notes with her free hand.

It took awhile, but she managed to loosen the knot without damage. Using her left index finger, she widened the opening as far as she could without destroying it, and shook out one the items inside. Instead of marbles like she figured, the thing that fell onto the counter looked vaguely like a bear crudely carved out of black shiny material that resembled ebony but was stone not wood. She held it up to the light and turned it every which way. Placing it on the paper, she grabbed her camera, photographing it and making notes on her computer. She would do this with each item in the bag.

Tipping the pouch again, a stone that looked like lapis lazuli fell into her palm. This one depicted a lizard. It quickly joined its brother on the counter. Ugh. She suppressed the fear clogging her throat with a giggle. Her disgust over lizards was totally irrational, but there it was. The next to drop out was a squiggly rock in a yellowish quartz-type stone. As it lay in her palm, it appeared to move. A little shiver skittered down her spine, and she hurriedly dropped the snake fetish next to the others.

Next came a turtle cut from a jade-like material. The fifth fetish was either a deer or an elk, carved from a brown and cream striated rock. Or maybe it was made from antler. She made a note to check the composition of each fetish. Holding that one up between her thumb and index finger, she studied it.

"Moose maybe?" she wondered aloud.

The last item wouldn't come out. With reluctance, Adele stuck two fingers into the blood-encrusted bag and fished for it. She finally snagged it and managed to pull it out. Carved from amber, there was no mistaking what animal this fetish represented. Dark eyes stared out from the wolf's face. She blinked. For a moment, she thought the wolf had blinked back. Carefully, and almost reluctantly, she set the fetish down.

The fetishes were somehow tied to Drew Parker's murder. There was just something about them—a creepy, heebie-jeebie something. Adele could feel their power even through latex gloves, but she hadn't felt anything when the stones were in the leather pouch. She tried an experiment in case there was some element in the stones triggered by exposure to light. Out of curiosity, she put the wolf back into the bag and inserted her index finger. As soon as the tip touched the fetish, it felt like she'd stuck it in an electrical socket. Strange. Removing her finger, she cupped the bag in one palm and used the same finger to poke at the wolf through the leather. Nothing. Even stranger. Leather seemed to block the effect. She needed to remember that.

She also needed to remember that she was approaching thirty-six hours with no sleep. Time to call it a day, get a good night's sleep, and tackle the question of the fetishes with a functioning brain. Sliding all the amulets back into the bag, she secured everything in the evidence bag and noted time and her initials. Sleep. She was desperate at this point. Time to call a cab because she'd fall asleep sitting at a stoplight if she drove.

The next morning, Adele pulled a leather work glove onto her right hand then fitted a latex glove over it. Okay, she might be overreacting, but while she'd slept for almost eight solid hours, she woke up feeling hungover with a nagging headache and wisps of remembered dreams leaving her chilled to the bone. She set up her work space and grabbed the evidence. Gingerly, she picked up the leather bag. It hadn't changed since the last time she'd looked at it. She set it down on fresh white paper. If the pouch contained any more trace evidence, she would find it.

Opening the sack, she carefully dumped the fetishes and poked them with her leather-sheathed finger. Nothing. She lined them up in the order they'd come out of the bag—bear, lizard, snake, turtle, deer, wolf. For a long moment, she stared at the wolf. While the other amulets were crudely wrought, the wolf was a work of art. He'd been finely carved with a sense of motion about him. She blinked and pursed her lips in thought. Him? None of the other idols gave her a sense of gender, but her gut rumbled and insisted the wolf was male. Physically, like a dog coming out of a pond, she shook off the hold the wolf seemed to have on her.

Carl looked up from the computer screen where he watched AFIS, the automated fingerprint identification system, compare prints she'd lifted at the Parker scene to those in the database. "Why do those things fascinate you so much, Addie? Are they haunted or something?" He laughed and rolled his eyes in her direction.

"Adele," she muttered under her breath then said louder, "You mean other than the fact they were stuffed in the crotch of a dead man? A dead man who was skinned and happened to be worth mega-millions." She hoped Carl picked up on the sarcasm.

He ignored her and crossed his eyes at her before returning to his own duties. Fine. She'd just ignore him back.

Turning her attention to the leather pouch, she stripped the gloves off, tore a new sheet of butcher paper, pulled on new latex, and picked up the bag. The victim's blood crusted it, stiffening and staining it. Patiently, she worked at the string, getting one knot untied so she could slip the turquoise bead off the end. With that task accomplished, she worked diligently on unlacing the drawstring. At some point Carl mentioned he was headed to an early lunch. She waved a distracted hand and continued working without looking up. The butcher paper was soon covered with rusty flecks—dried blood that would have to be collected and tested to make sure it all belonged to the victim.

Adele suppressed a shudder. Death and dead bodies didn't upset her. Like all good lab rats, she had long ago disassociated the body from the soul. The essence that made a person a "person" was long gone before she ever arrived on the scene. The husk left behind was simply evidence. Most people didn't get it. Most people thought she was cold and uncaring. Most people didn't last long as a forensic investigator if they didn't learn to make that distinction. This case was different though. She couldn't put her finger on the why of it, only that it was. There was a deep, dark something lurking out there just beyond normal perceptions and it gave her the willies.

Her computer dinged and a window popped open. Adele backed away from the counter, unwilling to turn her back on the amulets. Totally insane, but she just didn't trust them. She stripped off one glove and hit the accept icon on the Skype window. Adele smiled at the Indian-born forensic pathologist. "Hi, Dr. Jamnu.

What's up?"

"Hello, Adele. I have just finished the autopsy on Drew Parker. I will email my report, but there are facts you should know."

Uhm, okay? His serious expression and words both intrigued and worried her. "What did you find?"

"It is my professional opinion that the decedent was skinned alive."

She couldn't stop the shudder racing through her. "That's...wow."

"Yes. Wow in a very bad way. That is not all."

"It gets worse?"

"Yes."

"Ohh...kay?"

"I found no traces of cuts or nicks in the musculature."

"Uh... What does that mean?"

"Have you ever hunted? A large animal like a deer or elk?"

"No, but my dad does."

"Have you watched him skin an animal?"

"Yeah. He slits the hide down the middle of the belly and then sort of shaves it off the muscle with a sharp skinning knife."

"Yes. This is what I expected to find. Marks from a skinning knife."

Adele's brain caught up to what the doctor was implying. "Wait! Are you saying...what are you saying?"

"I believe the decedent's skin was removed in one piece, like one would peel a glove off a hand."

She couldn't wrap her head around what the doctor just said, but her gut did, and that last cup of coffee was not going to stay down. She bolted for the cleanup sink and emptied her stomach. Rinsing her mouth and spitting, then washing her face, she returned to her computer. Dr. Jamnu waited patiently, looking unsurprised by her precipitous exit.

"I'm sorry, Doc."

"Do not distress yourself. Several of us had the same reaction."

"Who does something like that?

"A monster."

CHAPTER SEVEN
DEATH IS A DIALOG

New Mexico Desert

MONSTERS. CALEB HAD MET his quota of them in his life and a fair share of them had been human. But this? Incinerating the two juvenile werewolves twisted him up. He wanted to turn feral, to hunt, to taste the blood of the creature that did this. Their deaths were needless and cruel.

Death and dying was not something Caleb normally contemplated on any given day. Contrary to pulp fiction, most werewolves led exemplary, if long-lived, lives. They grew up. They held jobs—most of the urban wolves anyway. They mated and had children. And they turned furry occasionally. They didn't kill humans. Usually. And they didn't think about death. Old age would eventually cut them down, as would more violent means. Wolves weren't immortal, but as a species, they were close enough that death wasn't a specter that dogged their trail.

Bringing those two kids back to their pack was one of the hardest things he'd ever done. And he didn't mean in terms of his own personal safety. True, his position was a bit tenuous at the moment because he was a pack outsider. Orrin went on the offensive, rallying his troops to go on the warpath. There had been a couple of older, cooler heads hanging back on the fringes who would talk some sense into the buggers once their hot blood cooled a bit. He'd told the Alpha he didn't know who had done it. The two drug runners Caleb followed and put out of business were involved, but there had been other scents as well. Two more

64

humans and some...*thing* he couldn't quite put his nose on.

That other scent was illusive—like a magical spell, but not. Spells had their own aromatic signature. And there was the cloying stench of magical death clinging to both bodies overlaying everything else. That burnt-fur acrid odor of ozone, the rotten eggs of sulfur, and a waft of copperhead snake nest, a stench immediately recognized by the spoiled cucumber smell. Like spells, magic practiced by the various races carried its own odor to the discerning nose. Just like a wine connoisseur could describe the bouquet and vintage of a good bottle of wine, a magick with a good nose could similarly discern the same about a spell.

When Caleb got a whiff, he knew who did the casting if he was familiar with the magick involved. If the spell caster was unfamiliar, he could tell what "ingredients" were used, like eye of newt, hair from a dead mandrake, that sort of thing. Only mumbo-jumbo touchy-feely fluff-bunny wannabes looked for and tried to conjure with such, turning their spells into a joke. Like the Nike commercial, real magicks "just do it."

A spell's odor depended on its use. Glamours smelled like the species. All magicks had a scent. Werewolves? They smelled like the outdoors—moldy leaves, juniper, fresh air with an underlying musk that is a dead giveaway. Vampires smelled of deep loam and the ocean, like tangy salt air. They didn't smell reptilian or like death at all. Why should they? They weren't dead...well, even though technically they were, they didn't smell dead. Walking in on a three-day old corpse? Yeah, to a werewolf death smelled like that, even moments after the event. Vampires didn't carry that stench.

Gargoyles smelled like old buildings—granite and dust, dry and slightly acrid but with a rich underlay there, like ripe grapes. And then there were the Fae. Just thinking about them made him sneeze. Werewolves were allergic to faerie dust. Fae left it everywhere they went. If a person could get past that, they smelled sort of...sweet. Like lilacs and rain but with the cloying, too-sweet scent of dying roses.

Caleb had a refined nose when it came to magic and spells. Once he traced a spell back to its caster, he was like an elephant. He never forgot that particular scent— or stench if that happened to be the case. And bad magic stunk like a pile of corpses with all sorts of other nasty odors thrown into the mix.

So he'd brought the boys home and got slobbered on by their mother while their dad pumped his hand. Orrin thumped his chest and vowed revenge. Mimi gave him the eye while all that went on, and he figured the little gal was looking to finagle another trip to the mall. Surprisingly, the Alpha remembered to pay him the rest of his fee. Before he got the bright idea to hire him to find whoever had killed the boys, Caleb got a call. Between the teens and that phone conversation, he found himself thinking about death on the drive to Colorado.

Caleb figured death was why the magical races couldn't reproduce with humans, and didn't often reproduce even with their own kind. The Universe, as fickle and absurd as it sometimes was, figured that one out. If magicks reproduced like humans, the whole place would be overrun, not that humans weren't doing a fairly good job of that anyway, but at least they died. The magicks stuck around for centuries sometimes.

As a kid, Caleb wanted to know everything about the magicks. Living in the household of master vampire Mathias DeVries didn't teach him to curb his curiosity. He got up his nerve one night to ask Aunt Polly why vampires didn't go around turning all their minions.

She'd been nipping brandy and was feeling garrulous. Aunt Polly's real name was Apollonia. Caleb didn't know if she had a last name. When she said she was older than dirt, he believed her. She was.

He'd discovered the ancient vampire in the front parlor one night and, as she had her tea cup of brandy-laced blood in her lap, he figured he didn't have much to lose by asking. She explained that if a vampire turned a human, the sire became responsible for his scion—forever. Literally. That would be like getting stuck in a bad marriage for eternity. He couldn't imagine anything worse. In addition, there was that whole power thing. Vampires were nothing if not arrogant. Caleb figured Judy Collins wrote "You're So Vain" not for Warren Beatty, but for a vampire.

The long ribbon of highway stretched to the horizon and Caleb couldn't stop the endless loop playing in his head. Peopled died, human people anyway. He understood why so many magicks refused to get involved with them. Death hurt. Just ask Bear Montoya's son. Well, not death so much as the act of saying goodbye. Werewolves only lived the equivalent of two or three human life spans. Vampires? Gargoyles? The Fae? They could live millenniums. How many humans did those magicks mourn in the course of their lifetimes?

How would he ever say goodbye to Sade when the time came? They would grow old together. Sort of. He'd eventually hit about fifty in human appearance and would look such until well past a hundred. Sade would continue to age, eventually grow old, and die. The only alternative was for Mathias to change her. Caleb didn't see a snowball's chance in hell that would happen. Mathias wouldn't do it. Sade wouldn't ask.

Yeah...Caleb could see why so many magicks had nothing to do with humans. And he understood why so many magicks became remote and uncaring.

After hours on the road, he hit his next stop—Pueblo, Colorado. He checked into a no-tell motel, found a diner that was open all night, and settled in with a good book—Dashiell Hammet's "The Thin Man"—and the blue plate special. The waitress flirted with him, but she flirted with everyone. Her voice sounded like tires on a gravel road. Her constant smoke breaks out in the alley probably had something to do with it. He didn't care so long as she kept his coffee cup filled.

Just after midnight, the last magick in the world he figured to see slid into the booth across from him. Caleb was there to meet someone, he just didn't expect Ariel. The King's Seducer was traveling far afield.

"Mutt."

"Glitter."

They stared at each other while the frowzy waitress sidled up to flirt and get Ariel's order. Caleb figured under normal conditions the fae would be considered handsome. He was too pretty for werewolf tastes. After the woman returned with tea for Ariel and moved off, Caleb leaned back, one arm draped over the back of the booth, looking for all the world like he was at ease. He wasn't. He and Ariel had a long and storied history, dating all the way back to Sade's sixteenth birthday.

Ariel opened the conversation. "I must admit you are the last person I expected to see here."

"Gotta say the same."

"I rather thought Sade would be on this case."

Caleb's instincts went into overdrive, but he didn't give anything away. "Why?"

"Given the nature of what was taken and the extremes to which those who lost these items are willing to go, I thought the FBI would send their best."

Yeah, he was definitely at a disadvantage here.

Director Bailey was going to get an early phone call once this meeting was over. "Nice try, fae. I can only figure you're here to seduce some poor woman."

A flicker of emotion flashed across Ariel's face. If Caleb didn't know the fae better, he'd figure it was hurt feelings. Nah, no way. The King's Seducer, and his reputation, had skin as thick as a gargoyle's.

"I am only here because an Anasazi shaman requested a favor from Oberon."

"You know anything about a pooka living in the New Mexico desert?"

"Why are you changing the subject, Mutt?"

"Because pookas, shamans, fae, and werewolves shouldn't have anything in common."

"You have a point."

"I usually do."

For the next hour, the two of them exchanged information. A pouch of magical items had been stolen from the Anasazi—a magical race born of the human realm, like the werewolves. In the wrong hands, the theft did not bode well for humans and magicks alike. Ariel didn't know what the items were or how they worked, only that they contained blood magic, were therefore dangerous, and in the wrong hands, very bad things would happen. Caleb explained about the two dead werewolf pups and the call sending him to Pueblo to see a pawn broker about a sale.

Ariel finished a piece of hot apple pie a la mode and leaned back. "Is she doing all right?" Caleb's snarl didn't surprise him. Ari would be the first to admit he and the werewolf had a love-hate relationship that centered on Sade Marquis. They both loved the human in their own way, and Ari was enough of a trickster that he enjoyed pulling the werewolf's tail when it came to Sade.

"She's fine. Stay away from her, and you'll stay fine too."

"Why not admit you love her and wish to get between her creamy thi—" Ariel didn't get the chance to finish the tease before Caleb's fist slammed into his face. Had he been human, he'd be dead. Instead, he had a bloody nose and cut lip. He retaliated by laughing.

"Shut up, Ariel. Yeah, I love Sade, but she's—"

"She's what?"

"Family. Something you can't understand. Sade's like my sister."

Ariel ignored the regret shimmering through him. He'd had a sister. Once. Before she tried to kill him. Family loyalty was a foreign concept in the Seelie Court of the Fae Realm. He pressed paper napkins to his face until the bleeding stopped. By the time he walked out of the diner, he'd be healed. Only iron could inflict serious injury or permanent damage to a fae. He leaned forward and lowered his voice.

"I love her too, Caleb." He held up his hand, cutting off the werewolf's retort. "Don't you think I know how special she is? How important she is to all the realms? I would lay down my life for her, just as you would. As would Roman. As that pesky dragon would."

Caleb rolled his eyes at the mention of Nikos Constantine, Drakon of the Kholikikos Dragon Clan. "Is that jackass still sniffing around her?"

Ariel laughed and nodded. "He sends her jewelry."

"No. Seriously? Jewelry? Sade?" Caleb's laughter snorted out. "I need to call her and give her shit about that."

"Yes, yes, you should. We both know the way to her heart, but it is amusing to watch the dragon stumble around like the love-sick wyrm he is."

"Yeah. You want to win Sade over? A bag of rare coffee. A rare antique pistol. A rare steak."

"And not necessarily in that order." Ariel met Caleb's gaze, and both of them burst out laughing.

70

"I'm really glad we had this dialog, Glitter."

"Back at you, Mutt."

"You coming to the pawn shop with me in the morning?"

"Alas, no. I must return to Las Vegas. I am simply the messenger." Ariel stared at Caleb, wondering if perhaps—a millennium from now—they could be friends. "Caleb, a word of warning. Whatever power is stirring is not to be trifled with." He took a chance and reached across the table to grip the werewolf's forearm. "I would not see Sade weeping over your good-for-nothing carcass." He added a twisted grin to take any perceived sting from his words.

"That's a two-way street, Ari. For some stupid reason, she likes you. Take care." Caleb should feel strange at the words, but he didn't. He didn't respect the fae warrior, but he liked him. A little. Or maybe it was the other way around. He respected Ariel but hated his guts. Either way, he could live with that.

CHAPTER EIGHT
THE MISSING PIECE

CBI Lab
"I CAN LIVE WITH THAT."

Adele glanced over at Carl to discover he was on the phone. He looked her way and rolled his eyes. His girlfriend must be making ultimatums about his RPG games again. The man spent hours with the on-line role-playing games. Returning her focus to the paperwork spread out on the counter, she stared at the page she'd been reading. She wasn't sure she could live with the conclusion made by the ME. Dr. Jamnu's report on Drew Parker still made her queasy. Like a magician pulling a tablecloth off leaving all the dinnerware in place, someone—some *thing*—had peeled Drew Parker's skin from his body. She'd seen a lot of horrific stuff in her career, but this case? This case was different. She could feel it in her bones.

She cut her eyes to the end of counter where she'd left the fetishes. Startled, she stared at them, wracking her brain. Hadn't she put the wolf down at the end of the line—the end of the line farthest from her? She blinked, shaking her head. Nope. The wolf was still closest to her. She rolled her eyes at her own folly and returned her attention to the leather pouch. With the drawstring removed, she discovered the pouch was almost a perfect circle. She carefully flattened it out on the butcher paper and measured. Just a tad over 12 inches across, the inside was almost as smooth as the outside.

Whoever had made the pouch had worked the rough side of the deerskin to smooth it. Adele took a marker and, careful not to touch the edge of the leather, drew the outline of it on the paper then photographed it. As an afterthought, she photographed the row of stone fetishes, too. Setting aside the camera, she snagged a biological sample kit. Taking the swab out, she dampened it with distilled water from the plastic squeeze bottle in her case. She rubbed the swab across the inside of the bag to get a sample. With well-rehearsed precision, she packaged and labeled the swab then put it aside. She'd run it over to the bio testing lab later. The bio lab did all of the DNA, blood and tissue typing, and hair sampling.

As a technical investigator, Adele's job was to process the evidence, not necessarily run lab tests on them. That was left to the chemists and biologists on staff. Once the results were known, the reports all came back to her, and she interpreted them in light of all the evidence and the crime scene itself. That analysis was a part of the job she did very, very well.

Using only her thumb and forefinger, she picked up the flattened pouch by one edge and turned it over. Reaching for a magnifying glass, she studied the outside of the bag, first by letting her practiced eye view the whole of it followed by a meticulous examination of it. The longer she stared at it, the more certain she became that there was something hiding beneath the blood. She picked up the leather piece again and shook it gently. More specs flaked off. She did this several times to make sure all the dried bits of blood had loosened and come off. Carefully holding the leather circle in her palm, she used her feet to propel her wheeled stool down the length of the counter to the group of microscopes sitting at the end of it.

Guiding the leather onto a microscope's stage, she pushed her glasses up on top of her head. Bending over the eyepiece, she adjusted focus with one hand while the other worked to adjust both an overhead light source and the microscope's illuminator. She could barely make out something beneath the blood, but there was a pattern of some sort that looked too deliberate to be a natural enhancement of the leather. Kicking her stool back down the counter, she grabbed a handful of bio kits and the bottle of distilled water. With the pouch still draped across the microscope's stage, she meticulously worked to remove the blood from the pattern, stopping to preserve and label each swab with utmost precision.

Adele didn't look up until her stomach growled. She tried to raise her head, but the crick in her neck locked her in place. With a groan, she pushed away from the counter so she could begin a series of stretches designed to loosen tight muscles and crimped vertebrae. Eventually, a loud snap followed by a crackle and a pop allowed her to raise her head. The big clock on the wall indicated it was 5:30. She groaned again. She tended to get lost in her work, but not like this. Her body urgently reminded her that she needed food, something to drink, and a bathroom, though not necessarily in that order. She trotted to the ladies room down the hall from her lab. Her gait wasn't very lady-like due to the urgency of the matter.

Entering the stall, she realized she still wore gloves. She peeled them off, turning them outside in just in case trace evidence remained. She dropped the gloves in the wide pocket of her lab coat. While washing her hands, Adele stared at her reflection in the mirror. She was pushing thirty, but tried not to think about the birthday looming in a couple of months. A natural blonde with blue eyes, she'd received a sprinkling of freckles from her redheaded mother. She blinked myopically before settling the black-framed glasses shoved to the top of head back onto her nose. She shrugged at her reflection. Her cheekbones were too high, her jaw too strong to ever be considered pretty. She wore her hair either in a tight braid or bunched up in a semi-messy clump held in place by an alligator clip. Down and loose, her hair kissed the bottom of her shoulder blades. She didn't go to a hairdresser. She told herself it was a waste of time and money. No one ever paid attention to her looks. She couldn't remember the last time she'd had a date because she'd given up. Her previous dates followed a pattern—the guy's reaction to her career, followed by a quick end to the evening, and no call back.

She could live with that because she liked her job. And she was good at what she did. Squaring her shoulders, she headed back to her office. She would put everything away, take the bio samples down to the lab, and check out for the night. She was craving a big steak, medium rare, with a loaded baked potato. She also wanted a margarita on the rocks with extra salt, but since she was her own designated driver, that wouldn't happen. Adele pushed through the door and headed back to her work area in the far corner. Her eyes swept the area, assessing what needed to be done so she could leave for the night. She noticed the fetishes first thing. Every last one of them was sitting in the circle she'd drawn on the butcher paper.

"Dammit, Carl," she barked. "That's not funny!" Her voice echoed in the empty room. Adele tried to ignore the fear ricocheting up and down her spine. Turning on her heel, she retraced her steps and grabbed the logbook by the door. Checking it, she realized that Carl had logged out at 1630—over an hour before. That persistent unease raised the hair on her arms.

"Okay…" she murmured to herself. "Haven't eaten today. Low blood sugar. Lack of sleep. My mind is playing tricks on me. That's all. I must have moved them. Yeah. That's what I did. I moved them to the circle to keep track of them."

She smoothed down the hair on her forearms with the palms of her hands then went to work. She pulled on a fresh pair of gloves, stuffed the ones in her pocket in a bag and marked it as evidence then gathered all the bio kits she'd used on the pouch. She covered the microscope, leaving the leather pouch in place on the stage. That would be her first task in the morning— mapping and photographing those lines she'd uncovered. Grabbing a small, brown paper sack, she started to scoop up the fetishes. Hesitating a moment, she snagged the leather glove, pulled it on, and then pushed the stones off the counter into the sack. She folded down the top, sealed it, and marked it with time, date, her initials and made note of the contents. She carefully rolled up the butcher paper covering the counter, bagged, and labeled it as well. She slipped out of her lab coat, hung it on a hook on the wall, grabbed the evidence sample carrier, and headed for the door.

Adele followed her check-out routine scrupulously, locking the door behind her. With purposeful strides, she headed down the hallway to the stairwell. The bio lab was one floor down and skipping down the stairs took less time than waiting for the elevator. She hip-bumped the push bar on the fire door to the stairwell and ducked through. This time of day, the stairs were dimly lit by emergency lighting, but she skipped down them with the assurance of someone who had made this trip hundreds, if not thousands, of times.

Jamie, the on-call bio tech, sat at his desk, feet propped up, watching a baseball game on the small TV set near his desk. She dropped the evidence carrier into the in basket and tilted her head to see who was playing. "Boston?" she snerked.

The lab tech offered a crooked grin. "Rockies don't play until later. Besides, I've got Big Papi on my fantasy team." He nodded toward the In-basket. "Those a rush?"

She nodded. "It's the Parker murder. Probably going to be his blood, but there's lots of samples just in case somebody else bled at the scene. If you can bump it up over regular rotation, I'd get the local LEOs and those jerks up on eight off my back." Regular rotation meant "first in-first out." Techs normally didn't deviate from that, but with a high profile case—and this one was, sometimes evidence got preferential treatment. Adele headed out but paused at the door. "Oh...before I forget. There's another sample in there. Came off a leather pouch. It's probably deerskin, but if you can manage some indicators to prove what critter the leather came from, I'd appreciate it."

"No prob," Jamie replied, obviously distracted as his player came up to bat. "I'll put 'em on to cook before I head home tonight.

"Thanks, Jamie." She headed out, shutting the lab door firmly behind her. This time, she headed to the elevators and punched the down button. A few moments later, the elevator doors slithered open and she stepped in. She was alone. She stabbed the button for the ground floor as the doors whispered shut. She was missing something. Something important. Maybe talking to an expert would help. Like a professor. She mulled that idea over. A trip to Colorado State University might be in order. CU was closer, but she was a CSU alum and maybe someone in either the art or anthropology department could supply the missing piece.

CHAPTER NINE
MAGIC IN THE AIR

THE MISSING PIECE? Adele hung up the phone and stared at it as if it were a dancing cobra about to strike. This was not the puzzle piece she expected and was definitely one she didn't want. Her eyes skittered to the pouch sitting on a fresh piece of white paper in the middle of her desk.

Carl breezed through the door, humming the Kansas song, "Dust in the Wind." He took one look at her face and stopped in his tracks. "Yo, Addie! You look like you've seen a ghost."

"Adele," she reminded him sharply, glancing up for only a moment before her eyes were pulled back to the pouch. "And I may have," she murmured.

Her lab partner snorted. "No such things as ghosts, girl." He sauntered over and hitched one hip on the corner of her desk. "Are you still messing around with that thing?" His reached over, grabbed it and bounced the bag in the palm of one hand. "Feels like shriveled up old balls," he joked, juggling it between his hands.

Adele's eyes widened in horror. She snatched the pouch in midair. "God, Carl. You have no idea!" she yelled. "Do you have any clue what this bag is made of? Do you? No. You don't." She clamped her mouth shut and forced a deep breath into her lungs to stem the rising hysteria. It took several before she could get a grip. "That pouch is made of human skin." She shuddered, dropping it onto her desk. The leather sack made a soft plop at it settled. "Human skin. Flayed off, dried, and made into this thing."

Carl's eyes widened and he look green around the

gills. "Oh, hell, Addie. That's not the vic's skin is it?" He stood up and backed away from her desk.

Shaking her head, she continued to stare at the pouch, completely horrified. "No. DNA lab checked. They said it might be at least a thousand years old. Maybe older. Like Mayan or Incan old."

He ran to the sink and scrubbed his hands. "Why didn't you tell me to glove up before I touched them? That's just fricking sick," he sputtered.

She nodded. "Yeah. You can say that again. And you didn't give me a chance. You just marched in here and snatched it up. Besides, you should know better. It's evidence." She managed to jerk her eyes away from the pouch to glance over at him. "You're going to think I've wigged out, but...I swear..." Adele took a deep breath. "I swear those things, the fetishes...there's something about them that's just...wrong."

Carl stared at her. "What do you mean wrong? What could be more wrong than the fact they're in a bag made of human skin?" He shuddered again.

She gulped in air and muttered something under her breath. "I swear I'm not crazy, but whenever I touch one of the fetishes, it's...it's like I get a shock or something. Like an electric buzz."

Furrowing his brow, he stared at her. "Nope." He sounded insistent and still watched her with a troubled expression. "That's just...that can't be. They're rocks, Addie. Just rocks." His eyes were drawn to the bag despite himself. "Just stupid, old rocks wrapped in...what they are wrapped in. It's your imagination, girl. That's all. Your imagination and this crazy case."

She was angry enough she ignored the diminutive of her name without rejoinder. "I know they're rocks, Carl. But I'm telling you, there is more to them than meets the eye!" She wanted to throw something at him. Like her fist. "Or the microscope," she added sarcastically.

She was a scientist. There was no room in her world for magical mumbo jumbo or weird things that went bump in the night. Those spooky sounds were just old pipes or creaky floors or the building settling on its foundation. And cold breezes meant bad insulation. Of course, since the Big Rip, humans had discovered they weren't the top of the food chain and unseen things were suddenly seen.

The Rip had been a shock to her system. The day after, she'd watched with avid curiosity as the President appeared in his true form, speaking live on all the TV stations. An elf. With pointy ears. Rhys Wynn, an honest-to-god elf, was the duly elected president of the United States. What a revelation that had been! But there wasn't much different about him other than those pointy ears and eyes that did a weird glowing thing occasionally. And he'd been reelected to a second term. The other party claimed voter fraud, of course. They went to the Supreme Court demanding the results be tossed out on the grounds magicks had bewitched the majority of the population into voting for one of their own.

Their argument didn't get very far because, about that time, they discovered the majority of their political war chest had been funded by magicks. They abruptly shut up and sat down. Since then, most normal people got used to the idea of magic in the air. A fundamentalist "pure human" group evolved and protested against the magicks. While not a fundamentalist, Adele had not embraced those races who fell through the rip in the Veil. She'd grown up with a grandmother who claimed to see *The Others*—ghosts, little people, space aliens. Her father, all law-and-order no-nonsense cold logic, had simply written the woman off as being senile, crazy or both. As a child, she'd loved listening to her grandmother's stories but as a teen, she'd cringed. The old lady lived with them and Adele's friends often teased her about the fanciful stories Nana told.

After the Veil ripped, she didn't know what to think. Nana had died before the magical races were unmasked. She'd often wondered if her grandmother actually had the sight or if she had been some poor deluded crazy lady talking to shadows just to hear her own voice. New laws had come out and new techniques for investigating magical crimes were developed, though it meant local jurisdictions turned their cases over to the Feds. That idea didn't sit well at all. This was her case, though she would admit that it technically belonged to the Evergreen Police Department and the CBI agent assigned to the case. She hoped Carl would keep his mouth shut. If the chain of command didn't get a whiff of magic, they wouldn't call the Feds.

Adele glanced at the pouch, grateful it hadn't moved. Every time she held them in her hand—bare skin to stone—her palm tingled. She knew she shouldn't touch them without gloves. Evidence, d'uh. But there was just this compelling pull no one else seemed to notice. Carl handled them like they were a kid's marbles. Or had before her revelation about the pouch.

She weighed her options, figured the time had come to talk to an expert. She glanced at her watch, grabbed the CD she'd burned with pictures of the fetishes and signed out. Carl never even looked up. That was good. What he didn't know wouldn't come back to bite either of them in the ass.

ADELE EASED BACK ON THE ACCELERATOR. She'd just wasted a trip to Fort Collins to meet with a bunch of professors—none of whom had any clue about her evidence. The brown bag containing the fetishes rode shotgun and she unleashed her frustration on them. She was going to get fired. She just knew it. When she left the lab earlier, all she'd had was the photo CD. Until she walked into the Anthropology Department and discovered the fricking pouch in her jacket pocket. If anyone found out she took evidence from the building without checking it out, she'd not only be fired, but she'd never work in forensics again.

Was she losing her mind? She still had no clue how it had gotten into her jacket pocket. She certainly hadn't put it there. The cold, logical part of her brain was still looking for a logical explanation for the occurrence even as it worried with the idea that someone would discover what had happened. If that occurred, either the evidence would be suppressed if the perpetrator was ever caught or, more likely, she'd be terminated. Getting fired from her dream job did not sound like a very appetizing idea. What magic did those damn "devil" stones have?

They were significant to the investigation. She knew that deep in her gut. Yet every time she tried to find out what they were or where they came from, she met with a dead end. Talk about a wild goose chase. She'd driven up to Fort Collins to talk to any professor in the anthropology department who had time then ended up talking to all of them. They were no help.

Neither were the cultural history professors, anyone in the art department, or the Native Student Association. Of course, she didn't show anyone the actual fetishes, just the evidence photos. One Ph.D type identified them as Apache. Another insisted they were Old Pueblo. One of the art professors complained Adele was wasting her time as they were crudely rendered modern pieces meant for the tourist trade and more than likely had been made in China—or maybe Mexico. She declared them made of plastic and scolded Adele for wasting her time.

Dr. Gardenhire, from the Cultural History Department, asked if he could see them in person. His eyes held an odd gleam when he saw the pictures, and Adele caught him caressing his computer monitor with a fingertip. She made an appointment for him to come down to Denver to see them. That was before she realized the damn things had jumped into her pocket for the road trip. Still, something about the man put her off a little so she was glad she didn't discover the pouch until she was already headed home.

Sitting in her apartment, she stared at her jacket, which was hung over the back of a chair. The pouch was still in the coat's pocket. The fetishes did weird things when they were out of the bag. They moved. Especially the wolf. Why was he so lifelike and the others appeared so crude? Her fingers itched to pull the wolf out and hold him in the palm of her hand.

Wait...What did Professor Gardenhire say? The snake. It was the picture of the snake he petted. He talked about the jewels in the eyes and how intricate the designs were on the thing's back. What was up with that? She'd have to ask him to clarify what he meant when he arrived. Surely he was talking about the wolf. When she looked at the wolf, his eyes gleamed. Oh, all right, she admitted. They sparkled, almost as if they were set with some sort of topaz, but she knew they weren't.

The darn things were just creepy. But why was she the only one who seemed to notice? Carl had handled them, not as much as she had, granted, but still. The ME's investigator touched them at the scene. Jamie in the bio lab. Jacobsen. No one, not one single solitary blasted one of them said anything in their reports about the fetishes being electric to touch.

She was positive the things were American Indian.

And old, despite what that art teacher said. They weren't stamped out of plastic in some third world slave factory, just a mass-produced item shipped to America for the tourist trade. And the leather pouch. Soft and supple and cut and made by hand and old. Really *really* old. And made of human skin. That was just freaking creepy all by itself.

She needed to find out everywhere these things had been. Where did Drew Parker get them? They were tucked between his legs, the pouch soaked in his blood, when he was found. They were significant. She just knew it. That rumble in her gut wasn't because she forgot lunch, and it was way past time for dinner.

Okay. She had a plan. Sort of. Tomorrow first thing she would call both the EPD homicide detective and Jacobsen to get more information. If push came to shove, she'd make the trip out to Parker's place to search his records. There would be a paper trail on the fetishes and she was bound and determined to find it. Oh, shoot. She'd already forgotten. That lame Dr. Gardenhire was coming tomorrow. Fine. She could still make the phone calls. If he showed up on time, she would head to Evergreen and Parker's house if the trip became necessary. That was her plan.

CHAPTER TEN
BEST LAID PLANS

ADELE'S PLAN FELL APART BY NINE A.M. Jacobsen had gone fishing. Literally. The Evergreen detective was in court testifying. The hours of the morning ticked away, marked by her frequently checking both her watch and the clock on the wall. By eleven she was pacing the close confines of the office and driving Carl to distraction.

"Dang, Addie. How much coffee did you have for breakfast?" he fussed.

She fumed and glowered at him. "That professor from Colorado State blew me off. He was supposed to be here at ten."

"So he's running late. What's the big deal?" Carl swiveled around in his desk chair. He smirked at her. "Don't tell me you have a hot lunch date or...something." The jerk waggled his brows.

"Oh, shut up, Carl." She growled under her breath and forced herself to sit down at her desk. "I want to go back to the Parker crime scene this afternoon, that's all. I'll be seriously PO'd if I'm stuck here waiting all day for this guy. He's the one who was all hot to trot to see the fetishes up close and personal."

When a new box of evidence arrived to be processed, Adele quietly seethed but turned her focus to the new case.

At noon, Carl slipped out for his normal lunch, shaking his head over his officemate. He knew that nine times out of ten, Addie skipped lunch simply because she was so deeply involved in her research she had no clue what time it was. He headed out of the building, walking briskly. The sandwich shop around the corner would have his phone-in order waiting when he got there. There was a TV up on a high corner shelf in the place and as Carl waited in line, he watched the noon report.

"In breaking news," the talking head exclaimed excitedly, "a professor from Colorado State University was found dead in his vehicle this morning."

Carl blinked up at the TV and shushed the couple chatting in line behind him. "Holy shit," he muttered, fishing in his pocket for his cell phone. Hitting a speed-dial number, he continued to mutter. "C'mon, girl. Pick...Addie! Turn on the news. Do it now....Channel Two." Through his cell phone, Carl could hear an echo of the news report he was listening to.

"The professor, who has not been identified pending notification of next of kin, apparently died of a heart attack while changing a flat tire. State police report that the vehicle was parked in Barbour State Park. The spokesman for the highway patrol speculated that the man was in the process of changing the damaged tire. The trunk was open and the jack had been placed under the rear passenger side. In other news..."

Carl tuned out the rest of the report. "Did you get all that, Addie? I'm betting that's your guy."

"Probably," Adele sadly agreed. "I'll call CHP and find out. Thanks for the heads up, Carl. Hey...is there any way you could bring me back a Reuben?" She rolled her eyes, listening to his retort. "Yes. I have cash and will pay you before you put it in my hands. I'll see you in a little bit."

Her conversation with the Colorado Highway Patrol did not go quite the way she expected. Philip Gardenhire was indeed the decedent found in the state park, but after the county coroner spoke to the professor's personal doctor, they were now planning an autopsy. Apparently, the man had an iron constitution, and as he'd just had a full physical, the doctor seriously doubted that Professor Gardenhire died of a heart attack. The problem, on initial examination, appeared to be no obvious signs of trauma or other causation. Adele called the Weld County Coroner's office in Greeley and explained her situation. She finally got connected to the coroner.

"Anything new?" she asked only halfway hopefully.

"I wish. It's a mystery," the coroner replied. "The doctor over at Fort Collins is convinced there is no way this guy would just drop dead. There are no bullet wounds, stab wounds, blunt force trauma, or other signs of injury. I have to run a full tox screen, and my budget is already bone dry for the year. Any chance I could kick this up to the state medical examiner's office?" His voice sounded even less hopeful than Adele's had.

She sighed. She would prefer to have the body at the ME's office, too. "Unless we have a crime, I don't see how."

"What?" the coroner asked, his voice sounding a little distant. "Are you kidding me? What the..."

"Hello?" She raised her voice. "Doctor?"

"Wha...?" His voice was still distant. "Miss McCoy...I...can I call you back? Something has come up here that needs my attention."

"What happened? One of your corpses came back to life?"

A long period of silence stretched between them. "Miss McCoy? I'm sorry. Actually, that would probably have been preferable. I think I just discovered Philip Gardenhire's cause of death. I'll be sending a toxicology sample down to Denver."

When the doctor didn't add anything for another bit, she cleared her throat. "Are you going to share?" she hinted. She heard rustling and indistinct voices through the phone line.

Finally, the coroner picked up the phone again. "Sorry about that. I had to go see for myself. Apparently, Professor Gardenhire was bitten by a snake. More than likely, a rattlesnake."

She blinked and clamped her jaw shut when she realized her mouth was hanging open. "Say that again, please?"

"Yeah," the doctor agreed. "Weird as it sounds, there are two fang marks on the guy's inside upper thigh. I'm betting he was lying down under the car and the snake crawled up to him."

That got a snort from her. "You're not from around here, are you, Doc?"

"I beg your pardon?" he retorted.

"Rattlesnakes don't go looking for trouble. If he'd rolled over on the snake or something, maybe. But I'm telling you, rattlesnakes do not go crawling around parking lots all willy-nilly looking to bite a human. And there's one other problem with this picture. It's October. We've had a couple of hard freezes and the daytime temps aren't staying above sixty degrees. Snakes have gone to ground. They're cold blooded." Adele took a breath. "Not to mention that most rattlesnake bites aren't immediately fatal. Do you have a time of death? Because the professor was supposed to be here for a meeting with me at ten this morning."

She closed her eyes against a sudden dizzy spell and gulped in another breath. When the vertigo passed, her mouth was dry though her stomach was heaving, and she was sitting in her desk chair, the phone clutched in one hand, the bag of fetishes fisted in her other. She let out a little scream and threw the bag onto her desk.

"Miss McCoy? Miss McCoy, are you all right?" The doctor's voice was insistent in her ear.

"I...uhm...yeah. I'll be fine...I think," she lied. She stared, horrified, at her desk. The pouch had opened and the snake fetish had fallen out, it's roughly wrought head facing her. "I'll...be in touch. Keep me posted on the autopsy, okay?" Her voice sounded distant and disembodied to her own ears. She hung up without give the coroner a chance to respond.

When Carl entered carrying a large brown paper sack, he dropped their lunches on his desk and rushed to her. "Addie?" He snapped his fingers in front of her ashen face. "Yo, Adele? Talk to me."

She pointed dumbly at the snake on her desk. "It *was* Gardenhire who died. But not from a heart attack." She sucked in a long, steadying breath.

"Stroke?" Carl asked.

She shook her head, eyes still glassy. "No," she whispered. "Snake bite."

Carl stared at her, his mouth gaping. Slowly, his eyes followed the path of hers, and he saw the snake on her desk. He snorted. "Oh, don't go all woo-woo on me again. That's a rock. An ugly rock that sort of looks like a snake, but it is just a rock. It isn't some mythological critter that can come to life, bite people, and kill them."

Nodding, Adele finally pulled her eyes away from the snake. "Do me a favor, though. Put on some gloves and stick that thing back in the pouch."

"Nuh uh. No way, Jose," Carl retorted. "I'm not feeding your phobia." He backed away from her desk. "Besides. I'm still on my lunch hour. I'm not even supposed to be here. I wouldn't be if you hadn't ordered that Reuben. I'm outta here." He turned, grabbed the sack, and dug through it. He pulled out the Styrofoam box containing the Reuben sandwich, tossed it on her desk, and backed out of the door, shutting it firmly behind him.

"Chicken!" Pushing off with her feet, she rolled her

desk chair across the floor to the work counters. Grabbing a couple of forceps, she wheeled back to her desk. She was not going to touch the fetishes or that horrific bag with her hands ever again. Deftly holding the bag open with the forceps in her left hand, she picked up the snake fetish with the forceps in held in her right. She dropped the icon into the bag and then used the forceps to tighten the drawstring. Still using the metal utensils, she snagged the bag and once more scooted across the floor to the workspace. She plucked a small brown paper bag from a drawer, snapped it open with a flick of her wrist, and dropped the pouch inside. Deftly folding the top of the bag, she stapled it, taped it and marked it as evidence.

Adele did this three more times. The skin pouch was carefully ensconced inside four heavy brown paper sacks. She placed the bundle into a cardboard "bankers box," closed the lid and wrapped the attached strings around the plastic holders on each end.

"There," she muttered as she patted the top of the box. "Let's see you guys get out of that."

With a resolute huff of breath, Adele pushed out of her chair and strode across the room to snag her Reuben. The thing was cold and the bread soggy, but she nigh on inhaled the sandwich. Once she had scooped the last shred of sauerkraut from the Styrofoam container, she dumped her trash, grabbed her kit and jacket then logged out. She had a crime scene to visit.

CHAPTER ELEVEN
TAKE CONTROL

CRIME SCENE TAPE FLUTTERED around the front door. Adele gave the Ford Explorer with New Mexico tags a cursory glance. More interesting was the uniform from Evergreen PD sitting in his patrol car, head back, snoring. She tapped on his window, and he jumped so hard he rammed his crotch into the steering wheel. She bit her lips to keep from laughing.

The guy glowered as he lowered his window. "What?"

She flashed her CBI ID and nodded toward the SUV. "Who's here?"

"FBI."

Dang it! She should have known this would happen, but how did the news leak?

"How long has she been here?" Everyone in law enforcement had heard of Special Agent Sade Marquis, head of some fancy FBI unit that dealt with the magicks.

"Don't know who you're talking about. It's some guy. He showed up at the station this morning to see the chief. After lunch, chief sent me out here with him to unlock the door. Fed told me to wait outside. Works for me. This place gives me the creeps."

Yeah, she knew that feeling. "Great. Fine. Log me as going into the scene."

"Copy that."

Adele pushed open the massive door and stepped inside. Her boots echoed on the granite floor with a dull thud. Standing in the living area, she debated where to start.

"Who are you?"

She screamed before she could catch herself and whirled to face the man standing in the archway that led downstairs. "Crickets on a cracker. You scared the bejeezus out of me. You must be the Fed."

"Guilty as charged. And you are?" He raised a bushy brow at her, a brow that got lost under a fringe of messy dark hair. His cheeks and rather chiseled jawline were covered with fine, dark scruff. Amber eyes watched her, unblinking, and her hind brain considered survival. Which meant running. Like crazy. But her human brain decided that was a bad idea. She wasn't prey.

"Adele McCoy. Colorado Bureau of Investigation."

"Ah, yes. The tech investigator."

She bristled but bit back a retort. "Turn about's fair play. You are?"

"Special Agent Caleb Jones."

Her libido sighed and fluttered eyelashes at him as he prowled closer. Adele froze while her inner hussy squeed. Wait? What? She had an inner hussy? Very Special Agent Caleb Jones was the enemy. Here to snatch her case away.

"I understand you have the scene evidence?"

"Uh huh." God, was she drooling? Not that he wasn't drool-worthy—all six musclely feet of him. Her fingers itched to brush the shaggy hair out of his eyes. Her lips actually tingled as he dropped his eyes to look at her mouth.

"You should breathe, Ms. McCoy."

"Uh huh." She *was* breathing. Wasn't she?

A smile crept across his face, and she wanted to bite his full, bottom lip. She was in so much trouble. He leaned down, and her breath caught in her lungs, which was bad because now his leather jacket tickled her breasts through her cashmere sweater.

"Do you have the evidence with you, or do we need to go to your office?"

She wanted to inhale again, to breathe the air from his words. She didn't. Instead, she exhaled with her third brilliant reply since his appearance. "Uhm…"

Caleb managed not to laugh. He was used to heightened interest from human women, but the crime scene tech's reaction was a little overboard. Or maybe she was just that dumb. Her brow furrowed as she thought then she pursed her lips. Everything that made him male woke up and saluted. What the hell? His hard-on fought with his zipper and wasn't that just fun and games. He stepped back before he did something completely out of character—like grab the woman, kiss her, take her to the floor, and to use Sade's term, fuck her blind. Oh yes. That was a really good idea. He liked it. A lot.

He stepped away. He had a job to do—a job further complicated by Ariel's request and his discovery that a very dead Drew Parker was apparently the last person to have handled the fetishes. Except for this very attractive woman. Caleb studied her in his own unique way. She was close to thirty, natural blonde with lively blue eyes. The sprinkling of freckles across her nose and the tops of her high cheekbones pointed to a redhead in the family tree. She settled black-framed glasses on the top of her head and clenched a jaw some might consider too strong. She'd pulled her hair back and bunched it up in a semi-tame clump held in place by an alligator clip.

Huh. He was probably the only guy in his Academy class who knew what an alligator clip was. Sade was fond of wearing them and he'd been subjected to all things girlie-girl when she'd gone through her pink phase at the age of eight. Adele looked utterly determined—if slightly bemused—and that made her utterly cute.

"The evidence?" She shook herself, mentally at least, and nodded. "Yes. It's back at the CBI lab in

Denver."

"Good. Let's go."

She balked. "Excuse me?"

"Still with the twenty questions? I've gleaned whatever I can from this scene. I need to see the photos and physical evidence you gathered." He waited for her to say something, and when she did nothing but stare at him, he added, "So...your office?"

Adele's temper simmered and she let it flick across him. "Yeah, my office. Because this is my case. There's no evidence of magick involvement so why are you here?"

"Because I have evidence this case ties into another I'm working." Caleb didn't expect her to be so single-minded on this. Most locals couldn't wait to hand off a case if there was even the barest whiff of magic involved.

"Fine. Whatever. I'll see you in Denver." She executed a precise about-face and marched to the door. She'd be a good little CBI soldier, but she darn well didn't have to like it.

Caleb hid his smirk, but the prickly tech investigator was punching far too many of his buttons. He was a werewolf. Werewolves had certain...appetites, and Little Miss Saucy could satisfy more than a few of them. He followed her out and gave a sharp whistle to get the Evergreen cop's attention. He tossed off a series of hand gestures to indicate the guy should lock up and take off.

Adele remained resolute as she stomped toward her vehicle. The guy could find his own way to the CBI building. She reached in her pocket to get her keys and stopped so suddenly, the Fed ran into her. If he hadn't circled her waist with his arm, she would have face-planted on the cobblestone driveway. Her hand still shoved in her pocket, she shuddered as her fingertips caressed what felt like deerskin but was human. This.

Was. Not. Possible.

"Ms. McCoy?" Caleb didn't like the way her face drained of color or her shallow breathing. If he didn't know better, he'd think she was bespelled. He inhaled and blinked several times. Not possible. He would have sensed any sort of magic around her when they were inside the house. When she pushed against his arm, he loosened his grip and let her go. His instincts didn't like it. Not one bit. But he wasn't just werewolf instincts. He was an educated man, not a wild wolf.

Adele fast dialed and held her cell to her ear. She didn't breathe until Carl answered on the fourth ring. She barely gave him time for a greeting before she started babbling.

"Carl. Check the Parker evidence box. Right now. Right this very minute. Drop whatever you're doing, go to the storage room and get that box. Open. Now, Carl. Now."

"Whoa, Addie. What's going on? Did you have some brilliant light-bulb moment or something?"

"Dang it, Carl. Just do what I ask. Get the box and open it. I need to know if the fetishes are still there."

Her voice dropped on that last, but Caleb had no trouble hearing her, or the voice of the man on the other end.

"Seriously, Addie? You still believe those dumb things teleport or something? They're just old rocks and they don't move on their own or kill people."

Addie? Seriously? Caleb rolled his eyes since she couldn't see him. She was so not an *Addie*. He hoped the nickname wasn't her idea. If it was, he'd have to disabuse her of that notion. His nostrils flared at the timbre of her voice when she insisted the guy do as she asked.

"Just do it, Carl."

"Don't have to."

She screeched, and Caleb winced, ears hurting from the pitch of her voice, and offered a little silent sympathy for the guy on the phone

"Look, Adele, I'm not the one who buried them under so much tape it took us thirty minutes to get them back out."

Whatever retort Adele had been about to make died in her throat. "Wha..? You took them out?"

"Yeah. Jacobson wanted to look at them again. He couldn't believe all the extra tape and crap you put on them." The derision in Carl's voice was obvious. "I didn't want to tell him that you were freaked out by them."

"Where are they now?" she whispered.

"He took them with him."

She didn't touch the pocket in her jacket. "You actually saw him pick them up and walk out with them after I'd gone?"

"Yeah. You'd logged out by the time I got back from lunch. Jacobson came in, wanted the pouch, and we pulled it out of the evidence box. He checked to make sure they were in the last of the *ten* paper bags, showed me, put them back, signed the log-out sheet and left holding them." Carl sounded puzzled. "SOP, Addie."

"Do me a favor." Her voice quivered, and she hated it. "Put me on hold, call Jacobson, and ask him to make sure he still has them."

Carl snorted. "Add...I swear."

"Dang it, Carl. Just. Do. It!" Her voice was filled with anger and rose in pitch with each word.

"Sure, kiddo. Whatever. A minute." Carl did as she requested.

While she was on hold, Adele opened the back of her Jeep and snagged her kit. Opening it, she grabbed Latex gloves and pulled both of them on one hand. She paused when Carl came back on the line.

"Stupid son of a bitch," Carl grumbled. "He lost them."

Her heart caught in her throat, and her chest was so tight she could barely breathe. She finally got up the nerve to pat her jacket pocket. The pouch was definitely there. Gingerly, she stuck her gloved hand in and withdrew the pouch. "No," she whispered. "It isn't lost."

"What the..." Carl sucked in a breath. "What do you mean, Addie?"

"I mean—" Her voice cracked. She cleared her throat and tried again. "I mean that I just pulled that cursed pouch out of my pocket."

"No. Fucking. Way," Carl denied.

"Yes, way."

Adele's phone would have hit pavement if Caleb hadn't snatched it mid-drop. He heard the man ranting as he swiped his finger across the screen to end the call. He reached into her jacket pocket with two fingers and withdrew the pouch. She gulped air, and he worried she'd hyperventilate.

"Gloves. That's evidence."

"You've already tested it." Caleb gritted his teeth against the bite of magic. "Human skin. You mentioned fetishes. How many?"

"Six."

"Do they look Native American?"

She nodded, her bottom lip trembling. A shudder rocked her hard, and she had to grab his arm to remain standing. Caleb noticed with one part of his brain that she'd shifted to put his body between her and the pouch.

"This has happened before?"

Her eyes were so wide and frightened when she looked up at him he wanted to fold her into his arms and keep her safe. He'd never felt that way before—not even about Sade. He had a protective streak a mile wide, but he normally didn't want to hold a woman and kiss her and make everything all right in her world. His nostrils flared at the stench of blood magic wafting from the pouch.

"Adele? Del? Has this happened before?"

She swallowed. Hard. Nodded. "Yeah. And...when they're out of the pouch, I swear they move. On their own."

"Okay, babe. It's okay. Get me an evidence bag. We'll secure them and go back to your lab. Okay?"

Eyes still terrified, she stiffened her shoulders. "Okay."

It wasn't okay. Nothing about this was okay, but she was Big Jim McCoy's daughter. She didn't turn tail and run. She would do her job. She moved away, with reluctance, and reached into her kit for a brown paper bag. With a deft flick, the bag popped open, and she held it out so Caleb could drop the pouch into the bag. He took it from her and folded the top over several times. She reached in, grabbed the stapler she kept in her kit, and secured the bag before indicating a side pocket of the duffel where he could secure the bag. She'd do her job, but if she never had to touch that thing again, it would be too soon.

WOULD IT BE TOO SOON to ask the lovely technical investigator out? Caleb worried the idea all the way down the mountains and into Denver. He'd been attracted to her at first sight, but after she'd touched him, after he'd read the fear in her eyes, he wanted to do more than work with her, or admire her from afar. He wanted far more. Wanted to be up close and personal. Very up close and very personal.

Wow. He really needed to get laid. He relaxed back into the driver's seat and followed, hot on her tail. He laughed, the sound a low rumble in his chest. And wasn't that just the whole point? As he drove, he mulled over the things Ari had told him and what might possibly be in that pouch. Del had mentioned fetishes. What kind? What did they depict? The thing reeked of age—ancient and powerful. It stank of blood magic. And even holding it by two fingers sent zings up his arm. That just wasn't right. Any of it.

He couldn't figure out why Adele hadn't called the MAGIC Unit once she realized her crime scene was tainted by magic. The Evergreen police chief, over a medium-rare burger, had waxed poetic about the state of the body—even though the man hadn't seen it in person. Skinning a human wasn't easy. Peeling the skin off a human like you peel off a sock? That was just...really bad ju-ju. Most humans were only too happy to pass the magical buck.

The locals weren't prepared for the power behind such a feat. If he were honest, *he* wasn't prepared for it. Once he nailed down the evidence, he'd have to put a call into

Director Bailey. But that would mean Sade getting assigned. Something whispered in the back of his brain. Those protective instincts that Adele stirred? Yeah, they were stomping on his last shred of good sense telling him to keep Sade as far away from this mess as possible. That meant going rogue.

ADELE PAID CAREFUL ATTENTION to her driving. In normal circumstances, she pushed the speed limit and the capabilities of her Jeep on the mountain turns. But this circumstance was far from normal. The good news? She wasn't crazy. The bad news? A devilish sexy FBI agent was there to take over the case she considered her own. Only it wasn't hers. She wasn't an agent or investigator in the traditional sense. She was a technical investigator. A CSI. Forensics. Evidence. The scientific stuff. But there was nothing scientific about this case.

If she was smart, she'd drop this case in the Fed's lap and run like devil himself was chasing her. Of course, the fact she'd rather drop herself into the Fed's lap wasn't helping her think clearly. She forced control on her erratic breathing. Hyperventilating would not help. So what if the guy was sex—She blinked. What the hey? He'd called her Del. Her brain had skipped right over that little bit of familiarity. And babe. He'd freaking called her *babe*! That was just...wrong, but it was nice. In a totally wrong way.

She gripped the steering wheel tighter and did her best to focus on her case. Cases. While they hadn't received the second one, she was already lumping the two together. Two dead bodies. One was found with the bag made of human flesh tucked between the thighs of his skinned body. The other had seen something in the pictures of the pouch and the fetishes—the ones she'd shown him.

"Oh double doo-doo. Does that make me an accessory to Professor Gardenhire's death?" She asked the question to empty air.

No. It didn't. It couldn't. She hadn't actually handed him the darn thing. She'd only shown him the photos. And it was only after she'd started home that she realized the pouch had...migrated into her possession. She used a technique her father often engaged in—the tried and true talking out loud to herself.

"So...he hears that thump-thump-thump that signals something wrong at highway speed. He pulls off... But why take the detour to drive into the park? Okay. Maybe the tire is just low, not flat. Or maybe he needs to take a potty break. There were restrooms near the parking lot. Okay. That's it. He needs to take a leak. So he stops. Gets out of the car. Does his business. Comes back. Realizes he has a flat tire. He pops the trunk, hauls out the jack and sticks it under the fender. Wait. Am I parked on a hill? I need to put a block under the tire in case the car rolls. Right?

"I need a rock. So I wander over to this pile of rocks. Bend over and squat down, spreading my legs because, you know, lift with the legs not the back. I grab the rock, disturb the snake, it strikes, fangs managing to get through my...What the hell was he wearing the day I saw him? Slacks? Jeans?...Jeans. He's middle-aged, but he wants to appear cool with the coeds. So he probably had on jeans. The snake is dead on, sinks his fangs through the denim and manages to inject a lethal dose of venom directly into the femoral artery of my leg. I stumble backwards, dropping the rock back on the pile, and get back to my car. Cell phone. I can call 9-1-1."

Adele drummed her fingers on the steering wheel. Why didn't he call 9-1-1? He would have had time. The scenario didn't make sense. But it also didn't make sense he fixated on the snake fetish, if that's what it even was. In reality, it was just a skinny, curvy rock that might be a snake. Maybe. Maybe not. But...he'd kept talking about the designs on the back of that plain ol' rock and how the eyes were set with jewels. That had been just creepy. The snake rock was just a rock. The wolf...now the wolf was different. She'd bet he was created later and added to the group. He was properly carved and had topaz chips set into his face for eyes. In fact, the wolf might even be modern. The eyes plastic and stuck in with glue.

"Yeah. That's it. See? Nothing otherworldly or magical about this. No need for that darn FBI agent to stick around!"

Except.

What the hell sort of thing skinned a man alive? Or had Parker been dead already, despite what Dr. Jamnu believed? Surely he was dead when it happened. But she still hadn't found the original crime scene. The man had definitely not been skinned inside his house.

She turned into the parking lot, still on autopilot as her thoughts did a spastic Hokey Pokey. The space next to her spot was empty for about five seconds before an Explorer parked. Oh, yeah. The Fed. Very Special Agent Caleb Jones and she darn sure needed to stop calling him that. She climbed out and met him at the back of her Jeep. He opened the hatch and reached in for her duffel.

"No. Leave it. Just need the evidence bag."

"Okay."

He pulled out the paper sack and showed no indication of any ill-effect. Then she had a completely, stomach-dropping thought. He knew the pouch was made of human skin without her telling him. Before she could process that, her mouth opened and the most bizarre thing she'd ever uttered tumbled out.

"How many of pouches could you make from a

human body? How much does skin shrink when it's dried?"

Caleb stared at her, his brow knit slightly. "Those are questions I've never needed the answer to. I bet you can Google it when we get up to your office."

Her lips pursed and she wandered off, distracted. Amused, he closed the hatch and followed, still holding the evidence bag containing the pouch by two fingers. Now that she'd asked, he admitted to a bit of curiosity. Disturbingly, he knew people who could answer her question off the top of their heads. What a world he lived in.

They entered the building through a door with a card reader. She used her ID and the door clicked open. Adele ignored him when he slipped in behind her. She took the stairs. Luckily, it was only a few floors—not that he couldn't have run up all the stairs to the top of the building and back again without getting winded. Just because he could, didn't mean he wanted to.

Adele logged them into her lab and he got his first look at the fussy man who shared her space. Caleb decided he didn't like Carl. Not one bit. When the guy refused to shake hands, Caleb figured the feeling was mutual. He could live with that. Del ducked around the long counter at the front of the room, peeling off her coat as she went. He wisely stayed on the public side. When she continued to ignore him, he held up the bag and cleared his throat.

"What?" Adele couldn't believe she'd just let the federal jerk follow her upstairs. She should have slammed the door behind her to make him go in the front entrance and have to follow protocol and do all the visiting big shots rigmarole.

He waggled the bag. "You want to do the honors, or do I get to open this particular little present?"

She stared at him a long moment, biting her lips

and trying to think. Oh. The fetishes. "Carl, put some paper down so Special Agent Bigwig can look at the fetishes."

"The what?" Carl backed up. "What are you saying? How did he get them?"

"*He* didn't get them, Carl. They came to me."

"Came *to* you. Yeah, right. Funny joke, Addie. You and Jacobsen are messing with me."

"Oh, I truly wish that was true. Now put down some paper."

She disappeared into the back storage room leaving Carl and Caleb to stare at each other. The lab rat postured, trying to mark his territory. Wanting to laugh, Caleb offered a curled lip and a push of alpha magic. Carl stumbled backwards, but he got himself together enough to put down paper to cover the work counter.

Adele reappeared carrying a box. She slid it onto the counter then glanced at Caleb. "Well? Open the sack and dump them out."

He started to run a finger under the folded rim of the bag when Carl yelled. "No. Nononono. Are you an idiot? Glove up for chrissakes. That's evidence. This is a lab. I should make you wear a hairnet!"

Caleb scratched his jaw. "At least I need one."

A snorting giggle burst through Adele's nose and she covered her mouth to stifle her laugh.

"Being follicle-ly challenged is a sign of high testosterone." Carl rocked up on the balls of his feet as he made the declaration.

The man reminded Caleb of the bantam roosters he used to chase as a pup. Scratching the thatch of hair just visible through the top buttons of his dress shirt, he offered a skeptical look. "Huh. You're the scientist. Guess you'd know." His voice conveyed an ocean of skepticism.

"Yes, yes I am. We rely on our intellect rather than

resorting to Neanderthal behavior."

Caleb flicked his gaze to Del. "Has he worked up the testosterone to ask you out yet?" Oh yeah, that was like dumping kerosene on a red ant hill. He let Carl sputter and blush and Del deny and dance away from the idea for a couple of minutes.

"Hate to break up the Dating Game, but where are the gloves? Some of us here are real investigators."

Adele glowered at him, one hand fisting on her hip. "Oh no you didn't. You did not just go there, buster!"

Really happy he'd learned to play poker from a millennium-old gargoyle who wore the original stone face, Caleb kept his face blank. He was chortling inside, though. By the gods she was fun to rile. Her color heightened, her freckles jumped out in stark relief, and those blue eyes of hers sparkled like snapdragons covered in morning dew. Mad looked good on her. While she ranted, he daydreamed about how she'd look beneath him, her face hardening with lust as he wound her up for her climax, then after she shattered, when her eyes softened with... Naw. He wouldn't go there. Love had no place in his life, especially not with a mundane. But sex? And mutual gratification? Oh, yeah. He was definitely going to get laid by Adele McCoy before this assignment was over.

He dumped out the fetishes. The two lab techs immediately shut up and stared at the countertop. Caleb recognized them immediately. Bear. Wolf. Lizard. Snake. Turtle. Deer. The ground rumbled beneath his feet. Or maybe that was his own equilibrium quaking at his thoughts. He'd never much trusted Fae. Ariel, like all his kind, was a law unto himself. After years of Sade standing between them, he'd finally begun giving Ari grudging respect. Now he didn't trust the glitterfly as far as he could throw him.

The magic swirling around these relics was ancient,

old as the First Bloods, and nasty as a ghoul's breath. All of them had landed right side up, standing on feet or, in the case of the snake, slithering on its belly. The bear looked sad rather than ferocious. The wolf stared back at him, accusations in its eyes. The lizard was all smug while the snake rattled its tail against the paper.

Caleb blinked. He'd been wrong. Not all of them had landed upright. The turtle lay on its back, rocking slightly on its rounded shell. The deer caught and held his attention. She looked skittish, and the aquamarine stones that were her eyes looked like they'd been crying. Oh yeah. These things had deep magic.

"What do you see?" He tore his gaze away from the charms to settle it on Adele. She inched her finger over, touched the ear of the wolf. Caleb fought the urge to scratch. What the hell? He snatched the wolf away from her and she snarled at him.

"Hey! What do you think you're doing? You put that back down right this instant."

The magic bit at him through the Latex. He sent a surge of his own power into his hand to surround the other. It didn't stop the magic. He wasn't that strong, but he could contain it long enough to figure out what was going on.

"I said put it back."

"And I asked what you see."

"Put it back and I'll tell you."

He tilted his head, werewolf senses surging within him. "What's the matter? Don't you trust me?"

"Not as far as I can throw you." She muttered his own thoughts back at him.

"Well, you'd better trust me when I say this case is above your pay grade."

CHAPTER THIRTEEN
SIMPLE MAN

Elbert County, Colorado
"THIS IS ABOVE MY PAY GRADE."

The deputy stood there with a thumb hooked in his gun belt and rubbing his chin. He had never in twenty years of law enforcement ever seen anything like this. Henry Larson had gone missing a week ago, but no one expected to find him like this. The deputy's radio crackled and he pulled his handheld out of its holder. "Sierra One-Niner," he answered.

"Sierra One Nine, you want to run all that by me again, Tuck?" a female voice crackled through the radio.

"I think I found Henry Larson. The body's wearin' his boots anyway, Dispatch."

Ol' Henry's hand-tooled boots were legendary all over this part of eastern Colorado. The old man had been a rancher for his entire adult life, raising cattle on the same land he had grown up on. Henry outlived two wives and several of his children, married and divorced a few more, and the old man had one vanity—custom-made cowboy boots, the fancier the stitching on the tops, the better. And Henry had enough money to do whatever the heck he pleased when it came to indulging in his passion. Truth be told, he had one pair in the closet that cost upwards of ten thousand dollars. He wore those strictly for important occasions—marryin', buryin', and the Western Heritage Awards at the National Cowboy Hall of Fame and Western Heritage Museum in Oklahoma City. He gathered up whichever current wife and kids were available and made the trek to Oklahoma each year so he could hobnob with the writers, actors, and artists who were being honored. He always came home with artwork and surprises for his family and ranch crew.

Deputy Tucker sighed. It looked like Henry wasn't going to make the trip this year.

"Body too decomposed to make a positive ID?" Dispatch inquired.

The deputy shook his head, even though the dispatcher couldn't see the gesture. "No...actually I think the body will be in pretty decent shape when they get him dug out."

"Repeat that?" Dispatch demanded.

"Dang it, Marva, you heard me the first time," he barked. "It looks like Henry fell into this stock pond. At least I think it used to be a pond. Since it's been so dry, the thing dried up and it is nothing more than a mud wallow now. Two of his hands found 'im this 108orning'."

"What am I supposed to tell the coroner?" Marva's retort came across the air sounding tart.

"Tell 'em the body looks like it's been covered in clay and baked dry." Tucker nudged at the dried mud with the toe of his boot. "This's the weirdest thing I have ever seen. He looks like one of those clay pots you find in an Indian tradin' post."

"You mean the fake ones they make in China?"

He shook his head, still forgetting she couldn't see him. "No. Like the pots that come from the pueblos—the ones that sort look like a human or an animal."

"Ohhhh!" Marva sounded excited now. "I know just the ones you're talking about—those little ones that folks collect to go on their knick-knack shelves."

The deputy heard other voices behind Marva's on the radio, and then the connection dropped. When his radio crackled again, the voice he heard belonged to the sheriff.

"Did the ol' man drown?"

"I guess, boss, but I don't rightly know as I'm not the coroner," he retorted. "Why don't you folks just come on out here and have a look see for yourselves. Those two hands who found the body already high-tailed it for the barn, their tails tucked between their legs and the whites showin' all the way around their eyes. Those boys were done spooked. I'm out here all by my lonesome, and I don't mind telling you this whole dang sitcheation is downright creepy. So you send me some backup, Sheriff, or come yourself, and get the dang coroner out here. Tell 'im he'll need four-wheel drive because I'm out here in the smack-dab middle of the cattle range."

The radio remained silent for a long moment. "How far are you from the house, Tucker?"

The deputy shaded his eyes and looked off toward the horizon. The sun picked that moment to come out from behind a fat cloud and its reflection glinted for a brief moment off the metal roof of the barn at the Larson Ranch home place. "I'm about four miles southwest of the big barn, as the crow flies. I can't see the house from here." He furrowed his brow as he considered things. He knew for a fact the old man didn't ride horseback anymore. A run-in with a green-broke mustang had cured him right quick of that notion. He either used his old Dodge truck or one of those four-wheeled all terrain vehicles. He pressed the button on his mike. "Sheriff? No sign of a vehicle and it's a darn sight far to walk for a man his age."

Once more, the silence from the radio was deafening. "You hold the fort, Tucker. I'm on my way." He could hear the sheriff take a deep breath. "That's probably gonna be a crime scene so don't go fuckin' it up, hear?"

"Ten-four." He stood for another few minutes

staring at the body. The arms extended almost straight out from the shoulders with the elbows bent at a ninety-degree angle and the hands roughly positioned on either side of the head. The legs were similarly positioned, though the thighs bent out at more of a forty-five degree angle from the torso. Shaking his head, Tucker retreated to his Chevy Suburban, climbed up into the passenger seat and settled in to wait.

The minutes ticked by slowly as the sun played peek-a-boo with the fluffy white clouds forming on the southern horizon before scudding across the sky like fat tugboats in the ocean. He checked the rearview mirrors on both sides. The Front Range of the Rocky Mountains loomed against the western sky. The view out his windshield stretched far and flat—a sea of waving grasses. When he was a boy, Tucker's father told him that if he climbed a small hill near their house, he'd be able to see all the way to Missouri. As his eyes searched the eastern vista, he could still believe it. He glanced out his window and stared at the body. From this angle, it looked like the clay had been heaped up and then rounded so the dried crust made the body look like it was wearing a turtle shell. The deputy took a deep breath and let it out slow. No good would come from this business. No good a'tall, he decided.

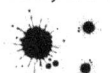

Denver: CBI HQ

ADELE STARED AT THE MAN lounging in the door of her boss's office. His brown eyes regarded her seriously, even though the wry smirk barely twitching at the corners of his mouth seemed to mock her. Pulling her eyes away, she rounded on her boss. "We don't need the Feds?" she insisted hotly. "We can handle this case. Just because Parker was some rich muckity-muck..." She paused to snatch a breath.

"It's still our case, Addie," the man in the polo shirt and dress slacks behind the uncluttered desk soothed, completely oblivious to her continued muttering. "Agent Jones is here as a consultant. That's all."

Caleb caught the muttered "It's Adele, *Dick*" and he chuckled. Del whipped around to glare at him, and he waggled his eyebrows at her. He held up one hand, palm toward her to hopefully quell her anger. "I'm just here to tag along and offer advice, Investigator McCoy." Caleb attempted to placate her. Before he could continue or Del could retort, the phone on the desk buzzed obnoxiously.

Her boss snagged the receiver and answered, "Richard Roberts." He listened. He hmmed. He hawed. He glanced from Adele to Caleb and back. "Sure thing, sheriff. I have a technical investigator and a special consultant here in my office even as we speak. I'll get someone headed your way A to the S-A-P." Roberts listened again. "That's what we're here for. Can I get directions?"

He listened again, scratching notes on a yellow legal pad. "My people are leaving here right now, sheriff. They'll be on scene in an hour or so." He hung up and stared at Adele. "Get your gear and head out to Elbert County." He ripped the lined paper from the pad and passed it across the desk. "Sheriff has a dead body."

Picking up the paper, Adele glanced at the directions and looked at her boss before jerking her head in Caleb's direction. "Why does he have to go?" She was quite pleased she hadn't snarled.

"Because the body looks like it's been wrapped in clay and baked...in the shape of a turtle," Roberts explained.

Her mouth opened and closed a couple of times, but no words came out. "Okay," she finally said, blinking rapidly. Her brain was doing somersaults so fast she felt dizzy. Taking a deep, steadying breath, she nodded. "I'm on it." Turning on her heel, she headed to the door.

Caleb didn't move for a moment, earning him a glare. He smiled and stepped back. "After you, Miz McCoy," he invited, a barely suppressed chuckle rippling beneath his words.

"Harrumph." Adele brushed passed him. She could feel his smile, and it only irritated her more. At the elevators, she stabbed both call buttons. "I've got to go up and get my kit. I'll meet you downstairs in the parking lot."

The green up arrow above one of the elevators dinged and lit up. The doors slithered open, and Adele stepped on board. Caleb was right behind her. He hit the button for her floor. "Nice try," he murmured.

"What?" Adele glowered at him. "I said I'd meet you outside."

"Yeah. Right." Caleb watched her, one brow cocked. "You left your go kit in your vehicle, Del."

She punched him on the arm. Hard. The man didn't even flinch, but she did. "Ow, ow, owwwww," she complained shaking her hand. "That hurt!" She snarled at him. "Why didn't you go downstairs and wait?"

"What? And get ditched? I didn't fall off the turnip truck yesterday, sweetheart."

"I am not your sweetheart."

Caleb laughed. "At least I don't call you Addie."

She shuddered, and the snarl turned into a growl. "I hate diminutives." The elevator doors opened and she stepped out. "I guess I'm stuck with you, huh?"

He nodded and held the door to her lab open. "Hey, I have to earn my paycheck too. And who knows, you might actually get used to me."

She stripped out of her lab coat and grabbed her jacket. She dug in her jean pockets for a key ring, found the key she needed, and unlocked a desk drawer. A nylon holster hugged a very serviceable 9mm Glock. Adele clipped the pistol to her belt, patted it, and grabbed a second black nylon duffel investigation kit. She slung it over her left shoulder, the same side as the gun on her hip, causing Caleb to shake his head. He thought about Sade. She would never have made such a rookie mistake—not even when she *was* a rookie.

"You don't spend much time around criminals, do you?" he asked as he held the office door for her. He didn't offer to carry the bag.

She made a lemon face at him. "What do you mean?"

"Never mind. Just remind me to hightail it out of range if you draw your weapon."

"Hey! I qualify on the range every year."

"Yeah? So does my grandmother, but I still wouldn't take her to a gunfight."

Miffed, Adele marched into the elevator as its doors opened and remained stonily silent all the way down to the first floor. She didn't wait for Caleb. As soon as the doors opened, she hit the exit and stomped off toward her vehicle. Caleb trailed behind enjoying her pique. She might not be much of a real cop, but he'd bet she was an excellent CSI—when she wasn't dealing with magic. Plus, she was certainly easy on the eyes. He grinned, adding another checkmark to his mental list. Adele McCoy had not said the word "like" once. Mimi's speech had been peppered with "Like ya know, I mean like yeah."

Caleb trailed her to her Jeep, examining it closely for the first time. The black paint had faded and there was bit of rust around the wheel wells. In snow country with salt and chemicals on the roads, that wasn't uncommon. She had the key chain in her hand, and with a flick of her thumb, she unlocked the doors. After stowing the additional bag in the back cargo area, she slid behind the wheel. Caleb made a show of fastening his seatbelt, trying not to laugh as his companion glared at him. It was almost pathetically easy to get under her skin—and far too entertaining to stop.

Ignoring her passenger, Adele concentrated on driving. Once they headed east toward Limon on I-70 and the traffic thinned, she loosened her grip on the wheel. She reached for the radio and jumped when Caleb cleared his throat. "What? You don't like music?" she goaded.

He tossed her an easy smile. "Depends on what you call music. Personally, I'd rather talk. Why did your spidey sense start tingling in your boss's office?"

She shot him a sideways glance before returning her eyes to the road. "Whatever are you referring to, Mr. Jones?" She changed lanes and passed a semi truck before adding, "And speaking of diminutives, do people call you Cal?"

"Not if they want to live," he replied, answering her second question first. "And I'm referring to the double blink, the widening of the eyes, and the increased breathing rate in Dick's office. If you weren't responding to the information about the case then you must have been turned on by my animal magnetism."

"I was not." Her fingers squeezed the steering wheel, and her lip twitched. The denial came out hot, despite her best attempts at nonchalance.

Caleb swiveled and braced his shoulders against the passenger door. "Me doth think the lady protests too much." He didn't hide his smirk and enjoyed the creeping flush tinting Del's cheeks, turning them a flattering shade of pink.

Clearing her throat, she turned her head to stare at him for a brief moment before the road captured her attention again. "Do you believe in magic?"

Caleb almost choked, coughing to cover his

surprise. He studied her profile while he considered the question. "Ah, I see," he finally said. "The quintessential scientist. You haven't balanced the two realities yet."

"You...you really believe all the mumbo jumbo?" She sputtered as her eyes darted between the windshield and his face. She didn't miss the rather wolfish grin spreading across his face.

"If you'd seen what I've seen, you'd believe too, sweetheart." He tilted his head to watch her, and his nostrils flared slightly. He remained silent for several minutes, but she didn't respond. He didn't know her well, but if his gibe hadn't gotten a rise out of her, something was seriously wrong. "What's going on, Del? What has you so spooked?"

"I'm not spooked." While insistent, she didn't sound very convinced.

Caleb leaned forward. "I'm waiting for the other shoe to drop. There was a *but* on the end of that statement."

She sighed then admitted, "But."

When she didn't explain, Caleb prodded her. "But what?"

"But my spidey sense is tingling. I have two unrelated murders...yet they are. Related, I mean. And now, there may be a third. And yeah. The evidence freaks me out."

"The evidence should freak you out."

She concentrated on her driving for awhile, and Caleb didn't push. He watched the foothills flatten out into rolling plains. This was cattle country, the land of huge ranches. Del wasn't the only one with a background in the sciences who wasn't quite ready to concede to the facts of mythical beings walking around in their midst. As far as he was concerned, the existence of atoms and quarks and the internet was far more magical than magic.

Silence stretched out between them, and while it wasn't companionable, it wasn't strained either. Caleb was a patient hunter. That's what made him a better interrogator than Sade. The times they'd teamed up and there'd been a need for good cop/bad cop, he'd always been the friendly quiet one. The irony of the situation never failed to amuse him. Sade was all balls to the wall, but he was the one who could rip out a bad guy's throat—not that she didn't have a mean right hook.

They followed I-70 east to State Highway 86 and then circled back west. Adele eventually turned south on State Highway 149 and headed toward Mathison. US-24 intersected the road they were on and she once more turned right and headed back toward the Front Range. They passed through a couple of small towns before turning south on a county road that was paved for about a block. Headed due south again, Adele took a deep breath, as if she'd finally made up her mind.

"We're almost there. I...I want you to see this scene cold. I want your impressions without prejudice. Only then will I explain what I think is going on...maybe going on...might be." She sighed. "Or not."

Caleb managed not to laugh. "I can live with that, Del. *Something* is going on...and magic is involved. I wouldn't be here otherwise. Trust me, the Director of the FBI doesn't call my cell phone just to say howdy."

She turned off onto an even rougher road and drove between two stone posts. "This is the place," she explained. "The body is out there on the range somewhere. We need to find the big barn and head south by southwest."

Caleb flashed a wry smile. "Isn't that a Hitchcock film?"

CHAPTER FOURTEEN
FEET OF CLAY

"HITCHCOCK FILM?" Adele put the Jeep in park and stared at the lone deputy sitting in his old Ford Bronco as she tried to make sense of the man beside her. "I don't think so. If there was snow out here, I'd say Fargo."

"Movie or TV show?" While Caleb had been trying to make a joke, by playing on the title "North by Northwest," he was now intrigued that she might be a fan of one of his favorite movies. He had a thing for the Coen brothers and their films.

"What?"

"Are you a fan of the Coens?"

"I have no idea what you're talking about." She opened her door and climbed out.

He followed. "Fargo. The original movie or the TV show."

"Oh. I don't watch much TV."

"Movies?"

"Not really."

Well, there went any chance of a lasting relationship. "So what do you do in your free time?"

She popped the rear hatch and hauled out her duffel. "I read. You should try it sometime."

He slapped his hand to his heart and offered her his best puppy-dog eyes—the look that always got to Sade. "Ow."

His performance only elicited rolling eyes from his intrepid companion. He slammed the hatch closed and followed her, wondering if he was amused by her brush-off, intrigued, or just pissed. He decided on amusement with a side of interest because...freckles. And she had a really nice hip sway when she marched across rough ground. Like a hound on a hot scent, he followed her, and almost tripped over a deep rut in the prairie.

Caleb wisely stood back, next to the local deputy, while Adele did her CSI thing. She was good at her job, and after his initial examination, he did not need to be close to the body. He picked up the same stench as he had with the two werewolf teens and at the house in Evergreen. While his eyes watched her work, his brain focused on the puzzle. What did two kids from a back-water pack in New Mexico have in common with the decadent heir of a mega-rich family in Colorado? And in turn, how did those three cross paths with a crotchety, albeit wealthy, rancher?

Transport from the local funeral home arrived and Caleb left the deputy to help with the body removal. Adele would want to be at the ME's office for the autopsy—including the process of chipping the rancher out of his coat of clay. Resigned to a boring afternoon while Adele got her crime scene geek on, he didn't want to get any closer to the magic than he already had. Deputy Tucker, other than being creeped out by the circumstances, didn't seem affected. Del, on the other hand, continuously rubbed the back of her neck, or smoothed a palm down her arms.

Putting the wait to good use, Caleb updated the director, Ari—and wasn't that a kick in the pants calling the glitterfly on purpose—and checking some data bases he could access on his phone for information about that upstart drug kingpin who now called himself El Diablo.

Adele sweated through her tee shirt despite the sharp winter wind kicking up across the plains. December had been a mild month so far. The ski resorts lamented the lack of snow, but she didn't mind. She hated driving in the stuff—not because she had problems but because of the other idiots on the road. Of course, December also meant Christmas was coming and she'd have to suck it up and spend time with her dad, and Big Jim's not-so-subtle condescension when it came to the topic of her job. She liked her job. She was good at it. But the big, retired cop and former hot-shot homicide detective made the holidays a chore.

She finished up, and brushed hair out of her eyes as she watched the coroner drive away with the body. She glanced at Caleb when he stepped up beside her.

"You'll want to watch."

He didn't ask, he assumed, and he was right. She did. "Evidence collection is my middle name."

"Let's go." He wasn't enthusiastic, but he nudged her toward her Jeep anyway.

"I'm driving."

"Of course you are."

Adele stopped and halfway turned toward him. "It doesn't bother you? Doesn't send up a man card SOS or anything?"

Caleb arched one eyebrow, deciding if she was serious, trying to be funny, or if this was an attempt at flirting. Not sure how he felt about that last one, he answered truthfully. "You haven't met my family." He didn't want to mention Sade by name, or the fact that she never let him drive. The woman was an absolute control freak. "Besides, this is your territory, not mine. Easier for you to drive than give me directions."

"Wow." She didn't say anything else as she continued to the Jeep.

A moment later, Caleb followed. He hadn't gotten a good read on the woman. Yet. He would. A sly grin curled his lips into his cheeks, and he was really glad Del was three steps ahead of him. He lengthened his stride and they settled into the front seat simultaneously. Adele froze, her hands white knuckled on the steering wheel.

"That is not freaking funny, wise guy." She hissed the complaint but didn't look at him.

"What's not—" His eyes finally translated what had upset her to his brain. The turtle fetish perched on the arch of the dashboard covering the speedometer. "How'd that get here?"

"Oh, right. As if you didn't know. This is soooo not funny."

"I didn't do it."

"Yeah, right. You probably palmed the darn fetish and laughed your buns off all the way out here while you planned to scare me." She whipped around in her seat to face him, finger wagging. "Well guess what, you federal jerk, I don't scare. Not by insipid, schoolboy pranks like this. Give me the evidence bag."

His gaze swung from her face to the turtle and back. "Adele, I'm telling you straight up. I. Did. Not. Put. The fetish there. I didn't take it. I didn't carry it around with me waiting for the most opportune time. And I certainly didn't put it there. It's evidence. It was in a sealed bag. This is a murder investigation with implications you haven't even begun to realize. There is no way in Hades' hell or on God's green earth that I would ever—I repeat *ever*—jeopardize an investigation."

Her eyes widened during the course of his denial, and a small, perverse part of his brain wondered if her eyes would look like the same as he enticed her toward a climax. He hoped so. He wanted to see her face flushed, her lips wet, eyes wide and dazed from him bringing her release. Damn but she was hot.

"Then how did it get here?" Adele really wanted to know what was going on in the handsome Fed's brain. Sort of. Maybe. His eyes had warmed from frozen coffee to melted caramel for a fraction of a moment. She was just curious enough to wonder what thoughts had chased through his mind and if she was in any of them.

"You're the CSI, you tell me."

"You're the big-time FBI expert. You explain it."

Caleb held her gaze for a minute then glanced to the fetish. "I'm not sure I can. But I know who to ask. Can you drop me back at CBI?"

"I...sure." Adele tried to pinpoint why she was hesitant. By all rights, getting rid of this guy was a main goal. At the same time, she wasn't quite ready to let him out of her sights. She didn't trust him. And he made her think of things she had no business thinking. Like if his abs were as rock hard as she pictured them. And what would his butt feel like if she cupped a cheek. And—And nothing. She jerked her thoughts back.

"Yeah. I can drop you off. It's on the way. Want to explain what's up?"

"I need to see a man about a horse."

His answer startled a giggle out of her. "Uhm...I can pull over beside the road. And I promise not to peek."

Caleb rolled his eyes at her. "Horse, not dog. And no, I don't need a potty break. I do need to head back to New Mexico. There's someone there who might be able to shed some light on all this."

"Are you going to share?"

He scratched his jaw, deciding not to shave before he headed south, while he considered his answer. Part of him wanted her very much involved because parts of him had definite plans for the sexy blonde. The more practical side demanded he get her out of this and far away from it before the spell imploded because his gut insisted it would—and sooner than later. "Del, are you sure you want to be in this mess?"

"Mess?" She put as much ire into that one word as she could manage.

Caleb huffed out a breath. "Look, darlin'. This is magic we're dealing with. Bad magic." He pulled his gaze from her to stare out the windshield and rub the back of his neck. "Blood magic, Del. That's as bad as it gets. And that kind of magic has a way of burning innocent people. I don't want to see that happen to you."

"Oh. Really." She added ice to her ire.

"You're human, Del. No offense meant and you shouldn't take any, but—"

"But what? You're human too. What makes you so special? The fact that you're some hot-shot Federal investigator and I'm just the local bumpkin?"

"But I'm *not* human."

When the Jeep swerved into the median, Adele over-corrected, shot across two lanes and ended up just off the shoulder, Caleb was glad to know his life hadn't flashed in front of his eyes and his shorts were still clean and dry. "Whoa, Del. What the hell?"

Adele managed to get the transmission into Park. She'd actually felt the blood drain from her face at Caleb's words and she was almost afraid to look at him, but she did. "What do you mean you're not human?"

And therein Caleb recognized his mistake. Del hadn't figured out he was one of the magicks. And not only that, she was totally freaked out that he might be. Oh yeah. That was a discussion for another day. Like *after* he got her into bed. His brain scrambled to come up with a plausible answer, which proved tough because his blood had all rushed to a different location. "Well...I'm FBI. Isn't the general consensus that we aren't human?"

He held his breath and crossed some mental fingers that she'd let this conversation lag.

"Oh...whatever."

Regrouping, he offered a contrite smile. "Look, in all honesty, I do have more experience with crimes like this. It's the whole reason the MAGIC unit was created.

There's stuff out there that boggles the mind, Del."

"And this is one of those things?"

He pointed to the brown paper bag sitting on the console between them. It had remained, as if rooted, despite the careening vehicle. "Those things are creepy. They carry deep magic. And, to reiterate, very bad magic. This is above even my pay grade, to a large extent. Being a member of MAGIC gives me contacts that normal humans don't have. I'm going back to New Mexico to tap into some of them. I believe the fetishes originated there. We need to figure out how they got from there to here. Right?"

Adele found herself nodding—and inordinately pleased that he'd said "we." "Okay. You're correct. I just...I want to see this to the end, Caleb. This is *my* case. Okay?"

"Okay."

When they arrived at CBI, Adele left him in the parking lot while she ran up to place the turtle back into the evidence box. Caleb knew he needed to get in his rental and get the heck out of town, but he waited. He wanted her to know he wasn't running out on her...and that they had unfinished business. Of the up-close and personal kind.

CHAPTER FIFTEEN
TICK TOCK

January, New Mexico Desert

CALEB MANAGED TO AVOID the up-close-and-personal part of the holidays by not returning to DC. Or Dallas. Not even Denver. Especially not Denver. The holidays, as celebrated by Mathias, were an ostentatious display of the vampire leader's power—whether magicks or mundanes were in attendance. He and Sade had suffered through the festivities as children, teens, and young adults. Since joining the FBI, they more often than not conspired to be "on assignment." Thing was, he really didn't want to see Sade either so he ignored her calls.

His head was in a weird place—even weirder than normal—and Christmas Eve had found him standing over Roy "Bear" Montoya's grave and wondering. About Bear's death. About his own life. About a human named Adele who occupied his thoughts way too much of the time. So he'd gone to ground. Hid out. But the time had come to answer the questions.

So now, in mid-January, winter finally blew into the mountains and desert. Better late than never, even in Gallup. Still, standing in a deserted parking lot at midnight, his collar turned up against the icy bitterness of the wind's fingers, he questioned his motivation. He'd been restless for years, always dogging Sade's steps, her faithful shadow. Thing was, he had no idea what he wanted to do. He'd been joined at the hip to his foster sister since he was a pup—literally. Werewolves wore fur until puberty. He'd been her faithful canine companion until his change. And wasn't that a real treat—sitting naked on her bed while her bad twelve-year-old self told him he could no longer lick his balls. As if!

Thunder rumbled in the distance and Caleb's magick meter pegged out. He'd been thinking about Sade at odd moments for the past week or so and he didn't like the creepy-crawly sensation in his gut whenever he did. The last time he'd checked in with Director Bailey, he learned Sade had been sent to Chicago. Something about a vampire, a dead senator's aide, and bad magic mojo. Much like what he had here, minus the vampire and dead aide.

He paced around his vehicle, all senses attuned to the night. Magic lines had started shifting last summer. No one commented on it, but the feeling left a dark and oily taste on the back of his tongue. Caleb, and the few magicks he trusted, hadn't felt this keyed up since the Big Rip. That thought rocked him back on his heels. The world couldn't handle another upheaval like that one. There were Realms beyond the Veil that needed to remain sealed—for the good of mundanes and magicks alike.

Caleb hated being basically undercover at times like this, even though he'd revealed his true identity to the CBI. He needed their cooperation and had the Old Man's blessing to do so. Another bad feeling rolled over him and he couldn't get Sade out of his mind. Giving in to the impulse, he pulled out his cell and called. She answered after a few moments, but he beat her to the opening.

"Please tell me you aren't using Steppenwolf for my ring tone."

"Okay. I won't. Where are you, Caleb?"

Yeah, he totally knew she would—and probably was. "I'm with a horse with no name. What's up with you?"

"A horse—" She bit off the rest to ask, "Still walking on the wild side?"

"I'm working. You didn't answer my question, Sade."

"I'm working too. Why?"

"Ripples."

"What the hell is that supposed to mean?"

"Whatever you have stirred up is creating ripples, Sade. Throughout the Veil."

She didn't say anything for a bit then seemed to choose her words carefully. "The pot was stirred before I got here, Caleb. Although, considering the preternatural activity in Chicago at the moment, I shouldn't be surprised. Crevan is here. Along with Ariel." She muttered something then added, "And that damn dragon."

He growled, loud and long, at that information. The freaking glitterfly was supposed to be meeting him—he glanced at his watch—right now. But if Ariel was in Chicago? "That should tell you something, Slim."

Slim. Caleb hadn't called her "Slim" in ages.

"Are you okay?" Her voice came through his cell all soft. And concerned.

"Nothing I can't handle, but you've been on my mind. You're thinking too hard."

"No, I'm not. I'm not thinking hard enough."

"Ripples, Sade. Sometimes you just have to follow them back to find the stone that was thrown in the first place." Shadowy movement jerked his attention to a spot across the lot and he held the phone to his chest as a man approached. Not too tall but broad-shouldered, features chiseled out of red sandstone capped by thick, dark hair. This had to be Ariel's shaman.

The man stopped several feet away and whispered in a voice that still raised the hair on Caleb's ruff.

"You are the wolf?"

Caleb nodded and brought the phone back to his ear. "I need to go. Duty calls and all that. Watch your six, Sade. I can't ride to the rescue if something bites you in the ass."

Before she could retort, he broke the connection.

"Caleb Jones." He didn't offer a hand to the Indian.

"Chaco. You have found the fetishes?"

"I think so, yes."

"Where are they?" Dark eyes snapped at him and Caleb fought their pull.

"They're evidence in a couple of murders."

"Not murders. Sacrifices." Chaco hunched his shoulders as cold wind whipped across the open parking lot. "Things are moving too fast."

"I think you need to talk to me. Tell me what's going on."

"You need to tell me of these murders. Who? How?"

Caleb shook his head. "They aren't my cases. I can't—"

Before he could finish, Chaco had ripped out a badge. "This is the badge I currently carry because it is necessary."

Leaning closer, Caleb read the words "Catron County Sheriff Office" on the gold star. "You carry more than one?"

The Indian allowed a hint of humor to dance at the corner of his mouth. "I am also a member of the Navajo Tribal police, out of Window Rock. If pushed, I can produce an ID naming me an officer of the Bureau of Indian Affairs Police as well."

"Handy."

"Yes." Chaco studied the lean man for a long moment. He almost smiled as Caleb returned the perusal.

"You carry the authority of the FBI yet they are not your pack. You also searched for pups for a pack not your own. I think we understand each other."

Before Caleb could respond, the atmosphere rippled and the moon brightened. A breath later, Ariel appeared.

"Sorry I'm late. My attention was needed elsewhere."

"Oh? I'm sure you won't be missed, Glitter."

Ari glanced at Caleb and couldn't help his gloat. "Ah, I see you've touched base with our girlfriend, Mutt." Ari laughed out loud when Caleb snarled at him, showing a hint of fang. "I do have to get back to her. Things are coming to a head in Chicago. I don't want to miss the fireworks, especially between Sade and that vampire."

Caleb did his best to look bored. "Yeah? She gonna stake his ass?"

"No. More likely, he's going to nail hers."

"Shut up. Just...shut up. I don't want to hear this." Caleb shook his whole body to get the thought out of his head. "If you can't get your head in the game here, then you need to get back to the Glitterdome and leave the important stuff to the real magicks."

Chaco watched the two unlikely friends. Even his kind had heard of the Child of Mortals and her ability to meld alliances between immortal enemies. Consideration for another time. He reminded the other magicks of the reason they had gathered. "The fetishes, wolf. I need to know."

"Three murders. One was skinned, and the pouch holding the fetishes was found tucked where his balls should have been."

Ariel winced. "Skinning is a painful process."

The shaman shook his head. "He was not skinned piecemeal, was he?" As Caleb nodded in assent, he continued. "Peeled, not skinned."

Caleb rubbed the back of his neck, staring down at

the dark pavement beneath his feet. He looked up as thunder once again rumbled in the distance. "Yeah. What sort of walker would take human skin?

"A *yeenaaldlooshii* has its own skin. This is not a skinwalker. The second sacrifice?"

"A college professor. Bitten by a rattle snake. And a rancher who basically drowned in mud. The turtle fetish showed up at the scene, despite being locked in an evidence box a hundred miles away."

"The werewolf pups you searched for?"

"I found them." He glanced at Ari. "You know of a pooka who lives out in the desert southwest of Albuquerque?"

The fae considered the question.

"Don't play around, Ari. No riddles. This is too important."

"I understand that, Caleb. I've heard the rumor of a pooka. Likes to run as a horse. He's not there by the King's permission. Nor by Titania's that I'm aware of. Pookas may be Fae by origin, but they play by their own rules. Why?"

"I met a horse with no name who showed me where I could find the pups' bodies. They'd been burned."

"In what order?" Chaco pulled Caleb's attention back. "I need to know."

"I found the kids first. Then, according to my CBI contact, the guy who was peeled, followed by the professor, and turtle man."

The shaman's brows furrowed, causing Caleb and Ari to exchange worried glances. "No. That cannot be. Bear first. Then lizard, snake, turtle, deer, and finally the wolf. The summoning cannot occur unless the sacrifices are made in order."

"Whoa, whoa, whoa. Back up. Summoning? What the hell is being summoned and by who?" Caleb did not like the way the conversation was going.

"I do not know the who. The fetishes were discovered and taken about a year ago. I suspect a man named Santos Santana."

"The drug lord?" Caleb growled the question and his gut churned like he'd eaten a bushel of raw ghost peppers. He sank down to hunker back on his heels. "Bear." He looked up at the other two magicks. "Roy Montoya. A Border Patrol agent and a friend of mine. His nickname was Bear. He died in the line of duty last summer. Killed by drug runners."

Chaco dipped his head and offered up a silent prayer for the soul of a good man. "And so it began."

"But what about the pups? You say they're in the wrong order." Ari's worried gaze flicked between the shaman and Caleb.

"Even two pups would not have enough magic." Chaco gazed down at Caleb. "But an alpha werewolf would."

Rocking back on his heels, Caleb stared at the shaman. "Me. The pups were to get me here."

"Yes."

Ari spewed a string of incomprehensible words in his native language. "So what's coming, Chaco?"

"I do not know for sure." Thunder rolled, sounding closer, while he stared toward the horizon. "The records do not say for sure. Something old. Something evil. This we know. As to what it is? Or how to kill it?" He turned his head to look at the other two. "This I do not know. I intend to find out."

Caleb pushed back to his feet. "How much time?"

"Again, I do not know. It stirs. But something else stirs as well." Chaco studied Ari. "You must return to Chicago. What happens there will have far-reaching consequences, can even perhaps stop things here. Or make them worse. Go."

Without conscious directions, Caleb's hand shot out

and clasped Ariel's arm. "Take care of her."

The fae nodded. "Always."

Caleb jerked his hand back as the air shimmered and Ari winked out. Facing Chaco, he rubbed his hand down his thigh. He'd have to wash both hand and jeans to get the faerie dust off, especially since he was allergic. "What do we do?"

"We must control the fetishes. The summoner must have two more sacrifices. I believe you are the one chosen to represent the wolf. That leaves the deer. We must determine the sacrifice and prevent it from happening."

Thunder and lightning flashed, close enough both men startled. A thunderstorm in January? Weird. Caleb almost laughed. Weird was relative at this point. "Okay. That means I'm headed back to Colorado. Do you need a ride?"

Chaco threw his head back, arms raised out to his sides, shoulder high. He drank in the storm, absorbing the sound and the fury. "Time, wolf. There is never enough." He lowered his arms but didn't look at Caleb. "You must retrieve the fetishes. They will come to you as the wolf is the leader. On your journey, hunt the deer. We would do well to have the sacrifice near."

"Can we prevent it from happening?"

"That is the goal. I will work from this end to locate the summoner and the summoned."

"Chaco? I think you know what it is."

"I suspect."

"What's coming?"

"A wendigo."

"They don't exist." Caleb tunneled his fingers through his hair. "Do they?"

"Not in this Realm."

"Well..."

"Yes, well. Get moving, wolf. Time is ticking away."

CHAPTER SIXTEEN
IF YOU ONLY KNEW

January, Denver
TIME TICKED AWAY. Adele survived Christmas and the not-so-subtle digs about her chosen career from her father.

"When you gonna take the test to be a real cop, girl?" was the central theme of Christmas Day. She survived. So she felt a little lonely. What else was new? Even if she had the urge to find a picture of a certain FBI agent, pin it to the wall, and throw darts at it. Humph. She didn't need him. Or want him.

When the New Year arrived, she felt no remorse for kicking the Old Year out the door. Winter finally showed up with a vengeance. Snow. Ice. Howling winds. Road crews worked around the clock to keep the roads clear. Ironically, the weather didn't keep criminals home where anyone with any sense would be.

Luckily, she'd been able to process the evidence that came in from a new Priority One case before midnight. Equally fortuitous, she followed the sand truck home and made it safe and sound in half the time she'd allotted. Exhausted yet wide awake, she opted for hot tea and a hotter bath in her old-fashioned tub. Rather than relaxing, the bath gave her time to think, to remember.

What did she know, really? Adele scrubbed water-wrinkled fingers through her sopping hair. So he was fascinating. Handsome. Sexy. Oh, yeah. Very sexy. But he was FBI and she was a just a local technical investigator—a point she'd made and he hadn't disputed. Jerk. As soon as this case was over, he'd be gone with the wind. Not that she expected him to come back. He'd left before Christmas. Weeks passed. No word. What did she care? Really.

Lying in the steaming-hot bubble bath, eyes closed, she thought about him. Caleb. An old-fashioned name but sexy. She *really* had to get past that sexy part. She remembered he smelled of English Leather. Or maybe Polo. Something decadent. And rich, like leather and polo ponies, but a little wild, too, like the wind whistling through a mountain canyon.

Adele gazed into his eyes. The color of hot coffee, they were fringed with thick lashes she would kill for. Why did men always get the long lashes? Mother Nature was a witch when it came to things like that. He spoke, his words murmured endearments. She could taste his voice—caramel flavored, buttery and smooth with just a hint of sweet. And his hands, long-fingered and strong, grazing her skin, leaving goose-bumps. She wanted his hand to touch her in other places, lower, more intimate, and when he did, she moaned in need. She implored him to join her with hands fisted in his dark hair.

Her phone buzzed. Dammit, she was on call tonight. When she opened her eyes, her memory of Caleb was gone.

"That's the trouble with dreams," she told the cat sitting on the toilet. "They die too soon." She snagged a towel to dry her hand and managed to hit the accept button before the call rolled to voice mail. "McCoy."

"Jones."

Speak of the devil. She hated her breathless, "Caleb" before she regained control. "Agent Jones. It's been awhile." Yes, there. That was frosty and professional.

"Too long. Get out of the tub, and come unlock the door. I'm too cold to pick the lock."

"What!" She screeched and clamored out of the tub, snatching a towel and her robe. She made it to the door of her duplex in record time and flipped on the outside light. Peeking through the peephole, she recognized the man standing there. Her heart thrummed in some primal beat that was all about hormones and alpha men.

She yelled through the door. "What are you doing here?"

"Let me in, Del. It's freaking cold out here and I'm tired."

"Then go get a hotel."

"Del..."

Her thighs clinched at the way her name rolled across his lips, at the humor twinkling in his chocolate brown eyes, at the way her hands itched to brush his shaggy hair off his forehead, her lips aching to kiss the stubble shadowing his jaw.

Before she realized what she'd done, the door was unlocked, opened, and Caleb stood in her living room.

"Uhm..."

His gaze flicked from her face to her chest and a knowing grin slid into place. "Are you cold or just happy to see me?"

She looked down. "Traitors," she mumbled and crossed her arms across her chest to hide her pebbled nipples. Louder, she added, "Cold. What are you doing here?"

"I missed you?"

"You never answer a question with a question, especially not that one."

"Okay. Do you have any coffee?"

"Of course I do, but it's after one in the morning. I'm not—hey!" She hustled toward the kitchen in his wake.

As if he'd been in her place a hundred times, he set up her coffee maker to brew a pot with minimal fuss and no comment to her.

"Make yourself at home," she groused.

He turned his most charming smile on her. "Thank you. I will." Caleb laughed as she glowered at him. "At least I didn't wake you." He reached for her, latched a hand around her biceps and eased her closer. "I missed you."

No question that time and the look on his face made her think he was as surprised by the admission as she was. "Why are you here, Caleb?"

He inhaled, filling his lungs with her scent. Old-fashioned aromas—lavender, chamomile, and something sharper, something distinctly her—a musk that swelled his dick. So she wasn't all about business tonight. Good. He had plans for the two of them and they didn't include rehashing the case.

"Came to see you." He cupped her cheek and brushed his thumb over the top of her cheekbone. "I know you feel it too."

Back up, get away. Her flight instincts fluttered deep inside, fighting with the equally primal instinct to mate. "No I don't."

Caleb smiled at her denial. "Okay." Then his mouth found hers.

She melted against him, her breasts fitting perfectly against his chest, their hips aligning like Mars and Venus in the most seductive convergence of two bodies ever. He held her face cupped in his big hands, angling her head for his assault on her mouth. His tongue swept aside all resistance as it teased between her lips.

Their breath mingled, their hearts beat in counterpoint, and she forced her brain to work, to form coherent thoughts. The cases. *Her* cases. No time for kissing. For sex. A part of her brain wondered if Caleb was any good at multitasking. She cleared her throat, managed to break their kiss.

"No."

Caleb dropped his forehead to rest on hers, but he remained tautly still. "No?"

What was wrong with her? Yes. Oh, yes. She wanted this more than she could fathom. "Not yet." Inhaling—a bad idea as her nipples brushed across the supple leather of his jacket—she attempted to put mental and physical distance between them. "Coffee. We need to talk."

The corner of his mouth quirked. "Okay. We can do that. I'm good at multitasking."

That's what she was afraid of. Slithering out of his embrace, she opened the fridge while he stripped out of his jacket. And his sweater. Down to an ab-hugging vee-neck tee shirt. Chest hair. And abs. And pecs. *Oh...my.* Adele licked her lips.

Caleb watched her tongue, the predator inside coming to life. He could talk. He could scare the bejeezus out of her over the cases and include her. Or he could lie like the dog he could be, keeping her out of it and safe. He didn't like either scenario. He reached for her again, pulled her against his chest, tipped her head back and took her mouth. *Mine.*

His hands and mouth were occupied in the most delightful ways so Adele was positive the man was an expert when it came to multitasking. His slow seduction heated her blood, setting her libido to slow boil. Whatever exhaustion she'd felt when she got home was scorched away by his touch. She arched against him from the sheer pleasure of touching him.

His mind went quiet, with single-minded focus, his blood hot, rushing into needful places. She leaned into him, reached for him, her mouth seeking his. He scooped her up, coffee forgotten, talking an item for later. He needed her now. The taste of her on his tongue, the feel of her surrounding him. With an unerring sense of direction, he aimed for her bedroom.

He made it to the bed, took her down with him, twisting at the last fraction of a second so she landed on top. A fast roll and she was beneath him.

Clothes. He had on too many. Standing, he stripped, his eyes devouring her lush curves, the tie of her fluffy robe barely hiding them from his sight. With preternatural speed, he shed his clothes and stalked up the bed to cage Adele against the headboard. He spread her legs, looked his fill. Lowering his head, he smiled wolfishly. "I do so enjoy a midnight snack."

And then he was between her legs, kissing, licking, nibbling. Adele gasped. Cried. Moaned. She grabbed his hair, tugged, not that her pulling did any good. His eyes caught hers, held them as he feasted on her. He grabbed her hips as she arched, her climax cascading like a mountain stream at the spring thaw.

The taste of their lovemaking, of her, seeped into him until he was drenched in her. He wanted to roll in her scent. Wanted to lick her entire body. With a final swipe of his tongue, he kissed his way up her rounded tummy. He caught one taut nipple with his lips, the other he pinched between thumb and forefinger. He wanted the feel of her skin, the rapid beat of her heart against his chest, the curve of her throat as she arched in welcome. Soft. Strong. Snug.

"Now," he demanded.

Yes, now, she thought. *Right now.*

It was sparks and a burning stretch when he plunged inside her, a glorious shock to her system when he took control. Her breath caught, released on a low hiss of approval as he pushed deep inside, her hips rising in demanding invitation.

Magicks couldn't mate with humans, nor did human diseases affect them. He'd have that conversation with her later. Now, with her soft body pressed against him, her hands gliding over his back, her nails lightly scratching at his skin, the feel of her seduced him. He slowed, settled, stroking long and sure in and out of her tight sex. As she moved with him, trembled for him, the need inside him that was never quite tamed leaped free.

Adele could see his eyes, watching her. Even in the dark of her bedroom they gleamed like some savage creature in the forest, wild and free. A tiny voice in the back of her brain warned her to be afraid, but her heart overruled the voice. She wanted him, just like this. Untamed. Demanding. Taking her. Driving her. Owning her.

Close. She was so close again. He changed the angle of his thrusts, and she couldn't breathe.

"Look at me, sweetheart."

She opened her eyes, unaware she'd closed them. She neared the crest of the wave poised to crash over her, to send her senses reeling into an ocean of sensations and thoughts and feelings she'd never before known.

"With me," Caleb growled. "Come with me."

His finger found her clit, pressed once, stroked a second time, and then his mouth crushed down on hers, and like riding a tsunami, she reached the peak, Caleb with her, falling, surfing, drowning in the tempest that was their shared climax.

"Breathe, beautiful."

She could do that. Maybe. She opened her mouth, sucked in air, filled her lungs to capacity. She might live now. Maybe.

Caleb rolled off, turned her, fitted her to his side. His breathing remained as ragged as hers. He concentrated on an act that should be automatic, but wasn't this time, as his system started a delayed reboot to normal. His heart drummed, pumping blood back to other extremities, but he heard it. Her heartbeat.

Syncing with his. As it should be.

She felt wonderfully sleepy now, and sated. Nothing beat good sex. Especially not the excellent sex she'd just had with the excellent man currently radiating heat. Adele snuggled in closer, dropped a kiss on the flat, brown nipple above his pounding heart. "As amazing as that was, it's never happening again."

He laughed. He couldn't help it. He was just getting started with her. "Never say never, sweetheart."

CALEB STOOD A LITTLE APART, legs braced, chin lifted, eyes glued to the horizon. He looked like one of her dad's retrievers locked in on a pheasant. Adele wanted to pet him. The man was beyond gorgeous and she was struck again at his wild, untamed appearance. Her fingers itched to brush the dark hair out of his melted-chocolate eyes, especially now that she was on intimate terms with the silken texture of that hair. She'd never met a man who quickened her pulse and sent her imagination to places like rumpled beds...or panting, hot-doggy sex in the parking lot.

Especially after spending the last two weeks with him. What was she thinking? Sex in the parking lot? Seriously? She didn't know this guy. Well, beyond a road trip to see a body, and lots of toe-curling sex. Caleb Jones. What kind of name was that? But there was something about him—something hard, unsettling—that hit her right in the pit of her stomach.

"I don't like him." Carl's hands were shoved in his coat pockets and his breath puffed out in the cold air. "And I don't trust him. I see the way you look at him, Addie. Like you could eat him with a spoon or something. What are you doing? The guy shows up claiming to be a Fed with intersecting cases? I don't buy it. Not at all."

"He's not claiming to be an FBI agent, Carl. He is one. It's verified."

"Well, those fetishes didn't start acting weird until he came on the scene and claimed magic is involved."

"Magic *is* involved, Carl." Since the Big Rip, the governor's office had a witch on staff. Adele, in a fit of frustration, broke down in December and had him look at the fetishes. After the man almost passed out, he ordered her out of his office with threats of cursing her, her children, and her children's children's children if she ever darkened his door again. His reaction scared her more than she wanted to admit. Magic wasn't science. Curses didn't exist. Yet, the President of the United States was an elf. Monsters lived under the bed. And the Fae were not Tinkerbell.

"Addie, are you listening to me? I think he might be involved, maybe even the perp. There's something just not...right about him. He could be the one."

"I wish." Adele swallowed her sigh, praying Carl hadn't heard her admission.

Caleb chose that moment to turn his head and stare at her partner, his gaze feral, until Carl looked away. Holy cow. Had he overheard their conversation? His gaze shifted to collide with hers and the corner of his mouth quirked in a wolfish smile. Crap. Could he read minds, too?

"I don't have to." Caleb's attention centered on her.

She was in so much trouble.

"Don't have to what?" Carl puffed out his chest but stepped back and behind her as Caleb approached.

She gave him the fish eye, and Caleb laughed. Spending the night and most of the day in bed with her had done wonders for his mood and general outlook. He stalked toward her, ignoring her lab partner. Adele glared and Caleb leashed the smirk hovering around his mouth. It wouldn't do to tip his hand. Not yet anyway.

Her partner looked like he wanted to run. Flicking his gaze in the man's direction halted the lab geek in his tracks.

"You are impossible."

He liked the way Adele's breath caught, pushing her breasts against that shapeless jacket with the CBI logo. She was way more turned on than she wanted him to know. But hey. Werewolf. He knew. "No, I'm not."

His lazy drawl created enough heat her cheeks flushed. He liked that too.

"You think you're so special. How do you put on your pants every morning?"

"You should know since you watched me this afternoon." Air hissed between her lips, and he fought the urge to kiss her. "Sadly, I also put them on the same way Carl does. One leg at a time, sweetheart."

"Don't call me that."

He unfurled the smirk, stepped into her space, and caught her gaze in his. "Thing is, sweetheart, if I call, you'll come."

Her pupils dilated then shrank to pinpoints. Her face drained of color before temper infused her skin with a cheeky red. And there was the reaction he wanted—her lips parted as her tongue darted out to moisten her full bottom lip. He would have this woman beneath him again, and soon.

The flare of her nostrils warned him just in time. He twisted to one side so her knee collided with his thigh rather than his balls. Oh yeah. The best thing you could do to an alpha werewolf was provoke a challenge. He smiled and uttered one word.

"Run."

Like an idiot, she did. All the way to his car. Laughing, she jerked the door open and jumped inside, but she didn't manage to click the locks. Not that it mattered when he dangled the key fob just outside her window.

Caleb glanced over his shoulder toward Carl. "She's off duty. You aren't. Back to work." Sliding into the driver's seat, he offered her a big smile. "I feel like steak."

"I DON'T TRUST HIM."

Adele closed her eyes and girded her virtual loins for another fight with her lab partner. "Carl, we've been over this. He had nothing to do with these murders. He was in New Mexico. Not to mention he's a decorated FBI agent."

"Don't care. There's something...wrong with him."

"Wrong?"

"Yeah. The guy is...off. I don't like you hanging around him."

She stared at the man she'd worked with for three years in the CBI lab. "Dude, you sound...jealous."

He muttered something under his breath that sounded suspiciously like, "He just wants in your pants...er..."

"Chemistry, Carl," she asserted. "You Skyped me to share the chemistry report on the mud where Mr. Larson was found."

The hair on the back her neck lifted, and she had just enough time to angle the laptop so Caleb didn't appear in the Skype window as lips brushed across the sensitive skin where her neck and shoulder met.

"I'll give you chemistry, sweet girl."

"Who's there, Addie? Is *he* there?" Carl's angry voice sounded tinny coming from the computer's speaker.

She couldn't prevent the sigh or the delicious full-body shiver as she ignored the questions. "Carl, I need that report. Like yesterday. Do you have it or not?"

He had the good graces to look embarrassed. "No. Jamie's still running the full spectrum, but he's convinced there's something extra in it—something not native to that area."

"Fine. Email it as soon as you get it. I have to go."

Adele closed the program before her partner could respond. Swiveling, her nose bumped Caleb's. "Dude, personal space."

"I like personal space." His lips brushed across hers as he spoke.

"Stop that."

"What's that they say? All work, no play?"

"We don't have time to play."

"Says you."

"Caleb—"

She didn't get the warning out as he kissed her deeply then growled. "Play now. Work later."

"Okay. That works."

Chapter Seventeen
Desperation

THIS WASN'T WORKING AT ALL. Caleb's head felt like a watermelon that had been smashed on concrete. He flexed his fingers, yanked at the restraints holding his wrists together. Metal. He was strong, but even werewolves were limited when it came to breaking steel manacles, especially when even more chain looped around his chest and arms, effectively hogtying him. Closing his eyes, he let his other senses roam free—and tried to remember how he ended up shackled in this bare room.

He'd gotten a lead. Returned to New Mexico from Denver. He let loose with an internal Sade-style string of obscenities and he ground his teeth. The memories wouldn't come. Taos. Yes. He'd gone to Taos. To the pueblos. A mountain road. Snow. Santa Fe. There was something in Santa Fe. Or someone. Who? What? And how had he ended up a prisoner? More important, who was his captor?

His head pounded, a deep throbbing worse than any subwoofer in a low-rider custom hot rod. Why couldn't he remember? Even a blow to the head should have healed, and his memory with it. Inhaling, he let his nose go to work.

Old. This place was old. Dust. Rats. An oily whiff of dissipated magic. Men. Four. One liked jalapenos. Another needed to shower more often. The third liked his tequila and the fourth...

Caleb's nostrils flared. He'd scented the fourth man before. Where? When? The man was human...but not. Not witch or wizard. Something...different. He opened his eyes, glancing around the space. It wasn't huge—like a warehouse—but the room felt large. And disused.

Footsteps echoed beyond the closed door. He tensed, waiting. For what, he wasn't sure. He couldn't fight—not tied up like he was. He'd survive whatever they threw at him, just so long as they didn't decapitate him, fill his heart with liquid silver—harder than it sounded, or burn him to a crisp. With luck, the one who was *other* wouldn't recognize Caleb's heritage.

The door banged open and two men entered, dragging someone between them. Adele! A third man followed, automatic rifle held ready across his body. Swallowing his anger and forcing his need to shift into the recesses of his consciousness, Caleb offered a sardonic smile instead.

"Of all the gin joints in all the towns in all the world, she walks into mine." Caleb didn't bother keeping his voice down as Adele was dumped beside him.

"Shut up!" The brute with the weapon glared while one of his buddies, the one who'd copped a feel before dropping Adele, smirked.

Caleb just managed to hold on to his humanity, hooding the feral gleam in his eyes from the guards by blinking. He glanced at the woman trussed up like a Thanksgiving turkey next to him. The gods really were crazy to have brought them by such circuitous routes to what looked like a final destination. The armed guard fingered his massive weapon. Again.

"Makes you wonder if he's over-compensating for something," Adele whispered *sotto voce*. "You know what they say about small men with big guns…"

"Ya think?" Caleb managed to give her a gentle shoulder bump. The show of solidarity was tough considering he was tied up tighter than she was.

"Shut up. Both of you. El Diablo will be here in a minute."

"El Diablo? Wasn't he a character in that movie starring Dennis Quaid and Kathleen Turner?"

Caleb cut his eyes her direction. "You mean 'Undercover Blues'?"

"Yeah. That one. Set in New Orleans. They kept making fun of the El Diablo guy."

"Naw, I think he kept saying his name was Muerte."

"Morty. Yes. That's the name."

"Shut up!" Bullets sprayed the ceiling, sending a curtain of dust and debris down around them.

They exchanged a look before turning their gazes toward the shooter. Adele pursed her lips and nodded. "Yes. Definitely overcompensating."

The other two men snapped to attention as a fourth man entered. Caleb wasn't sure what he expected, but this bantam rooster of a man wasn't it. He wore a white suit and red satin shirt circa "Saturday Night Fever"—complete with strands of gold chains, a huge, gold ID bracelet on one wrist, and an expensive watch on the other. His western boots had impossibly pointed toes, the leather died an eye-searing urine yellow. Human, he carried a hint of *Otherness* that perplexed Caleb.

El Diablo waived a hand in front of his face, stirring up both gunsmoke and dust. "Oye, cabrón. Por qué están disparando? Why are you shooting in here?"

"They wouldn't shut up, boss."

El Diablo closed his eyes and shook his head. "Ay yi yi. You make my head hurt, pendejo." When he opened them, his gaze slid over Adele.

Wanting to appear brave, she faced down the man, but still leaned a bit closer to Caleb. He couldn't help her. She knew that because it looked like fifty feet of chain was wrapped around him. Caleb leaned forward, giving her a little space to brace her shoulder behind him, his unspoken promise to protect her to the best of his ability.

"Sí, me gustan. Bueno sacrificio."

Caleb didn't need to speak Spanish to translate. El Diablo planned to sacrifice them for something. "Why, Santana?"

"I am not that person. Santos Santana no longer exists. I am El Diablo."

Adele giggled. She couldn't help it. She was terrified, cold, spoke Spanish and knew bad things were going to happen, but she could not get that movie character out of her head. When the giggles tipped over into tears with a touch of hysteria, she clamped her lips shut and rested her forehead against the point of Caleb's shoulder.

"We're gonna be fine, sweetheart." Caleb barely breathed the words. He needed to get the chains off. He was stronger in his half form, but fully shifted, he could slip his paws out of the manacles. It would hurt like hell because the shoulders of a wolf didn't allow for being wrenched behind the back, but he'd do it and heal—mostly—when he shifted back. At the same time, if the drug runners didn't know what he was, he needed every last vestige of surprise.

In a conversational tone, he asked, "What are you planning for us?"

"You are very curious. I don't blame you. Where are the fetishes?"

"What fetishes?"

Red suffused El Diablo's face. "Estupido! You know what fetishes. What have you done with them?"

Caleb attempted to shrug. "No clue, dude."

So angry spit came out with his words, El Diablo stalked closer. "You will tell me where they are!"

"Not here."

"I know this! Where are they?"

"Back in Denver. Under lock and key." He hoped. The damn things tended to have a mind of their own.

"No, no, no. This is not how this works. You were supposed to bring them with you."

"How did they get to Colorado?" That part had made Caleb scratch his head when he'd first started tracking them.

The big guy with the gun hunched his shoulders and studied his pointy-toed boots. Caleb had a suspicion, given the pawn shop he'd visited in Pueblo and the pawn ticket Adele found at the Parker scene. El Diablo fluttered his hands. "Idiotas. I am surrounded by them. One of my men pawned them."

Yeah. Two points to instincts and human nature. Caleb tilted his head. "Why are you doing this?"

"Por que? Because. The spirit made me do it." A broad smile creased El Diablo's cheeks.

Caleb's ear perked up. "The spirit?" If he could keep Santana talking, maybe he could figure out a way to escape. "Huh. Guess the spirit makes you willing but your flesh is weak. The spirit turn you down?"

"I make the sacrifices." El Diablo snarled and stepped closer. "I am the spirit's earthly vessel. I will be a god when your blood mixes with the sand of the desert."

"Golem?" Adele whispered the word.

"Don't think this thing is Jewish, hon."

El Diablo crept closer. "You will not make fun of me. Or of my spirit. He is great and powerful."

"Huh. Must be the Wizard of Oz."

Del giggled and, in her best Robin Williams' impersonation, said, "Are you a good witch or a bad witch?"

Their captor threw his hands in the air and gurgled his displeasure. Many deep breaths later, he found his voice. "I know this script. This is where I pistol whip you or something else to prove my manhood, but I shall not give you gringos the chance to be all defiant like that.

No. I shall simply sneer from here."

Arching a brow, Caleb coated his voice in sarcasm. "Well, rain check on the biting and spitting on you then."

"Yeah, I wouldn't want to peek behind the curtain, either," Adele added. "Another classic example of overcompensation."

Caleb really wanted to kiss her at that moment. They were very likely only minutes away from dying, and Adele was tossing quips like a closer threw fast balls in the ninth inning.

Tequila Breath struck before Caleb could react to protect Adele. He backhanded her, catching her cheekbone, and then he hauled her up. His hand cocked back, ready to deliver a closed-fist punch.

"No. The spirit, he does not like damaged goods. He has told me it is good you sent his fetishes away, Juan. He said three he needed would be found and the rest would come." El Diablo stared at Caleb, speculation in his eyes. "This has come to pass. But we need her to keep this one in line. If they will not take us to the fetishes, *he* will draw the fetishes. Take them to the desert."

Jalapeno Dude pulled a pistol from the back of his jeans. Two shots—a muted *pffft-pffft*. Yeah, that explained the headache and the memory blanks. Tranq gun. Darkness sucked him under, his last thought of Adele. And Sade.

SINJEN WATCHED HER THROUGH half-lowered lids. Long, lithe, she dressed with an economy of motion he found arousing. A man brutally honest about his own needs and desires, he admitted her presence alone was enough to stir his blood.

"Come here, Sade."

She paused, one hand on a hip as her bottle-green eyes flicked over him. With a smirk and rolling eyes, she returned to her packing. "I have to go."

"As do I, but I'm not ready to leave you."

"Don't have a choice in this, Slick."

"Agreed. Duty calls us both."

"No, duty dictates we get our asses in gear." She zipped her bag and sat on the edge of the bed to pull on leather boots. "You don't want to piss off the Conclave."

"I do not answer to the Conclave."

"No, you answer to Mathias. It's the same thing."

"You haven't asked why they demand my presence."

"Not my fu—" She bit off the rest before he chastised her. With another eye roll, she glowered. "I cuss, Sinjen. Get fucking used to it. As for the damn Vampyre Conclave, not my business. I have enough to worry about with Caleb's disappearance."

"The werewolf will take care of himself." Unable to resist, he stepped closer to her. She drew him like a magnet.

"And I'll take care of myself." Sade knew what this was about. Their relationship might be new, but she was learning to read the enigmatic vampire. He worried about her. For her. She'd come damn close to dying not long ago—in his arms. She still woke from the nightmares, his voice demanding she live for him, for them, reverberating in her memory. It wasn't like they were soul mates or anything. No such thing. But. He stirred feelings in her, emotions that were totally alien. She blinked, and he was right there in front of her.

He cupped her cheek, lowered his mouth to hers. He was learning to read her emotions, the way her feelings became etched on her face. This thing between them was tenuous, a fragile chrysalis easily shattered and the precious life within irretrievably lost.

"Not now, Sinjen." Her words whispered across his

lips. "We're already late."

"We are, yes. We will be even later. I want you."

"Again?" She glanced at her watch. "You have ten minutes."

"I don't need ten minutes."

The desperation was the same. It ached in him, a wound that didn't heal. He needed Sade more than he needed the night to survive.

She'd been a mass and maze of conflicting emotions the first time he'd seen her. He remembered everything. All heat and motion, driving him to frenzied want so that he'd burned to possess her, to cover her with his body, take her and spur them both toward release. But he'd wanted more. Even then, watching her stalk across the barren floor of his prison, he'd wanted more, wanted all.

He stripped her, stripped himself then gripped her hands, jerking her arms over her head, and she arched, pressing her hips to his.

"Inside me." Her eyes unfocused, emerald shimmering with forest shadows. "I want you inside me. Now." She shifted her legs, thighs cradling his hips. "Hard. Fast. I want to cover myself with you."

"Wait." He knew what she would feel like, knew intimately the hot, silken heat of her. He knew where they would take each other.

She freed one hand, brushed it down his side toward his cock. His control was a thin, taut thread. He captured her errant hand, drew it above her head, and cuffed her wrists with one hand. If she touched him now, his hard-won control would snap.

With her restrained, he could touch her. By all the gods, he had to touch her—the need like living fire in his blood. He wanted to watch her, to feel her body writhe and tremble from the assault of pleasure. He skimmed her damp skin with his free hand. A moan trembled on the tip of her tongue, tipped over, swelled to a hoarse cry as he plunged clever fingers into her.

He watched those eyes as sharp as broken glass go blind, reveled in the hammering of her heart, the throb of her pulse in the wrists he held. She sobbed her release, her body bowed before melting like candle wax beneath a flame.

"Again." His mouth came down on hers, frantic. Fierce. Yes, that sharp emotion in his chest was fierce. He wanted her. Again and again and again.

Then her arms were free and banded around him, and her hips arched, her long legs circling him. He was inside her and, as she'd demanded, he took her. Hard. Fast. Relentlessly.

Some part of her brain could still reason, could still make sense of the sensations raging through her, through him. Sade smiled, knowing that he'd gone over, gone to the place he so often sent her—that place beyond civilized, way past reason, where there was only greedy need. His. Hers. Control was impossible here and pleasure drowned thought, deluging both mind and body with pleasure.

Her body quivered, soared toward that last cliff, and she heard it. His breath hitched as if a lancing pain knifed through him. Wrapping around him she gave herself to him. "Now," she challenged, leaping and pulling him with her.

CHAPTER EIGHTEEN
RADIO SILENCE

———————————————

A LEAP OF FAITH had Sade pulling out her phone. Nothing. Determined to get to the bottom of things, she cruised through Denver's Stapleton Airport like an aircraft carrier headed to war. Smart people parted like the sea before her. Slow people spun out of the way like so much jetsam and flotsam. She passed the guy in the rumpled suit with barely a flick of her gaze. He spun around, his action caught in her peripheral vision, and legged it after her.

"Miss? Ma'am? Uh..." He panted at her side.

"Special Agent Sade Marquis."

"Oh, yeah. Well, listen up, Marquis."

She stopped so suddenly, the guy was four feet beyond her before his reflexes caught up. "You are?"

"Brad. Agent Brad Jacobsen. Colorado Bureau of Investigation."

"Uh huh." She started walking, and once again, he had to jog to keep up with her long legs.

Jacobsen grabbed her arm in an effort to either slow her down or stop her forward progress. It didn't work.

She stared at his hand. "Move it or lose it, Agent Jacobsen. I don't have time to play games. Keep up or go home. I need one stop at your headquarters to talk to a technical investigator named Adele McCoy, and then I'm out of here."

"Yeah, see, that's the problem."

Something in his voice got her attention. She halted, turned to face him, and arched a brow.

"Addie. She's missing too."

Well, shit. This wasn't good. "What about those

gawddamned fetish things?"

The CBI agent had the good graces to duck his head and toe the concourse as he mumbled, "Those are MIA too."

"Motherfuckingsonavabitchingfuckitalltohell. Please tell me you at least have some gawddamned crime scene photos."

His eyes widened at her string of curses, but he was smart enough to ignore her language. "Sure. We got those."

"Let's go, errand boy."

"Hey—"

"Don't got time, Brad." She whipped around and headed toward baggage claim. Her phone dinged—an email from Alice Cooper, the director's admin, with the info that the lab tech had been reported missing too. A day late and a dollar short.

Jacobsen huffed and puffed in her wake and cursed the tall Fed under his breath. Who did she think she was, dropping in here like she was God's gift to law enforcement? The director of CBI told him to play nice, give her what she wanted, and get her out of their hair. He was half-tempted to sic her on the director.

"Can you walk and think at the same time, Jacobsen?"

"Listen, Marquis—"

"I will when you have something useful to say." They arrived at the carousel and she pointed toward the exit doors. "Go get your car. I'll be right there."

"I don't take—" His eyes widened at the sudden appearance of the man standing behind Sade, and he forgot what he was going to say. Every hair on his body stood up, and he had to force his feet to remain where they were. Flight seemed way smarter than fighting.

"Gawddamn it. Nikos, what the fuck are you doing here?" Sade didn't need to turn around to know who was there.

"Hello, *khriso mou*, have you missed me?"

"Like a boil on my butt." She glowered at the CBI agent. "Jacobsen. Car. Now."

Nikos countermanded. "My car is right outside, Sade. I will take you where you need to go."

She whirled on him and jabbed his chest with her index finger. "Listen up, you overgrown, scaly pain in my ass, I have two words for you. Official. Investigation. Last time I looked, no dragons were involved. That means you can take your fancy Drakon rear and get the hell out of my space." She jerked her thumb over her shoulder. "Jacobsen. Car."

He didn't wait around to argue. Any bitch with the balls to take on a dragon shifter was tougher than he'd ever be. Jacobsen took off toward the exit.

"I've missed you too, darling," Nikos purred. He snapped his fingers and the dragon standing next to the baggage conveyor snagged the suitcase with Sade's name on it.

She peered around Nikos. "Damn. Stavros. I can't believe they let you back into the real world." Sade laughed when the dragon snarled at her. She fully expected to see steam shooting out his nose. They'd had a little confrontation a couple of years ago in New Orleans and Stavros had been punished for clobbering her. To say there was no love lost between them was the understatement of the year. "You make a good bellboy, though."

And there it was, the faint curl of smoke and waver in his glamour.

Nikos *tsked* at her. "Sade, have you not learned it is dangerous to tease a dragon?"

She brushed back her jacket to reveal the Beretta snugged in its holster under her arm. "I think I have a cure for that." She offered a toothy grin. "What the fuck are you doing here, Nikos?"

"I am looking into some mountain property for the Clan. Imagine my surprise to look up and see you strolling through the airport."

"I don't stroll, Nikos." She raised her hand toward Stavros. "I'll take my bag. I have an anxious CBI agent waiting for me."

Stavros ignored her as Nikos took her arm and led her toward the exit. "He did seem rather nervous."

Like a good dog, Nikos's second followed, dragging her roller bag with him. She really shouldn't jerk the dragon's tail, but it was just so much fun. When they hit the sidewalk outside, Jacobsen was standing there beside a standard-issue state sedan. Stavros shoved her suitcase into the rear seat and backed off, eyes narrowed, mouth quirked into a sardonic grin. He lifted one hand and moments later, a sleek, silver Range Rover slid up behind the sedan.

Nikos trailed his index finger across her cheekbone—the one Stavros had bruised with his fist back in New Orleans. "Can I not persuade you to change your mind, *khriso mou*?"

"Stop calling me that, and no. I'm not riding with you, not having dinner with you, and not sleeping with you. Ever." Her gaze flicked to Jacobsen. "You drivin' or what?"

Not to be put off, Nikos leaned close and whispered in her ear. "Ever is a very long time for a mortal, Sade. For one such as me? Barely a blink. I *will* have you, sooner than you think." He brushed his lips against her cheek and straightened. "Until we meet again, Agent Marquis."

She watched the arrogant dragon swagger off, ignoring his broad shoulders, tight ass, and how those tailored slacks caressed his muscular thighs. Before he could catch her looking, she ducked into the passenger seat of the sedan.

"You're either the bravest bitch I've ever met, or the stupidest."

Sade focused on the hapless CBI agent. "Excuse me?"

"Sorry. Shouldn't call visiting VIPs a bitch."

That made her laugh. "No, that's cool. I am a bitch. But I'm not stupid, asshole, so don't go there. The Drakon and I have a history." Her eyes narrowed at his speculative look. "Not *that* kind history."

Jacobsen pulled out into the line of cars jockeying for position and picked up speed once he hit the freeway leading from the airport to downtown Denver. The Fed didn't talk so he kept his thoughts to himself. He'd been as freaked out as the next guy when the bad nasties came out of the woodwork after the Veil ripped, but he'd educated himself. He could tell when a magick was around. He might not know what flavor, but he knew they were *Other*. With the Fed sitting beside him? Yeah, weird vibes. He figured he had nothing to lose by asking.

"So...what are you?"

Eyes the color of and glinting like faceted emeralds stared at him. He had to force his gaze back to the road.

"We've established I'm a special agent with the FBI. And a bitch. What are you asking, Jacobsen?"

"What flavor are you?"

Sade snorted and didn't hold back her laughter. "Flavor? You insinuating I'm a magick?"

"Aren't you?"

"Oh fucking hell no. I'm as human as you are." And she was. With a few minor alterations. Due to the long-standing feud between the master vampire who was her godfather and the Fae king of the Seelie court, she'd been marked by both sides while still a toddler. She'd grown up with a werewolf pup, had a gargoyle sentinel as a bodyguard, and a Fae seducer pursuing her virginity. A dragon enforcer wanted her in his fucking bed, she'd defeated a witch by swallowing her evil, and had fallen for a master vampire who'd once been a Templar knight. Yeah. She was human. Just a human way too aware of the worlds that existed beyond the Veil.

They rode to the CBI building in silence. Once inside, it took Sade less than an hour to review the crime scene photos, evidence, and terrorize McCoy's lab partner so badly he likely had to change his boxers. His fault for blaming McCoy's disappearance on Caleb—and his very vocal dislike of the werewolf she considered family. She was no closer to finding Caleb than she had been when she first got the call in Chicago.

Damn but she was angry with the flea-bitten cur. Bad enough that Director Bailey and Alice had kept his status a secret from her—letting her think he'd quit the Bureau and gone walkabout. The radio silence had killed her—and got worse after that cryptic phone call from him. She'd been standing in the middle of Chicago PD's homicide bullpen swamped by her current case when he'd called. And now? To be told he'd been undercover without backup? Without *her*? She and the Old Man would be having words once she was back in DC.

When she exited the CBI building, she shouldn't have been surprised to find an overbearing and imperious dragon leaning against his expensive SUV, ankles crossed, arms folded across his chest, ignoring all the feminine attention he was garnering.

"No."

"You don't even know what I am going to ask, Sade."

"The answer is still no. I don't have time for you or your games, Nikos. Go away,"

He reached for her and she backed up a step. Not a retreat, she reminded herself, but avoidance.

"You are not being fair."

"Don't have to be."

"But you do, *khriso mou*, if the rumors are true."

Her eyes slitted and her mouth thinned out. Nikos must be completely perverse to enjoy bedeviling her as he did. She wore her anger like most women wore diamonds and she was so utterly different from the females of his species and those human women he'd bedded through the ages.

"What are you insinuating, Nikos?"

He pressed his palm over the space where a human heart would rest in his chest. "I pray the wags are wrong, that you did not bed a certain vampire while in Chicago."

Her eyes glittered, and he was reminded once again of his favorite jewel. He would clothe her in emeralds to match her eyes if she would but allow him. Her cheeks flushed, and he could almost hear her teeth grinding. So the rumors were true. When Kristian St. John had teamed with his sire to rescue Sade from the witch, Nikos worried about the vampire's influence. Too many magicks underestimated his power, as St. John did not gather minions, nor did he flaunt his strength.

"That is none of your fucking business, Constantine." She offered a look of disdain and added her standard disclaimer. "I don't have time for magick games. Get the hell out of my life and stay out." She pivoted on her heel and glided away. If he didn't know her, hadn't studied her, he would believe her act. The set of her shoulders, the angle of her chin, and that angry glitter so similar to strong sunlight on broken bottle glass all confirmed he'd touched a nerve.

"Drakon?" Xan, his other *dankána*, held the door to the Rover open.

Nikos raised his hand to hold Xan in place. Tamping down his magic, he followed Sade to the end of the block. "Have you committed to him?"

She stopped dead, and one heartbeat later she turned to face him. "What part of none of your business do you not understand?"

"He is a vampire, Sade. An ancient one."

Sade snorted and gave him her d'uh face. "Uhm, pot. Kettle. Black."

"Yes, I am ancient, but I am a dragon. Passion burns inside us."

"You sure that's not heartburn from the last virgin sacrifice you ate?"

"Please, Sade, offer me the courtesy to hear what I have to say."

"Fucking fine. Spit it out."

"You may believe that since vampires begin as full human they retain their humanity. They do not."

"Gee, really? I had no idea."

"Sarcasm does not suit you."

"Fuck this, Nikos. You forget who I am. You forget who fucking raised me. You forget that those assholes Oberon and Mathias used my gawddamned toddler self as a pawn in their perverted games."

She got right up in his face, and he liked the fact he didn't have to look very far down to meet her gaze. Anxiety from his *dankánas* washed over him. He waved them back with a discrete flick of his fingers.

"I know exactly who and what vampires are. What *all* you magicks are. In the whole scheme of things, humans are at best pretty playthings and at worst, food."

He started to argue with her, but no words to refute her assertions would come. She was right. Like the apex predator he was in his soul, he studied her, assessing. The dragon smelled prey—interesting prey that would put up a fight to make things challenging. The heart of the dragon saw the human's heart—the lonely child who wished to be loved, the frightened child who saw real monsters in the world, the determined child who evolved into this warrior standing in front of him.

"The man who wins your heart will be a fortunate man indeed."

Sade rocked back on her heels, the sincerity of the dragon's words punching her in the stomach as hard as any blow she'd ever taken in a physical fight.

"Please guard it well and make sure the winner is worthy." He tucked his chin and placed a chaste kiss on her forehead. "Now, you are currently afoot and snow is about to fall. Xan will drive you where you wish to go." He placed his finger over her lips, keeping any protest bottled inside her. "No strings, Sade. He will stay in the Rover. I offer only a driver and vehicle for as long as you need."

She glared up and down the street but couldn't conjure a cab. Nikos was right. Big, fat flakes were drifting down from the dirty clouds hanging low over the city. "What about you?"

"I already have a second vehicle coming. Stavros and I will take it."

The silver Rover slid to a stop beside them. Nikos didn't give her chance to refuse. He opened the passenger door and ushered her inside. He ducked his head to peer at Xan. Something unspoken passed between them. Sade rolled her eyes at the secret dragon woo-woo. A second Rover, black this time, rolled up and a dragon she didn't recognize hopped out of the front passenger seat to open the rear door.

Nikos ignored the urge to kiss the distrust from Sade's expression. Instead, he offered his predatory smile. "Good hunting, *khriso mou*."

CHAPTER NINETEEN
WHERE ANGELS FEAR TO TREAD

"GOOD HUNTING."

Those words echoed in Caleb's head as he swam up out of the darkness to discover two things. Both the wall at his back and the floor under his ass was vibrating. And something soft pressed against his chest puffing soft breaths into his ear. His nostrils flared as he inhaled gingerly, keeping his eyes closed. Orange. A hint of vanilla. Burnt sugar. Adele. He inhaled deeply. Gasoline. Beer. Body odor.

The floor continued to thrum beneath him. His brain put the pieces of the puzzle together. Airplane. A small one from the sound of things. His back was braced against a bale of something. He sniffed again. Money. Wrapped in plastic. Well all righty then. He continued his mental exploration. The aromas he associated with Adele were closer and more intense. As was body heat and soft curves. His brain came on line. He was still handcuffed behind his back, but his arms were circled around Del and she was curled into his lap, her arms over his neck.

Her breathing changed, and her eyelashes fluttered then caught in his beard stubble. "Shhhh." He wasn't sure if he was trying to soothe her or alert her to their situation.

"Caleb?"

"Twenty minutes to the drop site." A voice from the front of plane rode just above the engine noise.

Opening his eyes just enough to assess the situation, he recognized Tequila Breath and Jalapeno Dude, both hunched over bundles near the cockpit. Caleb twisted his arms, squeezing Del's ribs. He couldn't avoid it.

"What are you doing?" Adele hissed at him, casting a furtive glance toward the front of the plane.

Yeah, that was the question of the moment. He couldn't exactly explain he was doing his best to shift just his hands and wrists into those of his wolf form. Caleb hoped to shed the handcuffs and give them a chance to escape—which was the other question of the day. He could probably jump out and survive. It would hurt way more than was fun, and there'd be a chance of permanent injury leaving him crippled. But it was a moot question. He was not about to abandon Del to the drug runners.

He did get his claws to come out before the men came for them but didn't have time to react before an inoculation gun was pressed to his neck. He felt a quick prick, and in moments, his vision went wonky as his claws retracted.

"That'll hold him. Get them apart and put the chute on him."

He heard Del scuffling with someone, followed by a sharp clap—skin on skin. Blood. Del's. He snarled, but his big bad wolf was down for the count. Damn drugs. He'd shake the effects off sooner than a human but not nearly fast enough to help. His arms dropped to his sides as the handcuffs were removed. One man hauled him to his feet and fitted his feet through straps before settling a pack on his back.

"Five minutes."

"Get her in place."

"Bitch." Another slap. "You better hang on to him because he's got the parachute."

Adele quieted. Her face stung, but both strikes had been open-handed slaps. Her head was clear now, adrenaline burning like wildfire through her veins. The men handcuffed Caleb's arms around her waist. Her wrists were still bound and they slipped her arms over his head. She looked into Caleb's eyes, hoping against hope that he was okay. Dilated pupils returned her gaze. Not good.

The man, dubbed Jalapeno Dude, who'd hit her wrestled with the door. Once he got it open, the other man shoved them closer to the opening. "You better hope your boyfriend shakes off the Ketamine because you ain't gonna be able to reach the rip cord to pull it."

He exchanged laughter and a high-five with the other man, and then they both pushed. She had time to grab a breath before she was free-falling, her arms tight around Caleb's neck. She instinctively wrapped her legs around his waist and screamed.

"Caleb! Caleb! Can you hear me! Oh, god, pleasepleasepleaseplease."

Her eyes teared up as she tried to judge how far they were from the ground. The desert floor was rushing toward them far too fast. She buried her face against Caleb's neck and prayed she was brave enough to move her arms from around him to dig between them for the cord. The Ketamine in his system would create a dissociative state. He wouldn't know what was happening and wouldn't have much—if any—control over his movements. Rescuing them was up to her, but she was terrified of heights and just knew that if she let go to pull the cord, she'd plummet to her death.

Caleb hated the sensation of falling. Had since he was a pup and was thrown off a cliff. Someone was clinging to him and crying. Del? He sniffed. Yeah, Del. He went to pat her back, realized he wore handcuffs. Wind whistled in his ears, and his hair whipped around his eyes. Everything came back in a rush. Oh hell no. He and Del were not going to die today.

"Del! Del, baby. Listen to me. I can't get to the rip cord. You have to. I'll hold you tight, but you have to let go of my neck and find the cord. Okay? Del!"

His arms tightened around her waist, and she lifted her head. His eyes still looked like black holes, but his expression carried awareness. "O-okay."

"Count of ten, sweetheart."

He counted down as she lifted her arms and tucked them between their bodies, her fingers scrabbling for the ring on the ripcord. "Got it!"

"Three. Two. Let 'er rip!"

She screamed as the parachute unfurled and jerked them up as it caught air. His arms tightened even more. "I've got you, sweetheart. We're gonna be fine."

"Promise?"

"Promise."

They hit hard, but Caleb made sure his body cushioned Adele. The chute dragged them about ten feet before he could get untangled from her and get it under control. He couldn't do much more than roll it into a messy ball until he escaped from the handcuffs. With his back to her, he concentrated, his face twisting into a grimace as the bones in his hands snapped, broke, and reshaped into paws. The cuffs dropped off, and he returned to his human form. He glanced over his shoulder. Del looked shell-shocked, not surprising given their circumstances. She was huddled in a ball, her knees drawn up to her chest. He could see her shivering and hear her teeth chattering. Yeah, free-falling through a winter night was not good for human physiology.

"Give me a minute, sweetheart. I'll get the parachute free and we can use it as a blanket."

"K-k-k-kay." Her teeth were chattering.

In a matter of minutes, he had the lines stripped, and he enfolded Del in the parachute. He ripped the pin from the main riser cord and used it to finagle the locks on the handcuffs still around her wrists. While he didn't want her shocky, it certainly helped that he didn't have to explain how he was able to do certain things. Gazing around, Caleb was glad they'd been dumped basically in flat desert, but their location was problematic. This was the desert in February. Temperatures would sink to freezing before morning. He needed to get Del up and moving—one, to help get her warm, and two, to keep moving until they found shelter.

A dark smudge shadowed the eastern horizon. Buttes. The rocks would hold some residual heat and maybe he could rig some sort of shelter using the parachute. Stuffing the lines and other bits he'd destroyed back into the deployment pack, Caleb slung it over one shoulder and held out his hand.

"C'mon, Del. Time to walk."

Her gaze flicked up to him, but she didn't move.

"On your feet, baby. You can't sit here all night. They tossed us out here for a reason. We need to move before whatever lives out here comes hunting."

As if to emphasize his words, a pack of coyotes howled in the distance. A full-body shiver raced through her, and she clutched the nylon parachute closer. She didn't believe she'd ever get warm again. "It's too dark."

"Moon will be up shortly. It's almost full. And until moonrise, I have excellent night vision."

She cocked her head. "Wait. They drugged you again. Ketamine. You shouldn't be functioning."

"Walk and talk, sweetheart. Walk and talk." He hauled her up, turned her to her left, and, holding her hand, led her across the empty desert.

"Why are we going this way?"

"High ground." He raised his arm and her eyes found the uneven horizon he pointed to.

"Oh." She stumbled along in his wake for a few minutes. "Why?"

"Why what?"

"Why high ground?"

"You never played army when you were a kid? Or cowboys and Indians?"

"Uhm. No. Not really. I was more a cops and robbers kind of kid."

"Oh? Why's that?"

"My dad." She stubbed her toe on a rock, but Caleb put his arm around her waist supporting her before she went down. "Before he retired, he had a hundred percent clearance rate on his homicides."

"Ah. Big Jim McCoy. I should have made the leap."

She sighed, but tried to cover it with a cough. "Yeah. Everybody has heard of him."

"Okay." Caleb's voice sounded noncommittal.

"What do you mean *okay*?"

He glanced at her and tried to read her expression. "I've heard of him mainly because no one who's ever studied crime statistics believes he cleared that many. How many of his cases are up on appeal?"

Del's temper rose, upset Caleb was denigrating her father, but beneath the temper was the technical investigator who wondered how accurate all the evidence had been and how truthful some of the guilty pleas. Deciding to sulk, she didn't answer, and while she wasn't so petty as to jerk away from him, she wasn't averse to the silent treatment.

After a few minutes of hearing nothing but their footsteps in the hard crust of the desert, Caleb's soft admission surprised her. "I got it. You have issues with him. Know the feeling. I have a hot-shot cop in my family too."

She didn't ask for an explanation, just kept trudging. She was thirsty. And tired. And her head hurt. And she was still cold, though not shivering like she'd been when they first landed. Adele glanced over at Caleb. He wore a long-sleeve tee shirt and jeans yet he didn't look cold at all. He'd insisted she put on his flannel shirt—a shirt that now enveloped her in a cocoon of scent overload. Especially since she was also wrapped in layers of parachute nylon.

When they'd been shoved out of the plane, she'd expected her life to flash in front of her eyes. Obviously, it was a myth. All she'd seen was the ground rushing far too fast toward her. All she'd felt was overwhelming panic. Trudging along, head down, she didn't realize Caleb had stopped. She slammed into his back.

"Ow."

"Easy, Del." Caleb fairly vibrated as he stared at the apparition.

"You again."

Del jerked her head up. A horse—an old paint, roan and white, with tangled mane and tail—watched them. The thing seemed to glow in the moonlight.

The horse whinnied and pawed the ground.

"Don't feel like playing twenty questions here."

The horse switched its tail as it's lips moved. "You brought me a playmate."

"Nope. The human is mine."

"Make you a deal."

"Nope."

"Then I'll give you advice."

"S'long as it's free."

"Bad times are coming."

"Tell me something I don't know." A thud behind him had Caleb looking over his shoulder.

"Del?"

Her knees had given out and she sat in the sand, staring and pointing. "That horse is talking."

"Not a horse, sweetheart. Not exactly. Pooka."

"Uh huh." She wrapped her arms around his leg.

"She's cute," the pooka said. He tossed his head again and whinnied softly. "You need to get out of the desert. I'm headed to greener pastures m'self." The horse turned in the direction of the rising moon and started walking. "Two things. There's an abandoned mine about two kilometers that way. There's water."

"And?"

"And I'd be lookin' for a sign, boyo. Aye, that I would."

The pooka shimmered and disappeared in a shower of golden glitter.

Caleb looked down at Del. "You can let go now, sweetheart. C'mon. We've got more walking in front of us."

"Oh. Okay."

One foot in front of the other. Easy peasy. Anything was possible. Because they'd just met a pooka. In the middle of the desert. A freaking *pooka*.

"Del?"

She looked up at Caleb's voice, realized she'd stopped walking. She lifted her right foot, put it down. Lifted her left, moved forward. "I can do this."

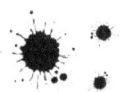

"I CAN'T DO THIS." She peered into the dark hole, shivering violently. Adele'd lost track of time as they walked though the moon rode high in the sky now. They'd reached an outcropping of rocks, and within a few minutes of their arrival, Caleb discovered the entrance to the old mine. She had two huge fears. Dark, enclosed spaces, and heights. She'd already faced one tonight. She wasn't ready for the other. Something rustled and she tensed. Okay. Add lizards to the list, though they were more creepy than a soul-sucking terror of the pee-in-her-pants phobia.

Caleb gripped Adele's biceps and gave her a gentle shake. "Stop, Del. You need to focus."

"I can't." Tears sparkled on her eyelashes, catching

light from the near-full moon.

"You can, and you will. We weren't given a choice when we bailed from the plane." He pulled her close, wrapping his arms around her shaking body, absorbing her fear through his very pores. "We do this or die, Adele. The temperature is going to plummet, and I have no way to build a fire."

She sniffled, brushing her face across his shirt.

"Great. Use me as a snot rag next time."

She hiccupped. That was a good sign. He rubbed her back, passing his warmth to her. The desert night would turn frigid before dawn. He had to get her sheltered. And that meant facing her fears.

"It's too dark. Too small."

"I can see in the dark."

She tilted her head to sneak a peek under his arm. "What about snakes?"

"It's February, Adele. They're hibernating."

"Yeah, in mines, d'uh. What about coyotes? Or wolves?"

He swallowed his laughter, biting his lips in case she glanced up and caught his smile. He was the biggest wolf in the neighborhood.

Her brow furrowed, and she frowned. "Ghosts."

Caleb blinked at that. "Ghosts?"

"Yeah. Old, abandoned mine? There must be ghosts. Or demons."

"Didn't I mention I was a ghost hunter in a previous life?"

She laughed. Another step in the right direction. Demons, though? He wished Roman was here. Gargoyles hunted demons. He sniffed the air. No sulfur.

"Congress is in session. All the demons are in Washington." He hoped. The idea of Santos Santana calling forth a demon scared the bejeezus out of him. What scared him more was that there were things worse

170

than demons floating around out there in other Realms. Adele choked and buried her face against his chest. He hoped it was laughter not sobs shaking her.

She wheezed in a breath and spoke. "The president is an elf. Why wouldn't there be demons in Congress? Makes so much sense."

He breathed deeply for the first time. Del was strong. She'd need to be to survive.

CHAPTER TWENTY
SHADOWS IN THE DARK

SURVIVAL. SADE WAS BEGINNING to wonder if it was overrated. After a quick call to the director's Admin, Alice, she'd caught a plane to Albuquerque. With no leads, she'd gone back to the beginning. She stood over the grave of Bear Montoya in Carlsbad. She read Caleb's emails. And here she was, bouncing along a sorry excuse for a road headed to a place called Buhmfuch. Seriously? Could her life get any more fucked up? She should have known better than to ask the Universe because, pulling up at the Teepee Motor Court, she discovered that yes, yes it could.

Two guys lounged on metal, shell-back lawn chairs near the front door. A furtive-eyed woman with scraggly gray hair slammed the motel office door shut as Sade climbed out of her rental SUV. The woman's shadow remained outlined on the tattered curtains on the window. Low-key, Alice had said. Nothing official. Yeah. Right.

Sade approached but stayed back about ten feet. Her reflexes were good, despite lack of sleep. She could take them down before they reached her, especially since her Beretta was loaded with silver bullets.

"Yo, dawgs."

"Bitch."

Okay. The big guy first. Sade stared him in the eye, but watched the second man in her peripheral vision. Multi-tasking. Always helpful when surviving a close encounter of the magicks kind.

"I see we've met. I want to talk to your Alpha."

"You're talkin'."

She laughed. Loud and long. Slapped her thigh. Wheezed in air. Then sobered immediately. "Yeah, right. *You're* the Alpha. Good one. You should be a comedian. Listen up, Benji. Orrin Johnson. Take me to him now or I'm calling in air support. Y'all won't like fighter jets buzzing the desert floor. Trust me."

"You don't got that power."

"Wanna bet?"

She slipped her phone from her jacket pocket and hoped like hell she had bars. When the guy blinked first, she gloated. She still had the best poker face to come out of Quantico.

"I gotta tell 'im who's comin'."

"Marquis. Sade Marquis."

The smaller guy beside him gulped. "Aw, hell, Buddy. Do you know who this is?"

"Sh'up, Moe. Don't know. Don't care."

"You should, man. You should."

Sade expected the short man to go belly up and pee himself. Buddy didn't seem at all impressed. She would disabuse him of that. Soon.

An hour's drive over a non-existent road later, she stood in the center of a ragtag community of campers, trailers, and an old school bus. The Alpha of the Johnson pack was everything she hated about werewolves. Thank the gods Caleb had grown up a Jones. The alpha of the Jones pack, Romulus Jones, was rough around the edges, a redneck of the first order, but the man had class.

She opened negotiations. "Caleb Jones."

Johnson scratched grimy fingers across a tobacco-juice-stained wife beater that might have been white. Once. A decade or two ago. "Don't know who you're talkin' about."

"Yeah, I think you do. Something about missing

werewolf pups? Ring a bell?"

"Nope."

"Where's Mimi?"

"Wha'chu want with her?"

"I hear Jones took her on a shopping trip."

Her eyes flicked to the largest trailer, caught a shadowy movement at the window. "Hey, Mimi! C'mon out and join the party."

"Leave my girl outta this."

Seething now, Sade demanded, "Where is he?"

The werewolf alpha scratched his chin. "Don't know."

"When did you last see him?"

"Couple months ago."

She wanted to scream in frustration. Or beat the crap out of the shifter. Neither was likely to happen. Warning growls from the pack trailed off and the cool desert night dropped a few degrees. Sinjen. Here. She could feel him. But how? Why? He was supposed to be in Chicago—or wherever the Vampire Conclave met.

"Come, Sade. They can do nothing."

His voice washed over her, touched lonely places she'd dammed up since leaving him. "I have to find Caleb."

"I know."

She whirled, fists clenched and ready for battle. The look on his face undid her. Like air seeping from a balloon, her tension deflated. His full lips curled into a knowing smile.

"Come with me." He held out his hand and she took it without thought. With a curt nod to the pack, he led her away.

Inside her SUV, Sinjen cupped her cheek and traced her lips with his thumb. "I've missed you."

"Me too you. Caleb's in trouble, Sinjen."

"Then I will help you. The monster under this bed is

unlike any you've faced before."

"I'll figure out a way to kill it."

"And I will figure out a way to protect you."

"Nice to know you have my back."

"And your front."

"No time to play, Sinjen."

"There is always time for this." The vampire kissed her, his lips branding her mouth. "There. That's better. Now let's go wolf hunting."

"If he's dead, I'm going to kill him."

"GODS BUT I HATE THE DESERT."

Sinjen wisely refrained from either smiling or replying. He kept his mouth clamped shut, a bland expression on his face as Sade waggled her finger at him.

"Yes. This is a gawddamn town. Sort of. But fuck it. Look—" She swept her arm out to encompass the jagged horizon and the clouds of stars in the night sky above them. "All that empty fucking space." She cocked a brow at him. "Wait. You're a city vamp. I mean...Chicago and all. How can you be comfortable out here? And the sun! Even this time of year there's so much fucking sun there's not enough damn sunscreen in the drugstore to make up for it."

Sinjen huffed out a breath. He sometimes wondered if Sade spiced up her language just to irritate him. He wouldn't be surprised, yet she'd had a foul mouth from the moment they'd met.

"Stop. Just fucking stop. I know what you're thinking. I am not going to quit cussing so you might as well just decide it's part of my charm or get the fucking hell out of my life."

He went preternaturally still, but was amused when Sade smoothed her palms down her arms. Thankfully, she had excellent instincts when it came to predators—at least recognizing them. Backing down from them? She still had a great deal to learn. Every day with her brought new terror into his life.

Magic washed across his awareness, bold, demanding, dragon. He stepped to put Sade behind him, but she ignored his efforts, staring instead at a man standing across the street. Impeccably dressed, the man tugged on his cuffs and the emeralds sparkling at his wrists winked in the pool of light cast by the streetlight.

"Ohgawddamnmotherfuckingjustshootmerightnow hell."

Without taking his eyes from the magick, Sinjen asked. "You are acquainted with the Drakon?"

Rather than answer Sinjen, Sadie yelled, "Yo, Nikos, what the hell?"

With a charming smile on his face, Nikos stepped into the street. He ignored squealing tires and shouted curses to join them on the sidewalk. Dragon and vampire sized each other up like a couple of junkyard dogs getting ready for a pissing contest. Sade refused to be the bone in this fight.

"You following me, Drakon?"

"No more than the bloodsucker."

She cut her eyes to Sinjen. "Yeah, about that. Why *did* you show up out there in the desert?"

"I have information for you, Sade." *And I missed you.* Sinjen would not voice that last aloud, especially in front of the dragon. He didn't need any sort of magical gift to understand what Constantine wanted. St. George he was not, but he would slay this dragon—risking war between the Conclave and the Clans—if Sade but asked.

She turned to him. "You couldn't tell me this on the drive to this gawddamned forsaken outpost of fucking humanity—"

"Sade, please—"

"Language, Sade—"

Dragon and vampire exchanged glances. Sade rolled her eyes. "I'm not a lady. I won't talk like one, walk like one, or dress like one. Y'all should just move along and forget you ever met me. Especially you, Nikos." She poked him in the chest, her eyes widening as a low growl raised the hair on the back her neck. Sinjen jealous? Well, hello there upper hand. She smiled despite the testosterone.

"What about you, oh scaley one? Why are you here again?"

"I received information as well." Nikos looked far too amused as he perused Sinjen.

"Okay. Waiting here." She looked at Nikos then Sinjen, anticipating one would speak. When neither did, she nudged. "You go first, Sinjen."

"Caleb met with a pooka out in the desert."

The crowd around them seemed to thicken, knots of people pushing past them on the sidewalk.

Nikos surveyed the area, unease settling on his shoulders. He exchanged another, more primal and understanding look with Sinjen. "We should discuss this later. Congregating on a corner surrounded by 177undane does not seem excessively intelligent to me."

Sade rolled her eyes at the dragon even as Sinjen stiffened beside her. "D'uh. Of course, it'd help if the two of you weren't so freaking sexy."

A lazy smile slid across Nikos's face though his eyes glittered as they cut in Sinjen's direction. The vampire curled a lip, offering a hint of fang.

"You think I am sexy, Lady Sade?"

"Swear to the gods if you call me that one more gawddamned time I'll tie your fucking tail into a fucking knot, Nikos."

Sinjen laughed, but didn't chide her about her

language as he usually did. Sade swore at least three women creamed their panties when they heard his laughter. Okay, four, though she would never admit the vampire played havoc with her libido. Not that he hadn't already figured it out during her stay with him in Chicago. He slipped his arm around her shoulder and tucked her into his side, much to Nikos's dismay. Damn but she was tired of the Neanderthal chest-thumping, but when dealing with an ancient Greek dragon and a master vampire who was once a Templar Knight, she didn't have much choice.

Ignoring the hormones, Sade stepped off the curb as the light changed. "We need to find a horse with no name. That means a trip to the desert."

"I can fly you, *kardia mou.*"

"You think I'm gonna climb on your scaly, slimy back? Nuh-uh. We're driving."

"You think I will sit in some tiny metal box with *him*?" Nikos sneered.

Sade halted on the opposite corner, pivoted to face the dragon, hands fisted on her hips. "I don't know why the hell you're even here sticking your gawddamned nose in an official fucking FBI investigation, Drakon. I think you need to get your damned dragon ass out of my fucking space because you got no business in it."

She heard Sinjen's soft snort of laughter. His laugh was followed by a soft *whuff* as she nailed him in the gut with her elbow. Whirling on the vampire, she shook her finger. "And that goes for you too, Slick."

Before she could continue chastising, the two men erupted. Sinjen jerked her to his chest and went to the ground with her. Nikos, gathering a glamour around him to hide his shift from man to dragon, shot into the sky, his wings sounding like a flock of pigeons beating against the cold, desert air.

"What the fucking hell?"

"Are you injured?" Sinjen's words slurred together.

"No. What the gawdamn motherfucking shit was that all—" Sade choked off her tirade when she saw the blood on Sinjen's face. "You better not be hurt!" She managed the threat despite him collapsing on top of her. Before she could react, the vampire's weight was lifted and Sade stared up at a massive gargoyle.

"Gotta go, Sade."

"Varrick?"

"Run now, talk later, babe. Magic kills. Remember that."

She did remember, and she'd be damned if she lost Sinjen to its ravages.

"SADE, STOP HOVERING. I'M FINE."

"You're fine? Sinjen, you were fucking bleeding. Look!" She gestured at her chest and three pairs of male eyes fixed on her breasts. "I have fucking vampire blood and other shit on me. You are not fine." She whirled to the 1500 pound gorilla in the room. "And you! What the fuck, Varrick?"

"Happy to see you too, Sade."

She glowered at the gargoyle sentinel, the dragon, and the vampire. "This is like a bad joke." The three men waited for her explanation so she enlightened them. "A vampire, a dragon, and a gargoyle walk into a bar..." Sade rolled her eyes when the men just continued staring at her. "Never mind. I want to know what the hell is going on. Somebody better start talking—"

The air in front of her shimmered and her ears popped. A moment later, Ariel materialized amid a shower of glittery faerie dust.

"Oh, goody. Isn't this fun? I'm obviously not in Kansas anymore." Sade pointed at the gargoyle, vampire, dragon, and fae in turn. "Look, the Tin Man, the Scarecrow, the Cowardly Lion, and a flying monkey. My life is now complete."

Ari glanced around the room. "Only one problem, Dorothy. Where's your little dog, Toto?"

"Missing, you glittering asshole. Why are *you* here?"

"What do you mean *missing*?"

Sade stared at the fae, shocked by the sincere look of concern on his face. "Caleb's missing, Ari. That's why I'm here. The director called and put me on his scent. As for the rest of this motley crew, I was just trying to determine their motives and reasons for sticking their noses in my investigation."

Nikos elbowed Ari out of his way and cupped Sade's cheek. Before he could speak, Sinjen was there, fangs extended, his eyes the color of a moonless, midnight sky.

"Enough!" Sade's sharp command cut the testosterone clogging the room. She stepped between the two, a hand on each of their chests and shoved. Amazingly, they stepped backwards. Sade was strong, but not strong enough to move both a dragon shifter and master vampire. "If it weren't for the two of you..."

"I came to help you," Nikos interrupted.

"No. You came to seduce her," Sinjen stepped forward and rammed into Sade's hand.

"Gods. You two drive me crazy. Stop the alpha-male chest-thumping. Caleb's out there somewhere. In danger. You want to help? Then cut the caveman crap. We need to locate him and that CBI tech who disappeared with him. And we need to figure out what the fucking hell is chasing them."

The men exchanged looks over the top of her head. She didn't miss the significance. "What are you not telling me?"

The air in the room compressed and shimmered. Sade's ears popped as an imposing figure teleported in.

She wasn't too surprised at the latest arrival. "Roman."

"Lady Sade." The gargoyle, hunched over to fit into the tiny motel room, quickly morphed into his human glamour. "I cannot stay, which is why I sent Varrick." He acknowledged each of the other magicks with a slight dip of chin.

"Maybe you'll give me a straight answer, Roman."

The gargoyle, one of her oldest friends, and once her protector, gazed into Sade's eyes without blinking. "You look well, but there are still dark shadows haunting you."

She shrugged off his concern. "Ding, dong, the witch is dead. That's all that matters. And I'm standing here despite her best effort. Takes more than a bitchy witch to take me down. Now tell me about Caleb."

"Something ancient has been roused."

Scrubbing her hands against her temples, Sade sat down on the edge of the bed. "Something wicked this way comes?"

"Yes. Very wicked and beyond evil." Roman glanced at the fae. "Ariel has more information. I cannot stay, Sade. There are other things demanding my attention. The rise of the witch created a chain of events that even now rips through the Realms. Though I leave Varrick here to assist, I fear even your protectors may not be enough." His gaze raked over each of the magicks, assessing motives and intentions. He hated that Sade, so wonderfully human, was once again ensnared in the evil leaking from the rip in the Veil. They'd come close to losing her barely a month hence, there in the icy cold of Chicago.

Each man surrounding her had reason to keep her safe—Sinjen out of love, Nikos out of covetousness, Ariel out of friendship and respect, Varrick out of duty. He prayed to all the gods they would be enough. Roman's gazed settled on Ariel. "Tell them what you suspect and what you know. You—" His eyes touched each one, including Sade. "—will have to find a way to defeat this enemy. Good hunting."

The air compressed and Sade's ears popped again as Roman disappeared. She eyed Ari. "Okay, Glitz, spill it."

Ariel didn't take long. He didn't know all that much. As he explained about the shaman, the fetishes, and the deaths in Colorado, Sade interrupted him.

"Wait. Name the fetishes again."

"Bear, lizard, snake, turtle, deer, and wolf." Ariel ticked them off.

"I've been backtracking Caleb. Last August, a friend of his in Border Patrol was killed in the line of duty. His nickname was Bear. Caleb came back to New Mexico last fall to search for two werewolf pups. He found them. They'd been burned beyond recognition. His notes mentioned a pooka and some character named El Diablo."

She pushed off the bed and paced the room. The men wisely got out of her way. "The three deaths in Colorado correlate to the lizard, snake, and turtle. That leaves the deer. We need to figure out who that is."

Stopping at the window, Sade gazed out across the parking lot toward the mountains in the distance. Lightning flickered above them. "Ari, I need to talk to the shaman."

"I will talk to him." Sinjen appeared at her back as he said the words.

Sade watched their reflections in the glass, caught the emotional undercurrents swirling through the room. She knew what they expected of her.

The gargoyle spoke for them all. "Go home, Sade. We will bring Caleb back to you."

"Like hell, Varrick."

"That is precisely what we face."

"Then I'm going to hell." This was Caleb. The

shadows couldn't have him.

Chapter Twenty-one
Change Is Coming

THE AIR THICKENED WITH SHADOWS, and chilled even more as the sun dipped slowly into a boiling sea of salmon, burgundy and lapis. Overhead, the sky darkened to blue velvet even as it faded on the horizon under the glow of the approaching moon. The abandoned mine was a day behind them. Caleb wanted to shift—needed to—but he refrained. He would, later. When Del was safe and asleep.

The outcropping of rocks Adele leaned against radiated heat absorbed during the day, and it felt good against her tired muscles. She glanced over at Caleb and resisted the urge to snarl. She was hot, dirty, and exhausted. He looked like he'd been to a picnic.

"How can you be so cool and collected about all this?" she groused, using the back of her hand to push her hair back off her forehead.

Caleb shrugged. "Practice?" He cocked a sardonic eyebrow. "You aren't used to field work, are you?"

Adele shook her head. "Guilty as charged. I'm a lab rat." She leaned her head back against the rock and closed her eyes, wanting nothing more than to sink down into a heap and cry herself to sleep. Pride wouldn't let her. She jerked when Caleb took her arm and urged her back onto the trail winding through rock cliffs.

"Well, Technical Investigator McCoy, try to stay on your feet for just a bit more. We need to find water. When we do, we'll rest for the night."

"That's *when* and not *if*, right?" she asked, trying hard not to whine.

"There's water ahead. It's just a matter of getting to it." Caleb was fairly certain, but his wolf would know faster.

Del nodded numbly, forcing one foot in front of the other. She couldn't say how long they'd been walking when she ran into Caleb's back. It felt like she'd smacked into a brick wall, and she just managed to stay on her feet.

"Oww," she complained rubbing her nose. "Why'd you stop?"

He held one finger up to his mouth and cut his eyes up the canyon. She leaned to look around him. A small spring bubbled from between two rocks, gathering in a hollowed-out stone basin. Water trickled over the edge to skip along a narrow trace for a few yards before it disappeared, every bit of moisture sucked dry by the thirsty sand and scrubby plants. Adele didn't really see any of that. The large mountain lion calmly staring at them, water dripping from its muzzle, held her complete attention.

The big cat sniffed the air curiously then dropped its head back to the pool and lapped, taking a long drink. When it finished, the lion raised its head to stare at the two humans again. It blinked once, its golden eyes covered for a millisecond. With a flick of its tail, the mountain lion turned and padded off a few feet. Leaping up to a rock shelf, the feline paused, silently regarding Caleb before turning and prowling along the shelf then gracefully leapt to another path higher in the rocks.

He didn't move until the mountain lion was completely out of sight. Glancing back at Del, he smirked. "You can let go now."

Adele stared at him then looked down. Her fingers had laced through his, and she was squeezing so tightly, her hand had gone numb from lack of blood flow.

"Oh. Sorry," she murmured, dropping his hand like

it was a hot coal. She looked around apprehensively even as Caleb boldly strolled up to the spring. "Are you sure that thing is gone?" She hated that her voice squeaked.

A low rumbling sound echoed in his chest. The man was laughing at her. "Yeah, city mouse, I'm sure." He stuck his hand into his back pocket and whipped out a white handkerchief. He held it out to her. "Here. You can use this to clean your face."

She took the cloth from him and sank to her knees beside the spring. Del dipped the cloth into the surprisingly warm water and wiped her face before cupping her hand and taking several long drinks. "Oh. Crap," she muttered. "This isn't going to make me sick is it?" She glanced up at Caleb.

He was scanning the area around them and didn't look at her. "It shouldn't." He waited until she'd had her fill and moved away. Caleb dropped to one knee and drank from his cupped hand too. When he'd had enough, he stood and glanced around. "Rest for a minute while I do some scouting."

Adele meant to stay vigilant—really she did—but within a few minutes of Caleb walking away, she was snoring softly. She had curled up in the fetal position, her head resting on one bent arm, knees tucked almost to her chest, the parachute draped over her shoulder.

That's the way Caleb found her when he returned and changed back into human form. He sighed, hating himself a little for what he was about to do. For a city girl, Adele McCoy was a pretty impressive specimen. His grin was sanguine as he murmured, "Definitely pretty." Since they'd been kidnapped, she'd kept her chin up, her wits about her and hadn't complained. Much. Hell, she'd been thrown out of an airplane at 5,000 feet, lived to tell about it, and was doggedly determined to get back to civilization so she could bring the drug runners to justice. He knew that would never happen. He would exact his own brand of justice on them long before human authorities ever got the chance. They needed to keep moving so he leaned over and touched Del's shoulder.

"C'mon, sleepyhead. We need to keep walking," he said quietly.

Startled, she jerked up. The top of her head connected soundly with Caleb's chin, and it felt like someone had hit her with a hammer. "Ow! Owowwwww," she whimpered, rubbing her head and hoping the stars dancing in front of her were really in the sky.

"Damn, girl," he growled. "You've got a hard head." He rubbed his chin ruefully. "We've got a bit of walking yet to do."

"No." Del sat up and rubbed her eyes, in the mood to argue. "You told me we'd rest when we got to water." She stabbed emphatically with her finger. "There's water."

He nodded. "And you've rested. Time to go."

She remained stubborn. "No."

"Fine," Caleb snorted. "I hope you don't mind cuddling with a mountain lion."

"Wha...?" She scrambled to her feet and looked around. "You told me that thing was gone."

"That one is. But this the main water hole around here. There will be all sorts of critters coming out of the rocks to get a drink." He looked around. "And this is rattlesnake country," Caleb added.

She let out a startled little "meep." "S-snakes?" Her eyes were wide enough that Caleb could see the whites all the way around her irises.

He nodded solemnly. "Yup. C'mon. I promise I won't make you walk all night. I scouted out a trail and there will be a place where we can sleep. But right now, we gotta keep moving."

Taking a step, she wobbled as the muscles in her legs protested. Caleb reached out and steadied her. Del leaned against him for a moment. "Sorry. Tired. I know that whole thing about the snakes is bull. It's February. They're hibernating."

"Busted. But we still need to get a move on, sweetheart." His arm remained around her back, and he urged her down the trail. After a short distance, he grinned down at her. "You watch cartoons?"

Adele tilted her head to look up at his face. "Cartoons? Why?" Her puzzled question got a chuckle but no explanation—just an arched eyebrow as Caleb waited for further clarification. "When I was a kid, yeah. Didn't we all?"

He shook his head. "No. Not all of us. So what was your favorite?"

Stumbling a little on the uneven ground, she was grateful his arm tightened across her back and his flattened palm splayed across her ribcage pressed gently to support her. "I sort of liked 'Josie and the Pussycats,' I suppose. Every little girl wanted to be them...or Barbie."

That admission drew a snort from him. "What about the classics? Bugs Bunny. Tom and Jerry. Roadrunner?"

She had to think about that for a moment. "I don't think I really enjoyed those. They just recycled the same tired story over and over. Bugs taunted Daffy Duck or Elmer Fudd and made them look stupid. The same with Tom and Jerry. Tom would always get blamed for the things Jerry did. And the Roadrunner? I hated that beep-beep. Poor Coyote. All those ridiculous traps he ordered from Acme, and they always backfired. I just felt sorry for the ones that always lost. It was sad. You knew they were never going to win."

"So," Caleb replied softly. "You do get them."

She stumbled again, stubbing her toe on an outcropping of rock buried in the sand. Caleb caught her with both hands and pulled her up sharply against him. "Easy now," he murmured. He looked around and Adele watched his nostrils flare as he sniffed the air.

"Crap." His head swiveled.

"What?"

"Here." He pulled her to the side of the canyon and pushed her down behind a rock fall. "Don't move until I get back. Understood?"

Adele shook her head. "No." A cold wind whistled down the canyon and she shivered.

"I didn't want to tell you this way, but there's no chance now." Caleb gripped her biceps and stared into her eyes. "You know those monsters you're afraid of?"

She gulped, nodded, but didn't speak.

"Well, I am one. I can't hunt what's tracking us in human form. I have to change."

"Ch-change? Change into what?"

"I'm a werewolf, Del. You probably don't want to watch. And I don't have time to be subtle about this. Not if I want to keep you alive."

Before she could react, he'd stripped. Her fingers curled at her sides, itching to touch him. Her memories of making love to him flooded her mind and she closed her eyes. Her brain held onto those images. She didn't open her eyes when a cold nose brushed her left hand, or when a low growl rumbled through the night.

Caleb mentally cursed but wheeled and trotted off into the darkness. There were too many sniffing along their back trail. The mountain lion was the least of his problems. The pack of werewolves and a big, bad black-hole of a nasty were of far more immediate concern. He couldn't worry about was going through Adele's head at the moment. He couldn't dwell on the fact that he'd fallen for her. Werewolves didn't mate with humans. They screwed them. Or made love if there was some affection there. But wolves did not get involved with humans on that level. Still, he'd give his life to protect Adele. Dying wasn't an option, though. Diversion. Intimidation. Retreat. In that order.

He tackled the lion first, literally. He dropped down to the ledge beside her and she toppled over the edge. Following her down, he growled and stalked her stiff-legged. The mountain lion was powerful and sleek, but he was twice her size and magick. She backed down the canyon, tail swishing, ears flattened against her skull, mouth scrunched in a snarling hiss.

Tangling with her claws would hurt and he wanted to avoid a physical confrontation. He continued to stalk her, pushing her deeper down the canyon toward a spot where a smaller ravine opened up. As he anticipated, she whirled and darted into it, big paws flying across the hard scrabble desert floor. He chased her for good measure, nipping her tail just enough to spur her on and keep her from coming back. There was easier game to catch and eat, and she would find it elsewhere.

With threat one disposed of, Caleb continued his hunt. The wild werewolves had circled around the rock fall where Adele hid. One remained in human form, one had shifted to a bipedal half-form, and the rest were fully wolf. Dropping to his belly, Caleb waited, assessing. Huh. Not an alpha in the bunch. He could change, get partially dressed, and take them on in human form. Luckily, he'd left his clothes tucked in a head-high crevice downwind from the pack.

Wearing his jeans worn low on his hips so he could jerk them off if he needed to shift, Caleb crept up on the wolves. Adele had climbed up on top of the rocks and brandished a thick cottonwood branch.

"Shoo. Go away. Bad dogs."

He almost fell over laughing at the expression on the intruders' faces.

"We ain't dogs, bitch."

"And I'm not one of your bitches, you jerk."

"Why don't you just come down here and play nice."

"You want to play?" Del broke a stick off the branch and waved it, holding the wolves' attention. When they were all riveted on her, she threw it. "Go fetch."

Three of the wolves broke ranks to chase it. The werewolf in human form yelled, the bipedal growled, and Caleb bent over trying to breathe through his cackling laughter. The wolves all became aware of him at the same time Adele did.

"Y'all need to back on off now." He kept his voice calm and reasonable but pushed a little power into it.

"You lookin' for trouble?"

Caleb favored their leader with a spreading grin. "You aimin' to find me some?"

"Our territory. You're an interloper."

Adele harrumphed. "Huh, I didn't see you guys peeing on anything."

Gods but he loved this woman—and that was bad. Very, very bad. "Del, honey, you just stay up there. I'll deal with these idiots."

"Uhm...Caleb?"

"Not now, honey." He focused on the human. "Tell your mutts to sit or I will." He unfurled a little more power. The most omega among them whined and prostrated on the ground, belly up.

"What the fuck? Who the hell are you?"

"Caleb Jones. You?"

"Jones? You part of the Texas Joneses?"

"Yup."

"You ain't their Alpha."

"Nope. That would be Romulus. He raised me."

"How come you ain't his beta or something?"

"Because I'm his...something." Caleb unfurled a toothy grin. "Just in case you haven't figured it out, the woman is mine. She so much as gets a scratch, she'll be sleeping on wolf pelts. Comprende?"

"Yeah, yeah. We're done here." The man snapped his fingers, and the wolves slunk toward him. He put his nose in the air and inhaled. "Besides, what's out there waitin' will take care of y'all."

Caleb waited until the group melted into the shadows before he stripped out of his jeans, shifted, and followed them just to be sure. Then he stopped and pissed on the rocks. Just to be sure the wild pack didn't come back. That's what he told himself anyway.

Prowling back to the rock fall, he stayed in wolf form, staring up at Adele. She hadn't climbed down. He wuffed at her, and with a swing of his head, indicated she should get down.

"No."

No? What did she mean no? He wuffed again, more demanding this time.

"I don't feel like playing Little Red Riding Hood. I'm not coming down until you have only two legs."

He sat down and contemplated their standoff. Then his ear itched so he lifted a back paw to scratch.

"Don't you dare!"

Huh? He stopped scratching and eyed her. What was it with human women? Did they think all men ever thought about was licking their balls? Males thought of other things. Like steak. Naps on the couch. Their girlfriends licking—

"Caleb, you change back right now or else."

He pulled on his magic and shifted. "Better?"

She stared at him—including his erection, which was a bi-product of the change—and gulped. "Uhm..."

"Del?"

"What?" Her voice squeaked around the word.

192

"C'mon down, city mouse. We need to get under cover before I can go hunting the bad nasty."

CHAPTER TWENTY-TWO
OF MICE AND WOLVES

SHE WAS NOT A MOUSE, despite the shivers running relays up and down her spine. Adele didn't know what sort of bad nasty Caleb thought they were hunting, but she kept reminding herself she must never forget what this man...this *thing* was. He was a predator, and he could eat her alive in a heartbeat. Despite her bravado, she was scared spitless. And she was still attracted, despite her best intentions.

Shadows cast by the buttes caught in the sun as it set. Darkness crept across the desert floor, searching for them, desperate in its hunger. Night felt like a living, breathing entity.

"Something's out there." Adele snagged his hand and tugged him to a stop, then jerked away from the contact she initiated.

How could he reassure her when she was right? There *was* something out there—a being older than time, far more deadly than any living creature, and it was calling. His name whispered on the wind, seductive, wild, and wrong on so many levels.

Del felt it too. She rubbed at her arm with her free hand in a vain attempt to control the fear dancing across her flesh.

Wendigo. Evil incarnate. And not a manitou or thunderbird in sight to contain it. If Caleb succumbed to the lure, he'd be lost. They might be lost anyway, Adele and him. It wanted him. As an alpha werewolf, his energy would feed it far longer than Adele's humanity. But if it took him, she'd be nothing more than dust. He refused to let that happen. He would get her out of this damn desert and back to safety.

"Caleb? Can you tell me what it is?" Worry leaked out in her voice, despite her best attempts to hide it. She raised her chin, determined to see this through to the end.

Del reminded him a lot of Sade in that regard. Only he never wanted to do the things with Sade he'd done and still wanted to do with Adele. He wondered if Sade was on their trail. If she was riding to the rescue, she'd need more than the cavalry for backup. He didn't think their usual little Scooby club could handle this big bad.

Caleb would never have believed there was anything in this realm or the others that a werewolf FBI agent, a gargoyle Sentinel, a fae warrior, and Sade couldn't defeat. Sade might be only human, but she always commanded every incident. He'd even settle for that jerk of a dragon Drakon at this point.

Too bad he was on his own this time. If it was only his life on the line, he'd just meet that sucker out in the dark and make his sacrifice worth the price. But not if it meant leaving Adele out here alone. She was not going to die. Not on his watch.

He gave her hand a squeeze. "How's your Native American mythology?"

"What? Is it a thunderbird or something?"

"I wish. Definitely in the *or something* category. I'm not positive, but I think it's a wendigo."

"Well...pistachios on a pita. That's not good."

Not good? Understatement of the year. "The *not good* train already left the station headed smack dab into *oh shit* territory."

"How do we fight it?"

There was the rub. Del was human. She couldn't fight her way out of a wet paper bag when it came to supernatural critters.

"*We* don't. You run. I fight."

195

"I'm not leaving you, Caleb. What did that pooka say? He told us to wait for a sign."

Yeah, and anybody who listened to a pooka deserved a sign. One that said STUPID! "A sign? Del, I don't think you get it. That damn horse with no name was on his way out of here. Wendigos don't just eat flesh, they eat souls. And they especially like human souls. I can shift and hold it long enough for you to get away."

"And go where? We're in the middle of the freaking desert, Caleb." She let go of his hand, parked that cute little butt of hers on a boulder, crossed her arms over her very lush chest—which crossed his eyes because...male, d'uh—and stared at him. "I'm listening. Where am I supposed to go?" She swept out one arm to encompass the vast emptiness. "No lights. No roads. No civilization."

A shadow drifted across the rising moon. He hoped that was a thunderbird, natural enemy of wendigos. Would it take on the monster? He watched massive wings beat against the updrafts before spreading like a black hole swallowing stars. Something roared. The thunderbird screamed in defiance. Damn, the pooka'd been right. This was a sign and it wasn't going to be stapled to his forehead.

Caleb grabbed Adele and pushed her toward the west, away from the fight.

"Time for Plan B, sweetheart."

"Plan B? What's Plan B?"

"We both run!" He didn't look back. Werewolves who beat feet lived to fight—and love—another day.

"C'MON, HON. Not much further and you can rest again," Caleb urged. He kept his arm tight around her waist, supporting her as he prodded her to keep moving.

True to his word, about a hundred yards on down the dim trail, the way opened up and leveled out to join a sandy wash. Grateful, Adele sank down to the sand, leaning her back against an outcropping of rock. Head back, eyes closed, she tried not to pant. "I don't want to be a wuss, Caleb," she muttered. "But I'm not sure how much further I can go."

"You'll go as far as you can and then I'll carry you the rest of the way, Del. I promise to get you out of here." His voice was rough, almost a growl.

She opened her eyes and shuddered again. There was a red light flickering in the depths of Caleb's eyes that made him look wild and feral.

"And I never break a promise," he added fervently. "You rest. I'll be back."

Her heart pounding, she started to get up. Despite his words—his promise—and her simmering fear of him, she was even more afraid he would leave her. Or worse, get injured or something and not come back. She knew with absolute certainty that she would die out here without him. In two smooth strides, Caleb suddenly stood in front of her.

"I'm not going far. I'm going to find something for you to eat and drink. 'Kay?" He gently pushed her back down. "Sweetheart, you're exhausted. There's water around here close and maybe I can scrounge some food."

"Yeah, easy for you to say. I bet raw rabbit is a delicacy in your world."

"Uh, eww." He waggled his brows then squatted in front of her and cupped her face in his hands. "Sweetheart, I promise. I'm not going far. I'll be close enough if something happens. And you need to eat."

Adele watched his face then slowly relaxed. "'Kay. I'm sure glad you aren't one of those cavemen types that insist on the little woman doing all of the food gathering." She made a "whatever" face and was rewarded with a broad grin and another waggle of his eyebrows. Too tired to do much more than lay her head back against the rock and close her eyes, she let his expression be the last word.

Caleb considered changing into a wolf and doing some hunting, but that would take precious time they didn't have and he had no way to cook whatever he caught, as Del had pointed out. Rabbit Tartar in wolf form? Good stuff. As a human, the only thing he enjoyed rare was steak. Humans tended to be a bit squeamish about how their food was cooked—as in meat HAD to be cooked.

He headed out and not too far away he found a patch of prickly pear cactus and gingerly broke off several pads of it. He took the time to carefully break off the spines then rolled them in the sand at the base of the patch to remove the smaller glochid spines that were as fine as hair and three times as nasty. They were hard to see, but broke off the plant easily and penetrated the skin. Once he could handle the stems safely, he tore off the fruit on the tops of the stems and "washed" them in sand as well. He then stripped out of his shirt, tucked his prize into it, and headed back to Adele. There would be enough moisture in the stems to sustain Del, and the fruit wasn't bad to eat once he peeled the outer skin off.

She must have dozed off. Adele sat straight up, her heart pounding. How long had Caleb been gone? Was he hurt? Lost? "Don't panic," she chided herself aloud.

"Why would you panic?" Caleb asked as he emerged from behind a rock.

Staring at him, she locked her jaw to keep her mouth from gaping. "Seriously? Let me count the ways. Uhm, kidnapped. Thrown out of a plane. Forced to spend the night in a haunted mine. Faced a mountain lion over a water hole. Got stalked by a pack of idiot werewolves." She plastered a prim expression on her face and straightened her shoulders. "Gee, you're right. Nothing to panic over."

Caleb, barely containing his laughter, hunkered down on his heels beside her and opened the pack he'd made of his shirt to reveal the cactus stems. He used a stick to stab down into the cut end of the stem and mushing the pulp. "Here," he said, holding one out. "Not the best tasting drink in the world, but it beats the alternative."

Taking the proffered stem dubiously, Adele simply held it while Caleb pulled out a couple of red-tinted nodules. He used a thumbnail to quickly peel them then handed one to her.

"Indian fig," he told her. "Otherwise known as the fruit of the prickly pear cactus. Eat up." To prove his point, he took a bite of the second one and chewed.

Still skeptical, Del took a hesitant bite. The fruit was tart. She screwed up her face, but chewed and swallowed then took another bite. She watched Caleb finish his off and then drink from a second cactus stem, though it was more like sucking the pulp out, chewing and then spitting it on the ground. When her tongue couldn't reach deeper, Caleb took the stem from her and sliced down the side, giving her access to the rest of the pulp inside.

"So," Caleb said after he'd finished his stem. "You got the point of cartoons without even realizing it."

She blinked a couple of times, her brain scrambling to catch up to his non sequitur. "What do you mean?"

"I mean, the road runner is a metaphor,"

Wrinkling her brow, she considered. "For what?"

Caleb answered with an easy shrug. "For chasing things which are elusive and yet ever just within your reach."

"So who or what is your roadrunner?"

"That would be like asking for help."

Her first thought was, *so what's wrong with asking for help?* She sighed. Sometimes getting information out of Caleb was like talking to the Oracle at Delphi—or pulling teeth with a pair of pliers. She could play Twenty Questions. "Helping you or helping me?"

Caleb's sardonic laughter echoed across the emptiness of the high desert. "Lady, I help myself."

Shaking her head, Adele attempted to decipher his meaning. Almost everything that came out of the man's mouth was a two-edged sword. The phrase *I help myself* could be taken several different ways. Tucking it away to be reviewed in the full context of the conversation, Adele forged ahead. "Okay, so help me. I'm nosy."

Smirking at her, Caleb replied, "As you're supposed to be. You're the investigator. I'm just the hired nose."

Pantomiming opening a satchel and pulling out a notebook and pen, she posed like she was taking notes. "So do your stuff. Sniff out the answers I need."

He looked her up and down, a very wolfish perusal. "You won't need a notebook for what I'm sniffing."

She could only stare at him for a moment and then her sense of self-preservation took over. Adele plastered a haughty look on her face and arched an eyebrow. "Why am I thinking I don't want to know the answer to that? And why am I going to ask anyway? What *are* you sniffing?"

Caleb pushed to his feet with easy grace and walked away. With a suppressed groan, Adele pushed off from the sand and managed to get to her feet, every muscle in her legs screaming in protest. She stumbled up the trail after him. Hearing her footsteps, Caleb turned to look at her, his eyebrows doing that irritating wig-wag dance with his shaggy bangs.

"Well, lots of things," he said. "You humans would

solve so many more crimes if you could smell fear. People get scared when they lie because they fear getting caught. Or they smell aggressive when you are challenging their truth."

Adele tilted her head to look up at him. "What else do you smell on people?"

Caleb did that thing she hated; he started circling her. "Mixtures of different things. Perfume or cologne doesn't so much mask the problem as make it like anchovies on a pizza. It's an added layer, but the underlying animal scents are still there."

She attempted to follow him with her eyes and head but found herself turning her whole body to keep him in front of her. A strained chuckle died in her suddenly dry mouth. "Should I start the Little Red Riding Hood routine about now?" She hated the quickening of her pulse and that shrill little *eep* in her voice. "You know the one...what big teeth you have, grandma?"

Caleb laughed, nudging her shoulder with his. "Well, it's not my big teeth you have to worry about." His suggestive smile was meant to keep her off balance. "And you know, they never go on about how big a schnozzle grandma had. It's too bad Red didn't have a nose. If she had, Red would have smelled the wolf and known that he'd fed on Granny, even if he'd been in human form. I think Red was a bit myopic. Too bad they didn't have LASIK back in the days of the Brothers Grimm."

If he could smell fear, he should be on sensory overload because she was far more terrified than she dared admit. Their plight. Him. Her heart thudded in her chest as instinct urged her to step away. She reacted and stumbled, automatically grabbing for his arm.

Caleb chuckled and held steady as she righted herself. He then stepped away before she could. "You asked for my help. You didn't ask me to eat you so I'm not going to do that." He offered a wolfish grin. "Not even if you ask nicely."

Her thoughts veered a totally different direction, toward a place filled with sexy things that he could—and had—done to her. Bad timing on her part so she shook the thought out of her head. She didn't realize she actually shook her whole body in the process. Time to change the topic.

"Okay, so help me." Her voice and expression were both tart, and Caleb fought against the instinct to take her to the ground and make love to her. Her mouth moved again as she spoke and he had to focus. "You're the one with the great nose for tracking. Track our butts out of this wilderness and back to civilization." She turned on her heel and marched away.

Choking back laughter, Caleb cleared his throat. "Ah, Del?" She stopped but didn't turn around. "Wrong direction, sweetheart."

"Grrrr." She pivoted and marched back, passing him with a lift of her chin.

Neither spoke as they trudged up the canyon. When they broke out of the ravine into wider spaces, the full moon hung on the horizon like a fat Japanese lantern.

"Oh, that's just great." Del jerked her head around to glare at him. "You're probably going to turn into a wolf, and I'll be talking to myself even more than I am now."

Passing her, he looked back over his shoulder. "The better to eat you, my dear."

She curled her lip at his back. "Yeah, and I bet you have fleas, too, you mangy dog," she muttered.

Caleb's laughter echoed back to her. "Oh, and I have better hearing than you do."

"You and your little dog, too," she spat.

He almost bounced across the valley floor, despite the crawling need to go to ground. Caleb admitted he was perverse because every time he provoked Adele into showing her sarcasm, he wanted to sing and dance. Like Gene Kelly. Something with a top hat and cane. Okay, maybe more Fred Astaire. He liked the classics.

The moon was setting before he halted for the night. He'd found a canyon with a stream. Water was a bigger concern than food at the moment, and following the creek would eventually take them to civilization. In the desert, where there was water, there were people.

Caleb lay on his back, arms tucked behind his head. Growing up near Dallas, he was used to city lights, not stars. But here, in the desert mountains, with the stream crooning a lullaby as it danced over the rocks strewn along its course, he wondered why he'd never looked for his wild roots. A shooting star blazed across the sky and Adele murmured at his side.

"Did you make a wish?"

She nodded, not revealing what she'd asked for. Wishes weren't supposed to be shared, which was stupid as far as he was concerned. If you didn't share a wish, how could someone make it come true? It wasn't like wishes were magic or anything. Not real magic. Which he could use some of at the moment. He had only a vague idea of their location and an even vaguer sense of where to find civilization. At the same time, he couldn't imagine being anywhere else but lying here, with Adele, staring at the stars, waiting for the next one to fall so they could make another wish. Together.

"Do you think someone is looking for us?"

He turned his head so she could see his face. "No." At her crestfallen expression, he touched her cheek. "I *know* they are."

CHAPTER TWENTY-THREE
GOOD MEDICINE

"I KNOW THEY ARE." Sade glowered at Varrick. "What sort of stupid question was that?"

The gargoyle refused to look chastised. "A fair one, Sade. They've been missing almost a week. While I have great faith in Caleb, he's not immortal and she's human. We shouldn't discount that this is a recovery mission."

"Shut up, Varrick. I'm positive they're still alive and I'm going to find them."

The gargoyle refused to give up the argument. "They were last seen in Denver. Why are we in New Mexico?"

"A plane chartered by Santos Santana took off from Santa Fe." She held up her index finger, effectively cutting off his rejoinder. "One of the ground agents reported seeing oddly-shaped bundles loaded on board, plus parachutes." Holding up a second then third finger, she added, "The flight plan filed with the FAA was false, and the plane dropped off radar somewhere southwest of Albuquerque."

She paced, marshaling her thoughts. "Santana's base of operation, according to the DEA, is in Catron County, New Mexico. Southwest of Albuquerque, in case you haven't figured that out. Caleb went undercover with the local werewolf pack at a greasy spot in the road called Buhmfuch, which is also in Catron County." She stabbed Ariel with her gaze and pinned him in place. "You met Caleb in Pueblo, Colorado and then in Gallup. Why?"

"We were both on the trail of the fetishes. We tracked them to a pawn shop in Pueblo."

"What is the deal with those fetishes, Ari? You've

been fucking tight-lipped about their significance and your role in this whole shitty mess. Other than you were—" She made air quotes. "—looking for them. Who exactly is this shaman?"

Ari knew when he was beat and Oberon hadn't exactly sworn him to secrecy. "A native shaman approached the king. The fetishes had been stolen, and he wanted them back. As they were in Oberon's demesne when taken, he ordered me to look into the situation. I put Caleb on their scent." He studied her for a long moment. "Then things heated up in Chicago. Right before the situation went to hell there, I met the shaman and Caleb in Gallup. Someone is using those festishes to make sacrifices for a summoning. Bear, lizard, snake, turtle, deer." He kept his gaze steady on her as he added, "And wolf."

Caleb. Sade didn't say his name out loud. "Is he the last one? Is he the only thing standing between us and whatever it is?"

"Wendigo. The shaman believes someone is summoning a wendigo."

Sinjen stiffened but remained silent as Varrick jumped to his feet and growled. "A native demon?"

"Is that a problem? I mean, isn't that what you gargoyles do? Fight demons?" Sade didn't like the way Varrick's face had paled.

"Yes. And no. A wendigo is a very specific demon, one not from the demon realm per se."

"Okay." She stretched out the word. "You didn't answer my question."

Nikos stretched his legs, neatly trapping Sade between where he sat and the wall. "The answer is no, Sade. Wendigos are extremely rare and not something most magicks are equipped to conquer. You need a shaman—one who is versed in this type of magic."

She stepped over the dragon's legs and received a

quirked smile for her trouble. "Then no problem, right? Ari, call your shaman buddy."

The fae raised his hands, palms forward in a not-so-fast gesture. "Not my buddy and I have no way to get in touch. I'll check with Oberon, but unless the guy decides to put in an appearance?" He ended on a question, leaving Sade to fill in the blank.

Sinjen snagged her hand as she passed the bed where he sat. "There is little we can do before full daylight. You are tired." He didn't give her time to argue, pulling her down beside him and cupping her face. "You are exhausted, Sade. I see it on your face, in your eyes, in the way your steps drag." He stared at each of the men in turn, settling last on the dragon, daring them to overrule him.

Varrick was the first to agree. "He's right, girlfriend. That witch stuff in Chicago knocked you on your butt."

Ari dropped to the floor from where he'd been sitting on the dresser. "Can't argue with the man's logic, sweets. We need your bad self at one hundred percent." He and Varrick met at the door. Nikos hadn't moved. Ari waited a few beats, watching dragon and vampire in their stare down. He cleared his throat. "Drakon, now is not the time."

With insolence born of arrogance, Nikos stood. He stalked across the room, a sardonic smiled hovering on his lips. He took Sade's hand and raised it to his mouth, though his gaze remained focused on Sinjen. Sapphire clashed with steel and tension spiked in the close confines of the motel room.

Sade jerked her hand away from Nikos and shouldered Sinjen to put space between them. "You're right. I need to sleep. Everybody out." She arched a brow at the dragon until he backed away then she turned to the vampire. "And I mean everybody."

He wanted to argue, but Sinjen would acquiesce this

time. Sade needed to appear strong in front of the magicks. He almost smiled at that thought. She was strong—the strongest human he'd ever encountered in his very long life. She might not want to admit she belonged to him—and she did—but he would not undermine her authority. Being a federal cop was essential to her being. It was his job to remind her that she was also a woman, one very desirable. She thought the dragon and the fae pursued her out of perversity. Not true. They were as attracted to her bright light—her sheer penchant for existence—as he was.

This woman, despite her human frailty, was a treasure any magick would find irresistible. It was her very mortality that drew them like the proverbial moths to her flame. And she was his. He was honest enough to know part of his desire came from an alpha male's need to possess the most coveted and ultimate prize. But the man he once was wanted only to claim her heart. And that humbled him.

Sinjen rose, his fingers trailing across her shoulder before tracing the line of her jaw, ending with a gentle tap against her beauty mark. He bent, pressed his lips there, and murmured. "You will be back in my arms soon enough, Sade."

Straightening, he ushered the dragon before him. At the door, he stopped, glanced back and offered her a knowing smile. She remained still, a bemused and dreamy expression in her eyes. Yes. He would possess her heart before all was said and done. He shut the door behind him and softly called through the metal. "Lock it, love."

THE NEXT AFTERNOON, with Sinjen in day sleep, Sade managed to shake off the dragon, the fae, and the gargoyle by sending them in three different directions on separate errands. With far more reluctance than she'd admit, she climbed into her SUV and headed for Reserve, New Mexico, county seat of Catron County.

About halfway between Datil and Reserve, she started to sweat. It was crazy. This was February. And there were mountains. With a dusting of snow. But here on the desert floor, the season might as well have been summer. She pulled up in front of the Catron County courthouse thirty minutes later. Parking, she stared at the two-story concrete block and red brick building. The blocks had been painted what was probably once an adobe red but had faded to a sort of rust-colored pink. Her eyes found the radio towers rising above the one-story gray block building adjoining the rear of the main courthouse. Bingo.

She pushed open the door, her FBI badge displayed prominently on her belt, along with her Beretta. The older woman at the front desk sat up, her mouth forming a little "O."

"Can I help you?"

"Special Agent Sade Marquis. I'd like to speak to the sheriff, if he has a moment."

"And this would be about?"

"An official investigation."

The woman's eyes widened as she blanched. She snagged her phone and hit a few buttons before swiveling her chair to speak into the receiver. Sade rolled her eyes at the woman's back but wore her bland official face when the woman turned around. "He'll be here in just a bit."

"I'll wait." She moved away from the door and leaned against a file cabinet, a position that let her watch the two entrances in the reception area as well as out the window to the parking lot.

Within two minutes, the lot was swarming with vehicles, all marked as belonging to the Catron County

Sheriff's Office. The occupants all hustled around the building and out of sight. Two minutes after that, a New Mexico State Police cruiser rolled in. The trooper used the front door. He cut his eyes her direction, his hand resting on the butt of his service revolver. Sade acknowledged him with a slight tuck of her chin. She'd been known to eat local law enforcement for breakfast, but since it was mid-afternoon, she'd wait.

"Agent."

"Officer."

"Official investigation, huh?"

"Yup."

"Problem with the sheriff?"

"Not yet." She glanced at her watch. "Another minute or so, maybe."

The door behind the secretary's desk opened and a compact man of Indian heritage gestured to her. She followed him down the hallway, stopping when he did. Two knuckle raps on the door, a muffled, "Yo," and she was in the sheriff's office—along with the Indian deputy and the state trooper.

The man sitting behind the desk had circles of sweat staining the armpits of his slate blue, short-sleeve shirt. Since it felt like 100 degrees outside and the AC unit wheezed like the Little Engine that Couldn't, Sade forgave him because sweat was trickling down her spine as well. Something was really wrong around here and she would get to the bottom of it.

The sheriff settled into his squeaky desk chair, steepled his fingers, and offered her his best attempt at a here-we-go-again expression. She just loved brushing up against local LEO ego. Not. She moved slightly to her right so she could keep all three men in view. There were very few people she trusted at her back, and one of those was missing at the moment.

"Sheriff, I'm Special Agent Sade Marquis of the

FBI's MAGIC unit."

"Yeah. So?"

"You gonna tell me that the fucking weather is a result of global warming?" Ah ha. Something flickered in his eyes. "Do you know anything about the Johnson Pack?"

That question got a sigh from the trooper. "What's old Orrin been up to now?"

Sade hit him with her perusal. "Nothing. Unless you consider the murders of two teenagers out in the desert."

Two men blanched at the news. The Indian didn't. He'd known. Interesting. "Any other deaths out that way?"

The trooper and the sheriff exchanged a glance. The deputy remained stoic. No one spoke. Their stubborn obstinacy was about to step on her last nerve. She inhaled, ready to verbally eviscerate them.

"There was a fire." The trooper looked uncomfortable as he made the admission. He also refused to look at the sheriff. "Looked like a drug lab. We found four bodies."

Sade folded her arms across her chest and waited. The sheriff deflated and nodded permission to the trooper.

"We'd been keeping an eye on the place. We couldn't prove the men or the lab belonged to a drug lord called El Diablo, but we suspected it."

"Uh huh. This would be Santos Santana?"

"If you already knew about this why you botherin' us?" The sheriff was full of bluster.

"Because an FBI agent is missing. One who was undercover with the Johnson Pack. And there are some suspicious murders up in Colorado we think might be tied to this Santana character."

The deputy cleared his throat with a quiet cough. "A

year ago, Santana was nobody. A low-level drug runner and coyote. Now he rules a three-state drug cartel, lives in a million dollar hacienda, and flies expensive aircraft."

Sade mulled over the information. "You believe magic is involved."

It wasn't a question, but the man answered anyway. "Yes. There is magic involved. Very old magic."

She studied the deputy and the hair on the back her neck and arms prickled. There was a whole lot more to the man than first appeared. She was far from a magical bloodhound, though she could see through glamours. This man did not wear one, but there was a subtle sense of power gathering around him. She took a stab in the dark. "And bad medicine?"

The sheriff banged on his desk before his deputy could reply. He glared at her as a nervous tic twitched in the corner of his right eye. "We been handling shit like this ever since that damn rip. We don't need the Feds."

"You have a missing FBI agent, four dead drug dealers, and five murdered civilians. But you don't need the Feds. What the hell do you need?" Sade uncurled her fists and smoothed her hands against her thighs.

"I need to know what the fuck is out there."

"Then I can help you."

"You?"

"Me, sheriff. What's out there is bigger and nastier than anything you've come up against. Trust me. I've seen really bad shit. Even I'm fucking scared of this one."

The deputy lounging against the wall straightened. Sade tried to guess his tribal affiliation and finally settled on Apache, despite this being Navajo country. "She's right."

The sheriff rolled his eyes. "Your medicine tell you this, Tonto?"

Sade planted both hands on the desk and leaned into the sheriff's personal space. "I can walk away and let it have your fat ass, or I can take your deputy here and go hunting."

The man grunted, but waved a hand in agreement and also to shoo them out of his office.

Outside, the deputy shook his head. "You are either brave or stupid."

"Or both. You ready to go hunting?"

"Guns won't kill it."

"No, but I have some heavy duty magical backup and I'll bet dollars to donuts you have good medicine that will."

"That is not a bet I would make."

"Are you questioning my judgment?"

"No. Only your sanity."

CHAPTER TWENTY-FOUR
MADE FOR THIS

ADELE HAD QUESTIONED HER SANITY for the past, silent hour. She suddenly halted and waited until Caleb realized she'd stopped and turned back to her before she confronted him. "Hey. I got a question for you, wolfman."

"Shoot."

"We've spent how many days walking in this desert because we were forced out of a perfectly good airplane. Why didn't you just, you know, wolf out and kill 'em all?"

Caleb shrugged. "Three reasons. One, I don't fight very well in close quarters. Wolves are harriers. We chase, nip at heels, rip through skin. Wear our enemies down. There's not a lot of room to dodge in an airplane."

"And the others?" She asked after a long moment with nothing else forthcoming from the man.

"Can you survive getting shot numerous times?"

She blinked and then exhaled a derisive snort. "Maybe." She rolled her eyes at his disbelieving stare. "Okay. Probably not."

"I can. Unless the bullets shred my heart or my brain. Even then, there's a chance I might regenerate. Unless the bullets have a high silver content. I wouldn't be happy if I survived and you didn't."

"That's very...noble of you."

He chuckled, a dry rustling sound full of innuendo. "I'm not noble. I have a vested interest in you." Caleb waggled his brows and leered at her.

"Down, boy. So that's two. What's the third reason?"

"Can you fly a plane?"

Del's mouth dropped open and she closed it before pursing her lips. Caleb's eyes locked on her mouth like a heat-seeking missile. She reminded herself to breathe before she answered. "That would be a negative."

"Neither can I. The only thing worse than being shoved out of an airplane with a parachute is trying to land said plane when neither of us knows how."

She nodded for a moment, considering, but then held up a finger. "Wait. How did you know I couldn't fly an airplane?"

"I've seen you drive."

Adele attempted to marshal an argument to refute his assertion then resorted to poking Caleb in the shoulder. "Dang it," she said, shaking her head. "I hate it when you're so smugly right."

Caleb walked a few steps away, whistling tunelessly. "Oh, that, and if you had been able to fly the thing, you would've been plotting to take over the plane as soon as we left the ground."

She trotted to catch up to him, rolling her eyes when she did. "I'm not all that blood-guts-and-glory when I've got my hands tied behind my back and they're the ones with the guns."

Caleb nodded. "Makes two of us. So, just as a rule, don't expect me to go all fangface at the drop of a hat because we're in trouble."

"Why not?"

"For one thing, it's hell on the clothing budget."

Adele had a retort on the tip of her tongue, but his upraised finger stopped her. "The alternative is that I strip down first. You really want to get that up close and personal in the heat of battle?"

Her breath caught and desire pooled low in her body. When heat suffused her face, she resisted the urge to fan it. Caleb's nostrils flared and a slow, sexy grin curling lips she really wanted to kiss.

"Well, all right then. Your wishes are duly noted, m'lady."

They trudged in companionable silence, and when the trail was wide enough, they walked side-by-side, holding hands.

"Can I ask you something?"

Caleb cut his eyes to her. "I don't know. Are you able to form a question?"

She slugged his arm with her free hand. "Smart ass. I'll rephrase. *May* I ask you a question?"

He stopped and turned to face her. He gazed deeply into her eyes for a long moment. "You can, and may, ask me anything, Adele."

Del remembered to breathe again. "Where were you when it happened?"

He furrowed his brow. "When what happened?"

"You know. The...thing." She twirled her free hand. "When the Veil ripped."

The Big Rip wasn't something people sat around discussing—215undane or magicks—even though the event had a profound effect on both. It wasn't like Kennedy's assassination or 9-11. People didn't remember precisely where they were, exactly what they were doing when the Veil between the human world and the magical Realms tore, spilling things best left hidden on humanity.

"I was living in a mansion in Dallas and studying pre-law at Princeton."

"Wait? You went to Princeton?"

"Well...yeah."

"They let a werewolf in?"

He dropped her hand. "Is that a touch of prejudice I'm detecting?"

"I..." She dropped her eyes. "I'm sorry. I just...I didn't handle it very well."

"Oh?" His voice held icicles.

"Yeah. Science versus magic and all that. And my father." She inhaled deeply, exhaled, and raised her head to meet his gaze. "He likes to hunt. And he doesn't like wolves."

"I see." He started walking again, and she trailed behind him.

"Caleb, I'm sorry."

"This is why we hid ourselves, Adele. Humans can't wrap their heads around what we are. And we aren't all that different in the whole scheme of things."

"Oh?"

"Yeah. We're born. We grow up. If we're lucky, we fall in love. We mate. We have kids. We go to work."

"Even the Fae?"

"Heh. You do realize that the Seelie Court owns ninety percent of Las Vegas, a good chunk of Hollywood, and you'd probably freak if you knew how many lived in Aspen. And that was *before* the Big Rip."

His hand found hers and he pulled her closer to his side. "I grew up in the household of a master vampire. My best friend was human. A gargoyle taught me how to fight. I'm allergic to faerie dust—as are most wolves—and right now, I really, *really* want to kiss you."

He did. His arms circled her, pulled her against his very hard and very warm chest. His mouth took hers like he was dying of thirst and she was the last drop of water on earth. When he stopped, they were both breathing hard.

"There's magic in your world, Del. Was even before the Veil ripped. Humans don't understand how special their world is, how amazing they are."

She studied him, head tilted, as she tried to piece together his meaning. "Seeing the world through your eyes makes my head spin some times."

Caleb gave her one of his open-mouthed grins that

would be a silent laugh on a real wolf. "Oh, trust me, I'm only just getting started."

Adele wrinkled her nose and he was hard pressed not to kiss it. "I don't know which scares me more, Caleb. The phrase *trust me* or *just getting started.*"

His laughter raised goosebumps. Before she could react, he'd led her to the top of a rocky outcropping—a spot high enough they could see across the desert floor and the splash of stars in the sky. She didn't have time to catch her breath before he had her all but naked and spread out on the parachute. She should have been cold, but the desert night remained warm and the rock at her back radiated heat.

Caleb heard her breath catch, felt her shiver. He swallowed her quiet moan when he slid his fingers just under the dainty edge of her panties. Dipping toward her heat and away again, teasing and stroking and arousing until she was slick and needy. His mouth dropped kisses along her jaw, her neck. Across her chest until he found a puckered nipple. He swirled his tongue, her heart kicking into a gallop under his relentless ministrations. Everything that was Adele melted into need beneath him.

His mouth found hers again, his kisses turned urgent as his hands roamed across her skin, took everything from her, sending her right to the edge. Adele hovered there. Waiting. Wanting. She didn't care they didn't have a condom. She didn't care that they were in danger. She didn't care about anything but the man poised above her, his beautiful cock teasing her entrance.

"Yes," she breathed. "Please."

Caleb tensed, his muscles locking up as he sank into her waiting heat. His body all but screamed in relief as her satin muscles wrapped around his dick, caressing him, welcoming him. He cupped her breast, brushed his thumb over her nipple. She cupped his face in her palms, leaned up, feasted on his mouth. Ah, the taste of her. He loved how she tasted, how she smelled. He broke their kiss and buried his nose in the soft juncture of her neck and shoulder. He would never have his fill of this woman. The way his body fit hers, the glide of sweat-slick skin over skin. He could spend an eternity right where he was, gorging on the magic he found with her.

Reckless. Clutching. Moving together on the shelf of rock, under the distant stars gleaming in the sky above them. He drove her higher and higher, tipped her over the edge, and her cry was one of wonder, of joy. *This*, he decided, this unity of body and soul, and her, this human woman would always delight him. Nourish him, his soul, his very existence. She was the peace he'd searched for all of his life. They were made for this. Brought together for this one, perfect moment, the magnificent enchantment of man and woman. And love.

Her eyes, silvered by moonlight, opened to his. Her lashes briefly shadowed her cheeks as she blinked, lips curving. Yes. Magic. An enchantment almost as old as time itself. He surged into her. Once. Twice. Thrice. The magical number three. Then he jumped over that shining edge with her, felt her spiraling out among the stars with him.

ADELE, ON HER BACK, her head resting on Caleb's hard thigh, stared at the wheel of stars above her head. "This is crazy."

He carefully wound a tendril of her hair around his index finger before loosening it and repeating the action. "How so?"

"Middle of the desert? Supposedly murdered by drug runners? And—" She choked off the next word. She didn't know what else was hunting them. Something big and bad. Something so evil her hind brain couldn't come close to comprehending it. Something a light-year away from reality. In the same way as the man currently toying with her hair was.

His finger tightened and tugged—gently—but it was enough to get her to shift her gaze to meet his.

"I'll handle it, Del. I'll keep you safe."

She curled up to sit and swiveled to face him. "How Caleb? How are you going to do that?" She fluttered her hands in haphazard circles. "Do you even know what's out there?"

Long moments later, Adele broke their staring contest first, her gaze sliding down and away. His rough palm cupped her cheek and urged her with gentle pressure to look at him again.

"Yeah, baby. I know what's out there. I expected trouble on the way to solving this case. I just didn't realize that little prick, El Diablo, was so stupid he'd release an ancient demon. And I damn sure didn't anticipate running into you and dragging your sweet ass into this mess."

Wait? He thought her ass was sweet? Before she could process that, his hand curled around the back of her neck and tugged her forward. His mouth met her halfway. She wasn't sure what she expected, but this kiss wasn't it. His lips teased her, his teeth nipped, and his tongue? It slid into her mouth when she unclenched her teeth with a breathless little, "Oh."

When she came up for air, she was straddling his lap. That was no gun in his pocket, though his weapon was definitely locked and loaded. For her. She didn't know much about werewolves beyond some tabloid reports that they were insatiable when it came to sexy times—as her past experience proved. Despite that, she knew instinctively that his erection was just for her, that he didn't kiss other women the way he kissed her. He was made her. She was made for him.

Caleb rested his forehead against hers. "Damn, baby. When we get back to civilization, we're checking into a five-star hotel and not coming out of our room for at least a week."

A nervous giggle erupted. "A week? I won't be able to walk."

That sexy grin she loved so much quirked the lips she'd just been kissing.

"I can live with that." He stiffened, all of his sense on high alert.

"Ca—"

"Shhh."

Caleb rolled her behind a boulder. "Trouble, baby. Stay put."

In a flash he was naked. In the slow blink of her eyes, his body contorted. Another blink and a wolf stood where a man had moments before.

Her bubble burst. Yeah, that was the crux of this whole situation. Their predicament crashed down on her. They had to survive before they could live the rest of their lives. The air changed, electrified. "What—"

The wolf raised his nose to the sky, testing the wind. He was perfectly silhouetted against the low-hung moon. The air thickened and drawing breath into her lungs became a labor. The worst stench she'd ever smelled shortened her breathing even more. Caleb stepped toward a coalescing whirl of blackness, and disappeared. His voice whispered in her head.

Run.

Del opened her mouth to scream, but heat seared her lungs. She did what Caleb ordered. Ran. Blindly. Then there was nothing.

CHAPTER TWENTY-FIVE
COLLISION COURSE

ADELE HELD HER BREATH, fervently wishing she wasn't human so she could stop breathing and her heart wouldn't thud against the walls of her chest like fists pounding on a closed casket. She couldn't remember scrambling off the rocks, or running through the canyon. Finding this narrow cave. Dark. So dark. And... She choked, unable to say his name.

"I am the hungry wolf at the door, the boogie man in the closet, the monster under the bed. I am every nightmare haunting the dreams of humans."

Something that might have been supernatural laughter bounced off the canyon walls sounding like echoes in the halls of the gods. Only there were no gods. Not in this world. There was only her, abject fear stripping away her humanity, leaving a brittle husk behind.

"Come out and play, little human."

Her skin prickled, the monster's magic crawling along her flesh like ants streaming to a picnic. Where was Caleb? Her breath caught in her chest as she remembered, choking on a sob. Gone. That thing out there had snatched him, torn him to pieces and flung the parts into the sky where the wind swept him away, beyond the horizon. She was alone. Defenseless. All she could do was remain huddled here in the back reaches of this narrow cave, the passage too small for the creature outside. Surely these ancient sandstone rocks could withstand the wendigo's assault. Surely the creature would tire of hunting her and would wander off in search of other prey.

No. She couldn't let it. As long as it stayed here, torturing her ears and her psyche, it wasn't out there, unleashing its power on people far more innocent than she. Something slithered over her foot and she scrabbled backwards, hands over her mouth to stifle the scream building in her soul. Snake. Or lizard. Something else scrapped across the sandy floor, brushed against her leg, something hard and round. She reached for it, found the hard shell. A turtle?

A hard shudder rattled her very bones. The fetishes. Lizard. Snake. Turtle. Bear. Wolf. Each had been a sacrifice. And now it was her turn. Deer. Forest dweller. Coy. Or rather McCoy—son of the forest, only not a son, a daughter. All the other victims had been male. She had to stay alive. And she had to figure out a way to kill that thing out there. Or stop the magic. Accomplishing one was about as plausible as the other.

She shared this claustrophobic space with a lizard, a snake, and a turtle. There wasn't room for the bear or the wolf and wouldn't that be just lovely? Maybe the predators would fight over which one got to eat her. Golden eyes blinked at her in the dark between her position and the mouth of the cave. A shaggy brindle wolf padded toward her, tongue lolling from the side of his mouth. Eyes far too knowledgeable watched her. Hope she didn't dare acknowledge flared, a match in the midnight depths of this night.

"Caleb?" The wolf pressed close, snuffled her cheek. "Please tell me you have a plan."

The beast licked her face then nosed her. He turned and prowled back toward the entrance. She didn't move. He turned to look at her and wuffed softly. She shook her head.

"No. I'm the last sacrifice. It can't manifest if it doesn't get me."

The wolf padded back, nipped the hem of her jeans

and tugged. He dragged her about six feet before she managed to kick him loose. "What are you doing? That...thing is out there."

Caleb growled and shook his head. His eyes narrowed and he nosed her again.

"Okay. Fine. I'm coming." She flipped over to hands and knees and crawled out after him.

Outside, the air was quiet, though storm clouds massed on the horizon and lightning flickered in their depths. Long moments later, thunder rolled over them. Caleb led her back to the rocks where they'd made love. The parachute was still there, along with his clothes. Within moments, Caleb was back in human form and dressing.

"What was that thing?"

He turned his head to gaze at her over his shoulder. "Wendigo. I think."

"The fetishes."

"Yes. They're blood sacrifices."

"You're the wolf."

"Yes."

"Why did it spit you out?"

"Because it wants you first." He left his shirt unbuttoned as he gathered her into his arms. "I won't let that happen, Del. You're mine. I won't give you up. Especially not to that thing."

Thunder hammered the air around them, lightning flashing even closer. Churning black clouds gobbled up the stars.

"We gotta go, babe."

Together, they scrambled back to the canyon. Del had to trot to keep up with Caleb's long strides. He led her on a twisting, turning path through the rocks. They suddenly spilled out of the rocks and Caleb halted. Del crashed into his back, her arms circling his waist to hold herself upright. In front of them, a wall of white obliterated the desert floor. Shadows moved in the bleak cloud, shapes moving closer. Caleb tensed, ready to fight.

Adele wasn't sure how to react. Five figures emerged. These *people*, walking through the wall of...mist? Smoke? Dust? Whatever filled the air, when they stepped through it, she could only think they were a band of superheroes or something out of a movie. Was that the deal? Had she and Caleb stumbled into the middle of some special effects extravaganza?

While she cringed back against the canyon wall, she watched a tall, gorgeous brunette stride up to Caleb and grab him in a crushing hug. Her heart twinged when he hugged her back. Neither spoke, just stood there clinging. He'd buried his nose in the woman's neck. Like he'd buried it against hers. She tore her gaze from them and decided she'd give anything to be a chameleon so she could just blend into the scenery. The men who stood in a loose semi-circle were the stuff of wet dreams and not one of them noticed her.

The hair on her arms prickled and she smoothed down the goosebumps forming on her skin. So much power swirled that she suddenly realized she was the only human there. She didn't know what those four men were, but they were definitely not mortal.

"Damn you, Caleb Jones. I was fucking ready to kill your sorry ass if you weren't already dead."

"Language, Sade."

"Shut the fuck up, asshole." Sade slugged Caleb's arm and he pretended to wince. "You scared the piss outta me. Do you fucking know what it's like to get a call in the middle of the night to hear the gawddamned director of the fucking FBI tell me you're missing?" She hit him again for good measure.

"I haven't exactly had access to a phone."

"And you couldn't do any magic fucking woo-woo to

get in touch with any of us?"

Caleb rubbed his jaw. Pretending he wasn't happy to see her was hard. That she brought some big guns to the fight was a relief. "Yeah, glad to see you too, Slim."

She thumped him in the chest. "Last time I ever whistle for you, dude."

He threw back his head and laughed. "You don't even know how to put your lips together and blow."

A throat cleared behind him and he glanced over his shoulder. A very amused master vampire returned his gaze. Sade stepped back, closer to the vamp, and Caleb did a double take, especially at the vamp's words.

"I think you know exactly how to put your lips together and blow, darling."

Sade glowered at tall, dark, and fanged before sending her glare back Caleb's direction. "You know Varrick, Nikos, and Ari, obviously. This is Kristian St. John. Sinjen, Caleb."

"Yes. I know who he is." Sinjen offered his hand for a shake.

Caleb stared at that hand like it might turn into a snake. Sade elbowed him so he returned the gesture. He added a chance to talk to Sade—alone—to his list of things to do. Like survive the night, the first item on said list. The vampire gave his hand a strong grip and a perfunctory shake, along with a side of knowing smile. What was up with that?

"And who do we have here?"

Uh oh. Caleb had momentarily forgotten about Adele and Sade just realized the other woman was there. "Adele McCoy, Sade. She with the Colorado Bureau of Investigation."

"So you two did run off together." Sade's voice gave no hint as to whether she was teasing or serious.

Adele straightened to her full height—which was hobbit-size compared to the others. Holy Batman and

Robin, did magicks all have to be so...tall? And so freaking gorgeous? Life just wasn't fair. She squared her shoulders and jutted her chin toward the woman. "We didn't run off. We were kidnapped and thrown out of an airplane."

"While it was flying?" Sade arched a brow at Caleb.

He shrugged and ducked his chin. "Sort of."

"Did you have parachutes?"

"One." He wouldn't meet her gaze.

"Uh huh." Sade stared at Caleb then cast her gaze over the other men as if hoping for divine guidance, or perhaps intervention. "You jumped out of a perfectly good airplane. With one parachute. That makes so much sense."

"Not quite like that, Sade. Bad guys. Guns. Drugs."

Sade opened her mouth to speak. Closed it. Opened it again. Closed it once more then shook her head. "I have no words. You owe me a beer and an explanation."

"Done. But later. We have a bad nasty to deal with first."

Sade threw her head back and laughed. "Don't we always?"

Sinjen watched Sade, hiding his worry. She still wasn't one hundred percent after dealing with the witch. She tired easily, her reflexes off when her energy ebbed. If he had any control over her, he would have left her in the hotel in Sonoma. He assessed their small band of warriors. Gargoyle and dragon could take to the air, ravage the wendigo from above, keep it grounded. That would give the fae, werewolf, and himself a chance to attack. He glanced at Sade and paled. She was checking her weapons.

"No."

"What the fuck do you mean *no*, Sinjen? You forget who is in charge here."

"No, Sade. You forget that you are human. This is

not something you can kill with human weapons."

"No, I can't kill it with bullets. But I can slow it down. And guess what, Mr. Knight to the Rescue, you fucking can't kill it either." She waved her hand at the rest of the magicks. "Varrick is the only one who might have a snowball's prayer in hell and he's already admitted he can't kill it. We need a fucking thunderbird." Sade jutted her chin and her eyes glittered like green glass in the moonlight. "You don't get to tell me what to do."

He lowered his voice, not that it mattered. Everyone, except maybe the human woman, would hear him. "You almost died, Sade. I sat there in the Chicago Morgue for hours waiting beside your body. I will not do that again."

"Wait! What?" Caleb pushed up beside her. "You almost died?" He was quivering with shock and anger. His hands fisted then unfisted when claws shot from the ends of his fingers. "Why didn't you tell me?"

"Why did you let me believe you'd gone fucking walkabout, you asshole?"

Human and werewolf stood nose to nose, steam all but rising from their skin. The magicks wisely backed away. While the argument raged, Sinjen planned battle strategy with the other magicks. Varrick and Nikos backed away, giving each other space. The gargoyle's change was like pulling a page of tracing paper from an illustration drawn on parchment. The human guise was drawn on the paper, the gargoyle form filled the parchment.

The dragon opted for a much showier shift. With a snort of fire and clouded in smoke, Nikos released his glamour.

Sade, her hair floating in a nimbus of static electricity, automatically stepped away, ending the argument with Caleb. She'd never seen Nikos in dragon form, but she'd felt his compressed magic while he appeared human. Wings of spun silver spread from the smoke—at least sixty feet across. His body was also silver, the tips of his trencher-sized scales dipped with burnished green. Massive haunches ended in claws almost as long as her body. Front legs with muscles as defined as a body builder. A long tail sporting spine ridges and a tip that looked like feather fletches on an arrow, only razor sharp. When the smoke cleared, Nikos was the size of a huge dump truck and a hundred times more lethal.

She gawked at the dragon's head. Long, narrow, a mouth full of teeth meant to rend and shred, twisting horns spiking from the top of the skull. Then she saw his eyes. She stared at stainless steel death. *Yeah, take that, you stupid wendigo!* Sade decided they might just have a chance. She had an ace in the hole, but the magicks had to get the wendigo here so the plan would fall into place.

Varrick and Nikos were both in their real forms. Ari released his glamour, the pretty playboy now a fae warrior in all his glory. Sinjen gathered darkness around him, ready to protect the human women, despite Sade's objections, which he cut off with a glower.

"No. We have discussed this. We have a plan and we will stick to it. You will stay behind me, take the shots you can, but even you, Lady Sade, with your dead-eye aim will be hard put to hit the target once the battle is engaged."

Sade huffed at him and curled her lip into a snarl. "Oh, whatever." She whirled on Caleb. "Why aren't you changed?"

Caleb stared at Sade, horrified.

"What?" She waved a negligent hand toward Adele. "If she hasn't seen you naked by now...dude! You are so falling down on the job. And these misfits? Locker room, dawg. Just sayin'."

He scratched the back of his neck, totally uncomfortable with this conversation. He needed to rein her in before things devolved to the point of no return. She didn't give him a chance.

"If you're worried about this becoming a measuring contest, trust me. These refugees from the Island of Misfit Toys got nothing on you."

He groaned as his chin thunked against his chest. "Sade."

"What? I've seen your skinny ass naked since I was twelve. We might not have played doctor—"

Choked-off laughter stopped the words spewing from her mouth. He didn't want to look up and he definitely didn't want to play biggest dick with a master vampire, a dragon enforcer, a gargoyle sentinel, and that damned fae known far and wide as the King's Seducer.

"Caleb, there are rocks over there."

Sinjen's quiet directive settled him. Well, that and the fact the vampire had his hand clamped over Sade's mouth.

Shaking his head, he explained. "I can't change." He opened his hand to reveal the wolf fetish perched on his palm. "I originally thought those pack teens were the sacrifice. They weren't. It wants me."

Adele touched his arm. "It can't have you. You're mine."

Something loosened in his chest. "Let's do this."

CHAPTER TWENTY-SIX
FINAL COUNTDOWN

"YEAH, LET'S DO THIS. Anybody have an idea of how to call this puppy out?" Sade gazed around the group, looking for inspiration.

Caleb nodded and moved away. This was the part he hated—using Adele for bait. "I have an idea." He schooled his expression, turned to face the women he cared about—his lover and his heart sister, and the vampire and fae who stood guard over them. "Protect them. No matter what."

Both magicks dipped their chins, a silent acknowledgment of his charge. He tilted his head back to watch the aerial acrobatics above him. Dragon and gargoyle flew dizzying patterns, feeling out the other, learning techniques and talents. Being in the wrong place, caught in something as simple as the backwash of a wing, could be disastrous.

He glanced back for one last look. Sade's gaze captured his, held, refusing to let go. "We have backup coming, but it's going to take awhile. We have to keep this thing busy until it gets here."

"Backup?" Four land-based voices chorused the word, varying shades of hope adding harmony to the chord.

Sade held Caleb's gaze. "Chaco."

Caleb cut his eyes to Ari. The fae nodded to him. "The shaman comes, but his magic is different from ours."

Lightning crackled across the desert, closer this time. "He needs to build the fucking storm, Caleb. We

230

have to hold that gawddamned native demon bastard until that happens." Sade's expression remained stoic, but her eyes told him everything. She was terrified—not for herself, but for him. "I'm not going to lose you. You understand me?"

He did and he also understood the irony of their reversed positions. Usually, it was Sade rushing into the midst of danger. Fearless. Determined. She was human. And the most insanely brave person he'd ever met. She knew she couldn't command this situation, understood she had no control. But he did. For once in his existence, lives and deaths came down to him. He couldn't fail. He wouldn't.

"Get ready," Caleb ordered, yelling so everyone heard. "If this works, no telling how quickly the thing will appear." The winged creatures offered wing dips in salute. His eyes sought, found, and fixed on Adele. He mouthed the words, "I'm sorry."

Adele darted to him, grabbed his cheeks and pressed her lips to his. "A kiss for luck." She clung for a long moment, her eyes fixed on his, unspoken emotion rampant in her expression as she pressed something into his hand. "Don't die."

Her actions and words caught him by surprise. Before he could react, she'd whirled and darted back to the others. Star Wars. Yeah, she'd do. His gaze caught Sade's and they exchanged a silent look that spoke volumes. The time had come, and all that jazz.

Raising his hands, palms up, Caleb offered the last two fetishes to the wendigo. He threw words into the teeth of the rising wind. "I have the deer. I am the wolf. Come and get me if you think you can."

Storm clouds rolled ever closer, but it was the swirling dust devil tearing across the desert that transfixed them all. It danced and spun, churning up the desert floor as it approached.

"Land!" Sinjen shouted to Varrick and Nikos. "Land before the wind tears your wings!"

The two hesitated a moment too long. The wind hit, ripped at bodies and shredded wings. The dragon fell first, one gossamer wing a skeletal caricature. He landed hard, unhurt beyond the damaged wing. Sade darted from behind Sinjen but fell back when the dragon snapped at her. Magic shimmered and the wing healed itself.

A shower of sand and plants exploded as the gargoyle plowed into the desert floor. He pushed off the ground, shook himself, and rolled his head to the accompanying sound of grating granite. "Right then, time for Plan B. Everyone take cover. I'll find the little mundane controlling this mother and pound him into a greasy spot in the sand."

Varrick launched into the sky, away from the whirlwind, before anyone else could countermand him.

"What's he talking about?" Del, holding her hair in one hand so it didn't whip across her face, had to scream above the wind.

"El Diablo aka Santos Santana. He's the one who conjured this thing." Sade had to yell as well. "Varrick thinks if he takes Santana out, the wendigo will collapse because it's conjured."

"Conjured? What does that even mean?" Adele's gaze darted over the magicks' faces looking for clarification.

Sinjen endeavored to explain. "We don't believe the wendigo is...real. Not in the sense of a summoned demon. It was conjured—called forth with native magic."

"I don't get the difference."

"Neither to do I," Sade interrupted. "Doesn't matter. We just gotta figure out how to kill it. Or send it back to hell."

Ari and Sinjen herded the women back against the cliff as Caleb remained where he was, almost a hundred yards away. Nikos paced back and forth behind the werewolf and snapped at the air as his deadly tail swished.

Sand swirled around him, a tornado abrading his skin. Caleb gritted his teeth, continued holding the wolf and deer fetishes in his palm, arm outstretched. His very nature screamed that he change, that he protect himself from the abuse being heaped upon his human form, but he knew on an instinctive level that he would be lost if he did so. He wasn't strictly human, but he was a man. And the woman he loved would die if he let go of his humanity.

Not on his watch.

The vortex slowed, the hulking figure inside the whipping winds still indistinct. Caleb wasn't sure what he expected to see as the sand settled. Movies and anime had nothing on the real deal. The monster was bigger than the dragon, and that was saying something. Covered in mottled and straggled hair, its long face looked like a mishmash of equine, bovine, and cervid features with teeth made to rend and tear, the thing sported a massive rack of sharp antlers. And opposable thumbs. Hooves were nothing to sneeze at, but hands with foot-long claws were worse. As the wind died, the hideous beast spread leathery wings, each joint tipped with a hooked barb.

"I am the hungry wolf at the door," the fiend growled. "The boogie man in the closet, the monster under the bed. I am every nightmare haunting the dreams of humans."

What? Caleb stared at the thing, noting its mouth hadn't moved. Maybe Varrick was on to something. Maybe this thing really was just a puppet.

"Here, little deer. Come to papa."

Was that an accent? Caleb watched the behemoth closely. Its gaze had fixed on the spot where Adele crouched behind the boulders with Sade. Sinjen and Ariel stood firm.

Adele shivered. "It said that before. Right before you guys got here, when I was trapped in the cave." Her eyes were drawn to the other woman and she watched Sade jab a syringe into a shotgun shell. "Uhm...do I want to ask?"

Sade glanced up briefly before returning her attention to the task at hand. "Probably not."

"Are you going after it?"

"Yeah."

"Why?"

"Because that's what I do." Sade glanced up and tilted her head toward the magicks. "They think they're immortal. They aren't. I'm going to fucking do whatever it takes to keep them alive, including that damned dragon."

Del folded her arms over her chest and pinched her face into a scowl. "Why you guys? Why Caleb?"

The breath Sade huffed out ruffled the dark strand of hair falling around her face. "It's our job, hon."

"Your job? Your job is to hunt demons from hell?"

"It's not technically a demon."

"Don't change the subject. Dammit. That thing could kill you. Kill Caleb. All of us."

With a great deal of self-control, Sade bit her tongue. This woman was important to Caleb. She could see it in his eyes, his protective stance. "It's still our job. We stand between the monsters and the 234undane, Adele."

She wanted to hit Sade. Or scream. Or run out there, grab Caleb, and drag him back. Hug him so tightly he wouldn't leave her. Ever. She'd never pegged herself as one of those overly dramatic chicks who swore they'd die if their man left them, but she just might—emotionally and physically.

Wrinkling her nose, she stepped closer. "What is that stuff?"

"You have to bring the right tool for the kill."

"Okay. I understand that. But what is it?"

Sade held the shell for a long moment, making sure it didn't leak. "Holy water and vinegar."

"Will it work?"

"Maybe."

"You better bring him back to me."

"Always. I love him too." Sade fed shells into the shotgun she held, and stood up behind Sinjen and Ari. She racked the shotgun, feeding a doctored shell into the breech.

"Sade—"

"Shut it, Sinjen. We have to hold this fucker until Varrick gets back and until Chaco arrives." She ducked under his arm and strode toward Caleb. "Yo, tall, dark, and ugly!"

The monster turned, ponderous in its movements. "You are not my deer."

"Nope. I'm your worst nightmare." Sade ran forward, ducked under the hand that swiped at her, laughing when the dragon chomped on the creature's arm and yanked so that it had to bend over. She pulled the trigger almost point blank at the monster's face. She tossed a combat knife. "Achilles, Caleb!"

He caught it by the handle as it flashed by, rolled beneath the thing's other hand and darted between its gigantic feet. Slash left, slash right. The knife bit into fur and skin and acidic blood spurted, but the creature didn't go down.

Ari joined the battle, his sword a silver streak as he sliced deep cuts into the wendigo's legs, reaching as high as he could leap to deliver the blows. Sade slipped on the uneven ground and the wendigo slapped at her, connecting and sending her flying. Sinjen sprinted to her, leaving Adele huddled behind the boulders, watching wide-eyed and terrified.

Somebody grabbed her from behind and she screamed before a hand covered her mouth. Everyone froze, including the horror intent on destroying them.

"Sheep. All of you." El Diablo sneered and held up the strand of fetishes around his neck. "I will not share, not with the angels, the gods. There is only the devil's cut in this deal. The power is all mine. I will make my cut, sacrificing this one, then the wolf. The world will bow before me! I am El Diablo. The Devil!"

Caleb snapped. He would give this devil his cut. He would dance with the devil in the most intimate way possible—to the death. He lunged forward, shifting on the fly.

"NO!" Myriad voices denied his actions. Sade. Her pale face flashed in his peripheral vision as he passed her. His massive paws scrabbled across the sand, his entire being focused on the smarmy drug lord and Adele. His muscles bunched, his mouth opened to reveal slathering jaws. He leaped.

"What the gawddamned fucking hell!" Sade squirmed out of Sinjen's hold, her Beretta in her hand, leveled on the man who still held Adele in front of him. The woman—Caleb's woman—appeared unconscious. Just as well. What she didn't see wouldn't scar her psyche.

The storm broke around them. Sade didn't care. She inhaled. Focused. Exhaled. Squeezed the trigger. A smaller, insignificant flash flickered amidst the sound and the fury of the storm. El Diablo stared at her as a shadow darted between the speeding bullet and her target. Caleb. The wolf jerked, absorbing the nine millimeter slug, but still rampaging toward the target.

The two humans went down beneath his onslaught.

Caleb's humanity was nonexistent. He barely acknowledged the burn of the bullet lodged near his spine as he sank teeth into the human's throat. Hot blood gushed and he swallowed the man's life force with great gulps. This human dared touch Caleb's mate. He would die for doing so.

Ariel and Sinjen braved the savaging wolf in an attempt to grab Adele and pull her free. Nikos's dragon form shimmered until he appeared human, his arm snaking around Sade's waist to keep her from rushing into the fight. Adele, fully conscious now, screamed, Sade's shout an echo. No one paid any attention to the wendigo.

The fiendish beast roared. One clawed hand snatched Sade and Nikos, brought them to its mouth. Sade fired into the nightmare's maw. The dragon shifted, taking damage as the wendigo's talons scraped human skin before armored scales could protect.

Varrick reappeared in winged-gargoyle guise. He'd located El Diablo but was unable to take out the summoner. He now left that to those on the ground as he attacked the wendigo's head. In moments, his shift complete, Nikos attacked with flame, claw, and vicious barbed tail. The thing dropped Sade and she hit the desert floor. Hard.

A man arose amidst the rocks, a man glowing from the power he contained. His words boomed out, shimmering in magic so they seemed written against the roiling clouds as if they'd been drawn by a child's sparkler. "*Yiweh! Nah'asdzan! K'adi!*"

A blinding flash. Deafening thunder. Caleb's body contracted, shuddered, hung suspended in midair. Darkness descended. He couldn't breathe. Couldn't think. Couldn't do anything but die. He'd failed. Caleb howled in the prison of light. Fought. Lost. Failed. Died.

And then all hell broke loose.

CHAPTER TWENTY-SEVEN
RESOLUTION

"WHAT THE HELL?" Sade pushed up on her hands, her face covered in grit from the sand where she'd taken a nosedive. Her vision was burned on the edges and her ears filtered sounds like she was underwater. The wendigo was rampaging, harried by gargoyle and dragon. Sinjen and Ariel looked worse for the wear as they sat up.

Her peripheral vision cleared enough she located a bloody pile of limbs. Scrambling on hands and knees, she got to Caleb and Adele at the same time as Sinjen. The woman seemed unhurt, if stunned. Caleb's jaws were locked around El Diablo's throat. Neither was breathing.

"Caleb!" She screamed his name, but nothing came out of her mouth as a dark shadow blocked out the sky.

Everyone froze—and not because they wanted to. Chaco, naked but for the necklace full of animal fetishes that had once adorned the throat of El Diablo, stood over them. He raised his hands, chanting. The ancient language wove magic around them, chaining them in place. The chant breathed for them, their hearts beating beneath the words like war drums. Varrick and Nikos dropped from the sky, helpless before the power of the Anasazi shaman.

The wendigo roared as Chaco stepped over and around humans and magicks. He reached for the storm, pulling lightning from the clouds and casting bolts against the creature. Thunder crashed, a continual roar drowning out Chaco's chant. The shaman gathered the tattered clouds, weaving their seething mass into a

239

black cloak he settled over his nakedness. Shadows danced, solidified, became flesh. Feathers. Wings. Massive beak and talons.

The thunderbird launched into the sky and the wendigo leaped after it, stretching hairy arms to grab the magical avian. It missed. With a bleating growl, the monster flapped its wings and lifted into the air, chasing after the wheeling thunderbird.

Sade managed to crawl to Caleb. Adele, fully cognizant now, had scuttled away and cringed against a boulder, eyes wide with shock, a silent scream painting her lips. Sade gave scant notice to the other woman, her entire focus centered on the man she considered her brother.

His body was twisted and... "No. No-no-no-no-nooooooo." Bile rose in Sade's throat. Caleb was caught between wolf and man—not his warrior half-form but part human, part animal. Tears slicked her cheeks as she cradled his bloody head in her lap. "No, Caleb. Nononononono." Her denial came out as one word. "You can't leave me. Not like this, you sorry sonavabitch. You come back to me. Gawddammitmotherfuckin' shitforbrains asshole. I love you. Don't you know that?"

Adele's heart broke as she watched the naked grief on Sade's face. She'd known there was something special between Caleb and the dark-haired woman. But this? Her own heartache was a single drop in the well of Sade's desolation.

The four magicks watched the aerial battle, staggered by the sheer power of the combatants. They were some of the most powerful entities of their kinds yet each one knew their combined capabilities would never have been enough.

Thunder and lightning still raged in the sky when their awe was finally ripped apart by sounds of grief.

Sinjen dropped to his knees beside Sade, her wrenching sobs shredding his self-control.

Ari peered over his shoulder. "Is he breathing?"

Sinjen checked. "Get Varrick. Caleb must be teleported now."

Nikos appeared, his silver eyes glinted, still those of a reptile. "It will do no good. I don't believe even the mages at the fae court can reverse this."

Sade's fist came out of nowhere, landing a hard uppercut to his jaw. "Don't fucking say that, Nikos. Just...gawddamn fucking no. This is Caleb. He can't die."

Ari caught her gaze. "Look at me, Sade. He's right. This is not fae magic." He glanced over his shoulder to check the battle.

"Both fae and dragon are correct, Sade." Sinjen added his voice to the chorus. "This is the same magic that gives life to the thunderbird and the wendigo."

Adele crept closer. Caleb wasn't hers, that was obvious now, but she still loved him. Still cared and hated that he was so terribly injured. Her tears fell to the sand, mixed with Caleb's blood already spilled there.

"Please," she whispered to the darkness. "Please help him."

The wind sighed around them, the storm having chased the battle toward the far horizon. A voice murmured in the night breeze. Adele's hair lifted. Deep in her hindbrain, spirits moved in answer. This devilry on the air's tongue was not hers. This magic was born of the desert, of the painted mesas, of the big sky.

"Please," Adele whispered again, ignored by the others. "I will give you anything to save him."

The wizened voice breathed into her ear. "Will you give your life?"

"Yes," she promised. "A thousand times yes."

The air shimmered and an old man appeared. His

eyes were all but lost in the wrinkles of his weather-beaten face. Eagle feathers adorned his long, gray hair. He wore a necklace of bear claws, and leather breeches. "I am Sotuknang, the First Spirit of Taiowa, the Creator." The man gazed down at Caleb. "The wolves are my children and I breathed life into them so they could walk as men."

Everyone now stared at him, entranced. The soft caresses of the wind dried the tears on the cheeks of the women. "My son is much loved. It is not his time though he seeks the door to the next level. I will breathe the life back into him so he may finish his journey in this world." His gaze locked on Adele. "I leave you your life but I will have your heart."

Sotuknang stretched out his left hand and crooked his finger. Adele shuddered, choked back a cry as she clutched at her chest. The Spirit raised his left palm to his mouth and blew. His breath, scented with sage, sweet grass, tobacco, and corn silk brushed across all of them, one at a time. First Caleb, then Adele. Sade and Sinjen. Ariel. Varrick. Nikos. They breathed deeply, taking the softly perfumed air deep into their lungs.

"It is good," Sotuknang proclaimed. In the distance, a coyote laughed and a crow cawed. An eagle screamed overhead and closer, a blue jay chattered. On the horizon, the storm raged—thunder growling and lightning a continuous display until Sotuknang blew another breath, this one picked up by the wind and sent into the heart of the tempest. A cry like a thousand eagles blasted their ears, and silhouetted by dancing fingers of lightning, the thunderbird ascended into the clouds. Moments later, all was quiet.

The ancient spirit was gone. A large turquoise stone rested where he'd stood. The flaws in the stone looked like a picture—of a wolf and a woman kneeling before the Great Spirit. Adele, her hand shaking, her chest still aching, picked it up and slipped it into her pocket.

Sade, calm now that Caleb was breathing and his bones were shifting into something more human, issued orders. Ari transported Adele while Varrick carried Caleb. Both returned to teleport Sade and Sinjen while Nikos guarded them until all arrived at the hospital in Albuquerque.

No one discussed the appearance of the native god. What was there to say, really? Ari and Varrick left, with promises from Sade to keep them updated on Caleb's condition. When she had to break up the fourth standoff between Nikos and Sinjen, she banned them both. Neither was happy, but both were well aware her threats were not idle.

Adele's injuries proved superficial, but she haunted the hospital halls, skulking just out of sight when Sade was there. More than once, Sade caught her sitting at Caleb's bedside, holding his hand and brushing hair off his forehead, talking softly or singing lullabies. Sade tried to make friends, got only grudging responses.

A week into Caleb's recovery, Sade watched Adele through the window for several minutes before returning her attention to Caleb, where he lay propped on pillows in the hospital bed. "She likes you."

He glanced up, eyebrows knitting over his nose. "Who?"

"Adele, you ass. I'd give odds she likes you a lot, in fact."

"How can you tell?"

"She keeps giving me these go-to-hell looks whenever we're in the same room." Studying Caleb's expression, she canted her head as the light bulb clicked on. "Jeez, Caleb. You didn't tell her, did you?"

"Tell her what? That I'm a werewolf?"

"No stupid. That I'm basically your sister."

He remained clueless. "What's that got to do with

anything?"

"Holy crap, Caleb. You are dumber than a fucking stump when it comes to women. She thinks there's something between us."

"Well, d'uh. There is."

"Well, d'uh, yeah. But not like she's thinking. Let me spell it out for you, dumb ass. Your pretty little CSI thinks we're lovers."

"Ewww."

"Precisely. She thinks I'm competition. You need to set her straight."

Caleb shifted his gaze to look outside. Adele sat on a bench, chin tucked to her chest, looking miserable. His heart constricted and he had to breathe around the pain. "Maybe that's for the best."

"What the fucking hell are you talking about?"

"She'd be better off with someone else."

"She doesn't want someone else. She's in love with you." Sade got right up in his face, hands on his shoulders so he had to look at her. "What are you going to do?"

Now there was a question filled with innuendo. Leave it to Sade to cut to the chase. Caleb had no good option in this matter. "I don't know."

"Liar."

"Leave it alone, Sade."

"The hell I will, Caleb."

He knew her. She'd pick at the scab until she made it—him—bleed. "I don't have a choice."

"We all have choices."

"Not this time."

He was a freaking werewolf. His kind didn't mate with humans. While he was saving Adele's life, she was all cool with his turning furry. But years from now? When she grew old? And he didn't—at least not at the same rate? When no kids came to their union?

"Do you love her?"

"What's that got to do with it?"

"Everything."

"What about you? Do you love Sinjen?"

"This isn't about me. It's about you. And resolving this thing between you and Adele. Answer my question. Do you love her?"

Yeah, that bottom line again. Break his heart? Or hers? He could live without her. Could she live with him? Resolution. Either way, it would hurt like hell. But gods help him, he couldn't—wouldn't—walk away.

"Yes."

"Then tell her." Sade bent and, after brushing his shaggy hair to the side, kissed Caleb's forehead. "I want an invite to the wedding." With a smile plastered on her face, she headed for the door. "I'll tell her you want to see her."

"Hey, Slim?" Caleb called after her. She paused but didn't look back. "I love you best."

Sade's mouth quirked into a smile. He caught it from her reflection in the window on the door. "Nuh-uh. I love you better than best."

Out in the courtyard, she schooled her expression and strode to where Adele still sat, shoulders hunched. "May I sit down?"

Adele refused to look up and lifted one shoulder in a show of uncaring.

"I'll take that as a yes." Sade settled, leaning back, long legs stretched in front of her, head back so her face was toward the sun. "We need to talk."

"There's nothing to say. I know he loves you." *More than me,* Adele reminded herself, the spot where her spiritual heart once resided aching.

"He does, but not in the same way he loves you."

"He doesn't love me."

"Au contraire, mon ami." Sade leaned forward

enough her shoulder could bump Adele's. "Let me ask you something." When Adele didn't respond, she bulled ahead. "Does it freak you out when Caleb shapeshifts?"

That got a reaction. Adele's head whipped around. "No. Of course not. Why would you even ask me that?"

Sade pressed her lips together to hide her smile. "The first time I saw him shift, he went from wolf to naked boy. In my bed." She curled her lips between her teeth when Adele stiffened. "I was twelve. It was his first shift. I gave him a blanket and told him not to lick his balls."

"Ewwww." Shocked, Adele swiveled to stare at Sade. "That's just...sick."

"I'd had Caleb since I was six. He was a puppy, wearing a big red bow, sitting under the Christmas tree. We love each other, Adele. He's...well, technically, I guess he's my foster brother, but he's so much more than that. He's my best friend. My partner. And he was the first member of my heart family." Sade found herself blinking moisture out of her eyes as her throat burned.

After a long silence, Adele replied in a small voice, "Oh."

"Yeah. He'd like to see you now. Tell him I'll see him when he reports back for duty in DC. I have a plane to catch, now that I know he's in good hands." Sade shoved to her feet and walked away.

Adele also stood, watching the other woman's back before turning toward the hospital door. Sade's parting shot drifted back to her.

"If you break his heart, I'll hunt you down and hurt you."

Feeling as if a huge load had been lifted from her, Adele all but skipped inside. She tapped timidly on the closed door to Caleb's room and pushed it open when he called, "Come in."

She stood there, staring at him. He'd almost healed

from the horrific injuries, but something...haunted remained in his eyes. She resisted the urge to shuffle her feet and instead, offered a tight smile and a shy, "Hi."

"Hey." Caleb didn't know what to say. He'd watched out the window when Sade spoke to Adele and really wished the glass wasn't soundproofed.

"Uhm...so..."

"I guess Sade sort of explained about us. Her and me, I mean."

"She did."

Okay. Now what was he supposed to say? What he really wanted was for Adele to crawl into bed with him so he could hold her and kiss her and show her how he felt about her. "Will you..." He swallowed around the lump clogging his throat and patted the bed. "Come sit?"

She dragged her feet. Just because Sade said Caleb loved her didn't mean he actually felt that way. But she was aching to touch him, to run her hands over his skin to make sure he was all there, in one piece, and healing. Whenever they were apart, the empty space in her chest—her heart—hurt so much she could barely breathe. But when she was near him, touching him, she felt...whole.

Her last few steps were a run. She hit the bed and he gathered her into his arms, dragged her up beside him and then he was kissing her. Her mouth. Her nose. Her face. Her neck. His hands prowled over her as she returned the gesture, making sure he was whole.

"Adele."

"Caleb."

Calling the other's name sounded like a duet, one not rehearsed but natural. Their words tumbled over each other, like puppies playing in the sunshine.

"I've missed you."

"I was so scared."

"I didn't protect—"

"Shush. I'm fine. Are you okay?"

"Werewolf. Hard to kill."

"Don't scare me like that again."

"I won't let anything ever hurt you."

"I love you."

"I love you."

And those were always the magic words. This was his mate, the woman he wanted to spend the rest of his life with. He didn't believe in that fated mate stuff. It was just an urban legend werewolf parents made up to scare their sons so they'd keep it in their pants. Werewolves didn't even mate for life. Usually. But for him? Caleb knew. There would never be another woman for him. Only Adele.

She owned his heart. With that admission, a memory returned. The First Spirit, Sotuknang. A low voice spoke in his head. "She gave her heart to save your humanity. You gave yours to keep her for the length of your life."

Caleb didn't know what that meant. Didn't dare hope that it meant they'd live their lives entwined and go together when the time came. He cupped Adele's face in his palms, realized she was crying. He brushed the shadow of her tears away with his thumbs. "Marry me, Adele."

"I...are you sure, Caleb?"

"Yes. It's crazy. I'm crazy. I hope you're as crazy as me. Just...say yes. Be mine. Now and always. We'll figure out all the I'm-a-werewolf-you're-human stuff. But you own my heart, darlin'. Don't break it."

Adele threw back her head and laughed, Caleb watching her intently. "That does it. I have to marry you."

"Have to?" He asked the question cautiously, his guard up.

"Your sister said she'd hunt me down and hurt me if I broke your heart."

Caleb kept a straight face for about a minute, and then laughter erupted in a series of snorting giggles through his nose. "No. Can't laugh. It hurts. Ah, it hurts so good. C'mere, baby." He gathered her close and kissed her temple. "S'long as you love me, we're good. You have nothing to worry about. Sade's bite is way worse than her bark."

"That's what I'm afraid of."

"I'll take care of you. Trust me."

"I do."

EPILOGUE

Washington DC, two months later

"I DO," SINJEN MUTTERED, pacing the confines of Sade's living room. The sun had set an hour ago and she'd yet to arrive. "What is so bloody hard about saying those two little words?"

The question was strictly rhetorical as he was alone. He wanted to hit something. Or wrap his hand around Sade's neck and crush her. He'd failed in every attempt to get her to talk to him. Something was bothering her, but she refused to trust him enough to share. He'd followed her back to Washington to make sure she healed completely. That was his reasoning, but he knew it for the lie it was. This woman had gotten under his skin, had burrowed into his heart and the thought of being apart left him melancholic and more than a little petulant. It was not a temperament that suited him.

Her phone rang and Sinjen almost jerked it out of the wall, but resisted. Instead, he muted the ring tone. He waited until the answering machine pinged. Listening to the message didn't make him feel guilty at all.

"It's Varrick, Sade. Have you heard the news from Paris? Ripples, babe. From the City of Light all the way to the Big Easy. He won't ask, and Le Viele would crucify him if he did, but Roman's gonna need you on this one. It's...big. And bad. So...call me."

Yes, ripples. As much as the magicks pretended all was copacetic since the Big Rip, wild magic still reared a malignant head. He'd heard rumors of some sort of unrest amongst the gargoyles. That Roman, the Legate of New Orleans, Sade's childhood protector, and right hand of Crevan, leader of the gargoyle Sentinels would be embroiled was unsurprising. That the gargoyles wished to draw Sade into the fray was troubling.

The quick tap-tap-tap of boot heels sounded out in the hall. Sade was home. Finally. He should have been disgusted at the way his heart lightened with her presence. He was an ancient vampire and that the heart and soul of this human stirred his blood should be troubling. Instead, he wallowed in the wash of emotions she brought to him.

She pushed through the front door, a large shipping box in her arms. "Oh my fucking god. They're doing it. A gawddamned wedding. Couldn't they just fucking elope to Las Vegas? Hell, Niagra Falls. Isn't that where people go if Vegas is too far away?"

His smile settled on his face. He took the box from her, set it aside. Pulling her into his arms, he kissed her soundly, smothering her curses and complaints.

"Welcome home, darling."

"Mmmm." Her hands fisted in his hair. "Less talking, more kissing."

There was much more kissing, less clothing, and a great deal of sex. The moon rode high in the sky before she listened to the message on her answering machine then opened the box from Caleb and his mate. Sinjen was unsure of which distressed Sade more. Choosing to give her time to settle, he fixed coffee and warmed leftover pizza, the only edible thing in her refrigerator.

A few minutes later, the woman he adored beyond all distraction appeared. Sade fisted her hands on her hips. Sinjen waited for her chin to thrust out in stubborn profile, and was rewarded almost immediately. Her green bottle-glass eyes glittered before they narrowed. He stilled, as patient as any predator.

"Why should I?" She pivoted on her heel, pacing

away from him. Sade paused at the window, staring out across the dark water of the Potomac River.

"Because it's important to him, Sade."

Her shoulders stiffened and he fought the urge to cross to her, to touch her, rub away the fear roiling beneath her angry surface.

"Why do you care? You don't even like Caleb."

"That is not true, Sade. Why does this upset you?"

"It..." Her nervous fingers uncurled and plucked at her robe. "He won't be mine anymore."

Ah, and there was the truth of it. Now he approached and slipped his arms around her rigid body, pulling her back against him. "He's not leaving you, my love." He turned her in his arms, kissed her forehead, and held her close again. "You need to learn to share."

"Just like you?"

Sinjen threw back his head, laughing. "I don't share. You'd do well to remember that."

"Is that a threat?"

"Yes."

Sade worked her arms up between them and leaned back. Then she thumped him with a fist. "Neanderthal." She glared through the bedroom's door at the frothy pile of satin and lace huddling on their bed.

"I am indeed." He gathered her hands in his, lifted them to his lips, and kissed each knuckle. "To stand with your brother's bride is an honor, Sade."

She shuddered and gulped. "But...why does it have to be so...pink!"

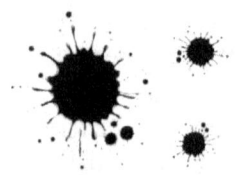

Dear Reader:

The world of the Penumbra Papers is one I've "lived" in for several years now. I'm always excited when Iffy, my Muse, insists we play in this world. When Sade first popped into my imagination, I had no idea who she would become, and where her story would go.

As originally envisioned, the books in this series would tell the story of the individual magicks in Sade's "inner circle." Each would receive a Happy Ever After. Well, leave it to Sade to disabuse me of that notion! She is such a force of nature that she insists on playing a part in every book. And after many attempts to keep her out of Caleb's story, I discovered I should listen to her, even as she informed me in her own inimitable way, "I fucking told you so!"

Music sets the mood when I'm writing the Penumbra Papers. Please keep reading to see the play list. If you are interested in listening while you read, check out the Spotify playlists on my website.

As an author, I'm always humbled when readers love my characters as much as I do. I live with these people during the course of their stories. They are very *real* to me and to know that they also live in readers' imaginations leaves me gobsmacked. Thank you for caring about them.

I would ask a favor before you go. Talking about a book is a priceless gift readers can give an author. When you like a book, please consider leaving a review and recommending it to your friends.

Again, thank you for visiting my worlds. The book is always open so don't be a stranger. Happy reading!

~Silver James

PLAY LIST

Prologue
When I'm Gone – Three Doors Down

Chp 1: Standing Outside the Fire
We Carry On – The Phantom feat. Amy Stroup

Chp 2: To Know a Man
Takes a Lot to Know a Man - Damien Rice

Chp 3: Talk is Cheap
Safe With Me - Joe Henry

Chp 4: Take My Body Home
The Mark - Cold Specks

Chp 5: Deadman's Hand
Breaking the Silence – Breaking Benjamin

Chp. 6: Monsters
Monsters - Angus Powell

Chp 7: Death is a Dialogue
Angels Fall – Breaking Benjamin

Chp 8: The Missing Piece
Don't You Remember - Adele

Chp 9: Magic in the Air
Bad Medicine – Bon Jovi

Chp 10: Best Laid Plans
Ruins – Melissa Etheridge

Chp 11: Take Control
Colors – Verite

Chp 12: Trust Issues
Don't Walk Away – Ryan Levine

Chp 13: Simple Man
Simple Man – Shinedown

Chp 14: Feet of Clay
Bury Me Alive – Breaking Benjamin

Chp 15: Tick Tock
Somewhere a Clock is Ticking – Snow Patrol

Chp 16: Never Say Never
Never Say Never – The Frey

Chp 17: Desperation
Surrender – Roxette

Chp 18: Radio Silence
I Don't Know What to Do With My Hands – Minor Alps

Chp 19: Where Angels Fear to Tread
We're Not Gonna Fall – Daughtry

Chp 20: Shadows in the Dark
Forty-Six and 2 by Tool – O'keefe Music Foundation cover version

Chp 21: Change is Coming
The Devil's Backbone – The Civil Wars

Chp 22: Of Mice and Wolves
Never Again – Breaking Benjamin

Chp 23: Good Medicine
Failure – Breaking Benjamin

Chp 24: Made For This
Letters From the Sky – Civil Twilight

Chp 25: Collision Course
Collide – Skillet

Chp 26: Final Countdown
Defeated – Breaking Benjamin

Chp 27: Resolution
The Great Divide – Breaking Benjamin

Epilogue: Dawn – Breaking Benjamin

Thank you!

Thank you for reading THE DEVIL'S CUT. I hope you enjoyed it. Reviews help other readers find books to read. I appreciate every review, good or bad. Please consider leaving one at Amazon or on Goodreads. If this is your first book from the Penumbra Papers world, please check out other books set in this world, and my other series and books, too.

THE PENUMBRA PAPERS
CASES FROM THE SHADOW'S EDGE

Penumbra: Etymology: New Latin, from Latin paene almost + umbra shadow

These "Cases from the Shadow's Edge" explore the forces of light and dark as they dance through shadows humans barely glimpsed prior to the Big Rip. Since then, all manner of preternatural magicks intermingle with humans in ways mysterious, magical and, in some cases, criminal. Much to humanity's surprise, there really are monsters under the bed and the things that go bump in the night are bigger and scarier than anyone ever imagined.

Vampires. Ghouls. Faeries. Ghosts. Werewolves. Creatures of legend and nightmares. Overnight, reality took on a whole new meaning. The world's best and brightest from every discipline—physics, theology, anthropology, chemistry, to name only a few—all tried to explain the rip in the cosmic curtain. Sade Marquis has her own theory. The monsters have been here all along, flying just under the radar of normal perception. They've been masquerading as mundanes—their term for humans. Of course, Sade knows the truth of the matter. She was raised by a master vampire and her pet "dog" shifted into a boy the night of her twelfth birthday. Sade's very good at keeping secrets. She has a lot of them.

This is where *Special Agent* Sade Marquis enters the mix. A human FBI agent with an X-Files mentality, Sade's been handpicked to fill a new slot within the Bureau—Preternatural Liaison Officer with the MAGIC Unit. The Magical Activity, Grievances, and Inhuman Crimes unit is in charge of investigations involving magicks. It's her job to deal with all the monsters, and she's very, very good at her job. That makes the magicks very, very afraid of her. As they should be...

THAT OL' BLACK MAGIC
PENUMBRA PAPERS #1

Along with her FBI partner—and werewolf best friend—Caleb Jones, Sade is sent to New Orleans to investigate the murders of several high-ranking magicks. The Big Easy is neutral territory so Sade must find and arrest the culprit before war breaks out between the Realms. Things look up when the gargoyle Sentinel, Roman, a permanent fixture in Sade's childhood, arrives to keep the peace. Maybe.

The investigation is hampered by Sade's faerie nemesis, Ariel—the King's Seducer. Oh, and then there's the new dragon in town, Nikolas Constantine. Sade can't decide whether to arrest his ass or admire it.

When guilt and innocence come to play in the French Quarter, it'll take Sade's brand of crazy to sort it all out.

2014 WINNER SHORT PARANORMAL NOVEL
INTERNATIONAL DIGITAL AWARDS

SEASON OF THE WITCH
PENUMBRA PAPERS #2

Sade Marquis. Her best friend turns furry. Her godfather is a master vampire. Her mother was once the mistress of Oberon, King of the Faerie Court.

When the Veil between the mortal and magical realms rips, FBI Special Agent Sade Marquis is in a unique position to head up the newly-formed MAGIC unit. She's the only human who knows exactly what goes bump in the night. When things go to hell in a handbasket and there's magic in the air, Sade is the agent FBI Director George Bailey wants in the trenches. She's savvy, snarky, and sexy, but she may have met her match when she's sent to Chicago to investigate the murder of a congressional aide.

Is the vampire, Kristian St. John, guilty as sin? Once a Templar knight, Sinjen now teaches history at the University of Chicago. He must rely on Sade to clear his name and track the real culprit.

Together, they unravel the clues to a mystery that began a thousand years before. If they don't solve the murders of six young women, the whole world—human *and* magick—will suffer the evil consequences.

2014 FINALIST LONG PARANORMAL NOVEL INTERNATIONAL DIGITAL AWARDS

MOONSTRUCK
THE AWARD-WINNING SERIES

AVAILABLE NOW:
MOONSTRUCK: SECRETS

The existence of Wolves has remained a secret for over 200 years. Now, the members of Army Special SciOps Unit 69 are about to be exposed. When a covert operation behind enemy lines goes wrong, Sergeant

Major Ian McIntire must trust Major Hannah Jackson to save his men—and his heart. She's already privy most of his secrets, but the one she doesn't know about the moonstruck alpha werewolf may get them all killed. She has one chance to get them undercover and safe, but it may already be too late.

Ten years later, former Army sniper Michael Lightfoot's life as a forest ranger fits his need to run wild when the moon is full—until two wild wolf pups are kidnapped, along with Dr. Liz Graham, the wildlife biologist who makes him want to howl. The last thing he expects when he rescues the feisty doctor is to be moonstruck. With her life in danger, he must reveal his true self—and risk losing her—in order to save her from the shady corporation stalking the Wolves.

Warning: Secrets, lies, and betrayals are more personal under the full moon, but when a Wolf loves a woman, he'll do whatever it takes to keep her safe.

Welcome back to the Moonstruck world with this first full length Moonstruck novel containing new chapters and deleted scenes in addition to the first two novellas, **BLOOD MOON** and **BAD MOON.**

STILL AVAILABLE
THE ORIGINAL MOONSTRUCK NOVELLAS

BLOOD MOON
(MOONSTRUCK – BOOK 1)

Army Major Hannah Jackson knows where the skeletons are hidden at the Pentagon and now she's been tasked with keeping the secrets of Army Special Sci Ops Unit 69—the Wolves—and their secret is a doozy. That a civilian corporation wants to exploit the Wolves is a matter of pressing concern.

Sergeant Major Ian McIntire doesn't trust Hannah as far as he can throw her—and that's quite a ways considering he's an alpha werewolf. The woman is a pain in his butt and with the Blood Moon coming, the unit needs to complete their mission and get home before tempers flare. While she might know most of their secrets, the one she doesn't know about the moonstruck Wolf might just get them all killed.

When a covert operation goes wrong, Mac must trust Hannah to save his men—and his heart. Secrets, lies, and betrayals are more personal under the full moon, but when a Wolf loves a woman, he'll do whatever it takes to keep her safe.

Warning: Pursue an alpha Wolf at your own risk. Hot sex, bad words, and action of the blood and guts kind will ensue.
2013 WINNER SHORT PARANORMAL NOVEL
INTERNATIONAL DIGITAL AWARDS

BAD MOON
(MOONSTRUCK –BOOK 2)

Former Army sniper Michael Lightfoot lives a simple life as a forest ranger in Wyoming. The job fits his need to run wild when the moon is full—until two special wolf pups are kidnapped, along with Dr. Liz Graham, the wildlife biologist who makes him want to howl.

The last thing Michael expects when he meets the feisty doctor is to be moonstruck, but the alpha Wolf has more on his plate than just convincing Dr. Liz to love him for who he is. She's being stalked by mercenaries who stole two wolf pups for an unknown faction. Now, with her life in danger, he must reveal his true self to save her. Reuniting with some of his old Army Special SciOps unit, Michael takes on the corporate raiders who want more than just his hide—and Liz's expertise.

Secrets, lies, and betrayals are more personal under

the full moon, but when a Wolf loves a woman, he'll risk heart and soul to keep her.

Warning: When a moonstruck Wolf meets his mate, hot sex will ensue. If his mate is threatened, bad words and violence of the blood and guts variety will definitely occur.

HUNTER'S MOON
(MOONSTRUCK –BOOK 3)

Dr. Jacey Randolph just might be crazy. A rescued wolf is more than he seems and his ability to get into her head—literally—makes her doubt her sanity. After the death of her husband in the Gulf War, she returned to the family ranch to run an animal sanctuary. Bad enough she has to fend off advances from the local sheriff, but now she's turning into some sort of Dr. Doolittle. Except she doesn't talk to animals, dammit.

When Colonel Joshua Harjo, an old friend of her husband's, shows up on her doorstep with a wild tale that the wolf is actually Marine Captain Nathaniel Connor, Jacey must make a leap of faith—and jeopardize her heart—to get involved with the wolf and a group of former Army SciOps soldiers in full rescue operation mode.

Secrets, lies, and betrayals are more personal under the full moon, but when a woman loves a Wolf, he can do no wrong. And Jacey Randolph is not about to let a little thing like a band of mercenaries keep her from the Wolf she loves.

Warning: Explosions, death, and sex go hand in hand when a group of Wolves and their women fight for their existence.

WOLF MOON
(MOONSTRUCK BOOK 4)

Sean Donaldson, former combat medic and

demolition expert, answers an SOS from an old Army buddy and rides smack dab into the middle of a conspiracy. Murder and kidnapping are just the tip of the iceberg. Going undercover with a biker gang seems the quickest solution, but Sean's best intentions are complicated by Annie Simmons and her son, Cody.

Annie is a waitress at the Half Dollar Bar and Grill just scraping by to provide a better life for her son. She doesn't want a man in her life, especially a scary dude like "Boomer," the big biker who steals a part of her heart. What she doesn't know about the lies he's told can hurt her...and put Cody in danger.

Secrets, lies, and betrayals are more personal under the full moon, but when a Wolf fights for his heart, he'll risk his life to make sure the family he loves survives.

Warning: When it's the month of the Wolf Moon, anybody who gets between a moonstruck Wolf and his mate deserves what they get. Blood, sex, and four-letter words dead ahead.

BRIDE'S MOON
(MOONSTRUCK BOOK 5)

When the remnants of Special SciOps Unit 69, the Wolves, reunited to save a group of soldiers used as lab rats in a secret experiment, Colonel Joshua Harjo never expected to command the covert government unit again. Someone near the top wants the 69th back on active duty and Harjo is tasked with making it happen, along with keeping the men the Wolves rescued top secret.

Amy Rouse is the best "cat herder" around and she's recruited for administrative duties with the new unit, a job with perks—Wolves and their commanding officer, Joshua Hargo, the man of her dreams. Amy didn't count on murder, mayhem, and a redheaded Deputy US Marshal to complicate her life.

Secrets, lies, and betrayals are more personal under

the full moon, but when a man loves a woman, nothing will stop him from tying the knot.

Warning: The road to romance is never smooth and a runaway bride might just jinx a highly sensitive operation.

ROGUE MOON
(MOONSTRUCK BOOK 6)

Rudek Tornjak is a Wolf without a pack. A man scarred by his past, he prefers it that way. While living in the shadows of the French Quarter, whispers of treachery and betrayal reach his ears—along with accusations implicating him in unthinkable acts. He comes out of hiding to confront his accusers only to discover he's under a death sentence. On the run, he encounters Isabelle Fontaine, a woman with a past of her own she'd rather keep hidden.

Family is everything to Izzy and she'll do whatever it takes to keep hers safe. Crossing paths with a shadowy corporation and a rogue Wolf puts the people she cares about in jeopardy—not to mention her own life and heart.

Secrets, lies, and betrayals are more personal under the full moon, but when a betrayed Wolf fights for his honor, no one is safe—not even the woman he loves.

Warning: Doubt a Wolf's honor and you'll get a serving of hot blood and guts to go.

CHRISTMAS MOON
(MOONSTRUCK BOOK 7)

The Wolves have been busy since blowing up half of Louisiana. Thanks to the government, there's a bounty on their heads so they're living off the grid. But Christmas is here and the kids want to know if Santa will find them this year. Not a problem until the phone call asking them to find and rescue a pregnant girl. On

December 20th. In New Mexico. Piece of fruit cake, right?

Walking into a firefight with a drug cartel is never easy, but with Hannah's wrath and Liam's first change on the line, Mac and the Wolves face a harder choice—save the girl or save Christmas.

Secrets, lies, and betrayals are more personal under the Christmas moon, and it might just take the magic of Santa to help the Wolves save the day and make it home to their families in time. Because in the end, it's all about family.

Warning: Santa's making his list and when the Wolves go into action, they'll find out who's naughty and who's nice.

2014 FINALIST SHORT PARANORMAL NOVEL INTERNATIONAL DIGITAL AWARDS

BLUE MOON
(MOONSTRUCK BOOK 8)

DJ Collier is a manhunter. As a Deputy US Marshal, she'll go after any fugitive, but the names in the secret file dumped on her desk must be ghosts considering the lack of information she can gather. Where better to hunt them than in the last place she encountered the elusive group of military Special Operators? She never expected to find death, destruction, and a sexy Wolf determined to make her his in the Louisiana bayous.

Antoine Fontaine has lived in the bayous all his life. Always standing on the outside of his close-knit Cajun family, he thinks he's one of a kind. He never expected to discover another like himself, much less a whole group of SpecOps Wolves who welcome him into their pack. He has no idea what it means to be moonstruck until he rescues a feisty Deputy US Marshal. Now, he'll fight to the death to keep her.

Once in a Blue Moon, a Wolf finds his mate and

even if he's up to his ass in alligators, he'll keep her safe. Warning: Hot sex, explosions, and mayhem of the blood and guts kind dead ahead.

2015 WINNER SHORT PARANORMAL NOVEL INTERNATIONAL DIGITAL AWARDS

MOON SHOT
(MOONSTRUCK BOOK 9)
A MOONSTRUCK/HARD TARGET CROSSOVER NOVEL

Scorched earth. The Wolves are damn tired of being hunted. They've licked their wounds and now it's time to take the fight to the enemy. They're moving on up—all the way to the hallowed halls of government. Intelligence reports indicate their enemies are getting closer—and more personal. Assassination of the Wolves and their families is on the menu and SEAL Team Atlantis has the kill order.

Unexpected allies, a new baby, and the healing of old wounds give the Wolves something to live—and fight—for. Every last one of them is ready for a Happy Ever After.

Retribution. There are three things a Wolf holds sacred—his mate, his pups, and his pack. Threaten any one of them and you'd better be checking your six. Threaten all three? Just remember—secrets, lies, and betrayals demand payback and the Wolves are ready to hunt.

Warning: Wolves don't hold a grudge, they get even.

ALSO SET IN THE MOONSTRUCK WORLD

NIGHTRIDERS MOTORCYCLE CLUB

Welcome to the darkest side of the Moonstruck world. Not every Wolf walks the straight and narrow like the Wolves of the 69th. Gritty, earthy, and violent, rogue Wolves run on the criminal side of society. Gun running, strip clubs, bounty hunters, the Nightriders live their lives in the outlaw 1%. There's sex, violence, and violent sex, and sometimes, a Wolf smacks up against the woman destined to turn him moonstruck...

NIGHT SHIFT
(NIGHTRIDERS MC #1)

Everybody knows you don't mess with a big, bad Wolf. Well, everyone except Samantha Prescott...

He's Easy...

Elijah "Easy" Cross works the night shift for the Nightriders MC, collecting pay-offs, protection money, and "policing" their properties. "Live to ride, ride to live" takes on a whole new meaning when members of a rival MC—the Hell Dogs— shoot him and give chase with the intent to kill. Easy ends up on the front porch of a single mom hiding deadly secrets from the same people after him. When she's brutally murdered by the Hell Dogs, he feels responsible and promises to protect her two kids. Easy and his Nightrider brothers might ride on the far side of the law but hell, yeah their honor is worth dying for, and a promise is a promise.

And she's not...

Samantha "Sam" Prescott only wants two things

from the Nightriders—her niece and nephew. It's bad enough her twin got involved with an outlaw motorcycle gang—and was murdered—but now Sam is desperate to extricate herself and the kids. To do that, she has to escape Easy, the sexy biker with boy-next-door dimples and killer instincts. It's that whole killer thing she must keep in mind when the moonstruck Wolf is determined to make her his mate. Her instincts scream, "RUN!" Her hormones want to get down and dirty with the man who turns her boneless with a kiss.

When Sam is kidnapped and tortured by the Hell Dogs, Easy must decide to either keep his promise to ride through the fires of hell to find her or let her go for good, even if it kills him.

Warning: Lots of down and dirty sex, extreme violence—including against women—of the blood and guts kind, alpha MC members, and a moonstruck Wolf shifter with dimples. This is the dark side of the Moonstruck world where sex is rough, death is brutal, and laws don't mean jack.

2015 FINALIST EROTIC NOVEL
INTERNATIONAL DIGITAL AWARDS

THE HARD TARGET TEAM:
JUDGE, JURY, EXECUTIONER...

The multinational Hard Target special operators hunt the worst of the worst, and each brings their own brand of special to the mix. Genetically enhanced Navy

SEALs. Wolf shifters from the SAS and Irish Marines. An Israeli Oketz officer. And a team of former USAF pilots and pararescue jumpers whose humanity doesn't keep them out of the fight. All corralled by Mother Goose, who commands the undercover group with steel-toed combat boots and cold beer.

DOUBLE CROSS
(HARD TARGET #1)

Double-crossed...

Duke Reagan's mission went to hell. His SEAL teammates dead, abandoned by Command in the middle of an African warlord's territory, he's wounded, blind, and on the run with a terrified American, Coreen Prince, a doctor who was supposed to be collateral damage. Somehow, they survive, but not before they lose a bit of their hearts to each other.

Dr. Coreen Prince struggled to put her life back together after her African ordeal, but a slight detour one night in Key West offers her the chance to apologize to the man who saved her at such great cost to himself. Too bad Duke didn't recognize her.

It takes a year to restore Duke's vision, and the return of his sight comes with the opportunity to join the Hard Target team, a not-quite white hat organization doing what government coalitions can't. His first mission as the team's sniper puts a drug cartel boss in his sights, but a face that's haunted Duke since Africa crowds the scope.

On special assignment in South America, Cory once again finds herself in the wrong place at the wrong time. Rescue comes from the last man she expects to see, the one man she can't forget. Will they get a second chance at love or will he just see her as another double cross...

****

FROM HARLEQUIN DESIRE: RED DIRT ROYALTY

THESE OKLAHOMA BILLIONAIRES WORK HARD AND PLAY HARDER!

COWGIRL'S DON'T CRY

The wealthiest of enemies may seduce the ranch right out from under her!

Cassidy Morgan wasn't raised a crybaby. So when her father dies and leaves the family ranch vulnerable to takeover by an Okie gazillionaire with a grudge, she doesn't shed a tear—she fights back.

But Chance Barron, the son of said gazillionaire, is a too-sexy adversary. In fact, it isn't until Cassidy falls head over heels for the sexy cowboy-hat-wearing attorney that she even finds out he's the enemy. Now she needs a plucky plan to save her birthright. But Chance has another trick up his sleeve, putting family loyalties—and passion—to the ultimate test.

THE COWGIRL'S LITTLE SECRET

She's back at his ranch...with baby in tow.

When nurse Jolie Davis comes home, she knows it's only a matter of time before she runs into Cord Barron—the Barrons own this town. In fact, it was their oil business rivalry with her father that caused her break up with Cord in the first place. But no amount of family meddling can deny the fact that she had his secret son. Now, four years later, as her ex is wheeled into the ER—while she's on duty!—it's time to come clean. Because it quickly becomes clear that Cord is determined to reclaim her...

COMING IN 2016
The Boss and His Cowgirl (June)
RDR#4

ALSO COMING IN 2016

THE FULL-LENGTH MOONSTRUCK NOVELS

Moonstruck: Lies
Moonstruck: Betrayal
Moonstruck: Retribution

AND SET IN THE MOONSTRUCK WORLD
Nightriders Book #2
Hard Target Book #2
Moonstruck Christmas Novella

PENUMBRA PAPERS
Penumbra Papers #4

ABOUT THE AUTHOR

Silver likes walking on the wild side and coffee. Okay. She loves coffee. LOTS of coffee. Warning: Her Muse, Iffy, runs with scissors and can be quite dangerous. An award-winning author, she's been a military officer's wife, mother, state appellate court marshal, airport rescue firefighter and forensic fire photographer, crime analyst, technical crime scene investigator, and writer of magic and mystery. Now retired from the "real world," she lives in Oklahoma and spends her days at the computer with two Newfoundland dogs, the cat who rules them all, and myriad characters all clamoring for attention. She writes dark urban fantasy thrillers, time travel romance, and sexy contemporary romance.

If you're ready to walk on the wild side or want to find out more about Silver and her books, you can connect with her on social media.

WEBSITE: www.silverjames.com
FACEBOOK: AuthorSilverJames
TWITTER: @SilverJames_

Be sure to sign up for Silver's newsletter (instructions on her website) to get first looks at upcoming projects, fan-only contests, and other sooper sekrit stuffs.

TITLES BY SILVER JAMES

MOONSTRUCK
*Blood Moon – #1
*Bad Moon – #2
*Hunter's Moon – # 3
*Wolf Moon – # 4
*Bride's Moon – #%
*Rogue Moon – Book 6
*Christmas Moon (A Moonstruck Novella – #7)
*Blue Moon – #8
*Moon Shot – #9 (A Moonstruck/Hard Target
Crossover Novel)
Moonstruck: Secrets

NIGHTRIDERS MC
Night Shift (Nightriders MC #1)

HARD TARGET
Double Cross (Hard Target #1)

PENUMBRA PAPERS
That Ol' Black Magic
Season of the Witch
The Devil's Cut

FROM HARLEQUIN DESIRE
RED DIRT ROYALTY
Cowgirls Don't Cry
The Cowgirl's Little Secret
The Boss and His Cowgirl (June 2016)

FROM THE WILD ROSE PRESS
Faerie Fate
Faerie Fire
Faerie Fool
*Faerie Faith (Twelve Brides of Christmas)
(novella)
*Faerie Reign (Boxed set containing the three full-length novels at a special price)
Twelve Brides of Christmas Vol. 3 (Contains 3
novellas, including Faerie Faith)

CLASS OF '85 REUNION SERIES
*Fairy Tales Can Come True
*Promises, Promises

Dearly Beloved Series
*Best Laid Plans

OTHER NOVELLA FROM SILVER JAMES BOOKS
CRIME NOIR
*Café Midnight

*Available in digital format only